his other wife

(a stella fall psychological suspense thriller—book 1)

ava strong

Ava Strong

Debut author Ava Strong is author of the REMI LAURENT mystery series, comprising three books (and counting); of the ILSE BECK mystery series, comprising four books (and counting); and of the STELLA FALL psychological suspense thriller series, comprising three books (and counting).

An avid reader and lifelong fan of the mystery and thriller genres, Ava loves to hear from you, so please feel free to visit www.avastrongauthor.com to learn more and stay in touch.

ISBN: 978-1-0943-7490-1

BOOKS BY AVA STRONG

REMI LAURENT FBI SUSPENSE THRILLER
THE DEATH CODE (Book #1)
THE MURDER CODE (Book #2)
THE MALICE CODE (Book #3)

ILSE BECK FBI SUSPENSE THRILLER
NOT LIKE US (Book #1)
NOT LIKE HE SEEMED (Book #2)
NOT LIKE YESTERDAY (Book #3)
NOT LIKE THIS (Book #4)

STELLA FALL PSYCHOLOGICAL SUSPENSE THRILLER
HIS OTHER WIFE (Book #1)
HIS OTHER LIE (Book #2)
HIS OTHER SECRET (Book #3)

CHAPTER ONE

Stella Fall jogged up the worn concrete stairs to her third-floor apartment. Her legs were tired from the eight-mile run, and her dark hair, tied back in a ponytail, was damp with sweat. She'd taken a longer route than she'd planned through the streets of Evanston, needing to push herself, craving the distraction.

Now, it was five-thirty p.m. Below the gray veil of cloud, the sun was setting in a crimson haze, and goose bumps prickled her skin as the cool breeze intensified.

Five-thirty p.m. meant close of business. Didn't it?

"Let there be an offer. Please," she said aloud, closing the front door behind her and heading eagerly over to her laptop on the table in the cozy lounge. As she jiggled the mouse, the anxiety that she'd put out of her mind during the run came flooding back.

Today was the deadline for the job she wanted most. The junior position as a jury consultant, working for a top legal firm, would be the gateway to a dream career. It was an opportunity she'd never believed would come her way.

She'd already had a few impersonal 'we will not be offering you an interview' replies to other applications. At the moment, her future felt scarily uncertain, and the tenuous comfort zone she'd settled into seemed as fragile as a spider web.

The screen refreshed and Stella looked down, holding her breath.

Two more rejections from other companies. Her heart sank. No positive word back from anywhere and no response at all from the law firm.

She stared around the apartment with a mixture of longing and panic. In ten days, her lease would be up for renewal, and the landlord had increased the rent. She desperately wanted to stay on here, but to afford it, she needed a full-time job.

This was the first place she'd ever lived that felt like home. In the past months, she'd made happy memories here. Nights of studying, nestled up to the heater with hot chocolate and her playlist. Dinners for two with her boyfriend, Vaughn, which were romantic and memorable despite her lack of cooking skills. Intensive sessions working on her master's thesis with her mentor, Clem.

1

Her phone rang, jolting her out of her worried thoughts. She was pleased to see Clem on the line.

"Hey!" she answered. She guessed Clem – a tall, energetic man who looked ten years younger than his age of sixty-seven - would be pacing up and down the balcony of his apartment overlooking the Chicago River.

"You were waiting for an answer on a job today. You got it yet?" Clem wasn't one for small talk.

Stella made a disappointed face as she rechecked her inbox once again. How she wished she had positive news for him.

"Nothing. They haven't gotten back to me, although they promised to by the end of the day."

"Which job is it?" he asked.

"It's the jury consultant job. This law firm has their own in-house consulting team that does pre-trial research, jury selection, witness evaluation and preparation, and development of trial strategy." Stella felt breathless with excitement and nerves as she thought about it. "It sounds fascinating, and there's so much room for growth."

"So they've interviewed you?"

"Last week. I think it went well. They said my forensic psychology degree was relevant, and they were definitely impressed by my master's thesis," she said, allowing herself a moment of hope.

"I was impressed by it, too. It showed great insight. It's going to redefine the approach and perception of serial killer mentality."

"That's thanks to your guidance, Clem." If it hadn't been for him, Stella knew she would never have graduated *summa cum laude* with her master's degree.

"You should be a top candidate for the job then," he encouraged her.

"Not necessarily. Because, as they mentioned in the interview, I don't have any relevant work experience," she said.

She glanced hopefully at the laptop screen again. Nope, no new emails had arrived during the past thirty seconds. With a sigh, she turned away, and headed to the tiny kitchen to pour some water.

Clem refused to be sidetracked. "Don't underestimate yourself. You have many months of work experience in other fields. I've seen how many different jobs you've had to juggle to pay your way over the years – waitressing, tutoring, front-desk work, research assistance. You've been determined and resourceful, and never once let your employers down."

"I don't –" she protested, but he continued firmly.

2

"Plus, you have a brilliant mind. Your grades were phenomenal. But you need to work in a place where your talents will be most needed. I still think you should apply to join the FBI. Even if they offer you the job at the legal firm, treat it as a second choice."

Clem himself had retired ten years ago after a stellar career as an FBI profiler. It had taken him around the USA and to many other parts of the world.

But she wasn't Clem. Even though she had always felt drawn to the field of law enforcement – hence the topic she'd chosen for her thesis – she didn't think she was ready to apply.

"Is that really why you aren't considering the FBI? Or is it because of all the times your mother told you that you weren't good enough?" the voice of honesty inside her head asked, demanding answers.

As she poured a glass of water from the jug in the fridge, Stella knew she couldn't answer that question.

"Or is it because of what happened to your father?" the voice continued.

Stella refused to listen to her internal voice a moment longer. Slamming the fridge door, she quickly replied to Clem.

"I'd rather have some relevant work mileage first. Plus, I need to start earning, and the jury consultancy salary is excellent."

Clem sighed. "I guess so. Experience in the legal field will be a plus when you approach the FBI. And I get that you need to start earning," he admitted reluctantly.

With nobody to finance her studies or support her, she'd had to pay her way through college herself. But, since meeting the handsome Vaughn four months ago, Stella had cut back on all the part-time work that had been her financial lifeline and prioritized seeing him instead. She'd justified it as a mini vacation, a well-deserved break before getting her final grades and starting the job hunt. Even so, she'd been dismayed by how fast she'd blown through her meager savings.

Falling in love had been a whirlwind journey of fun and excitement, but now, the only way of avoiding financial disaster was the lifeline a well-paying job would provide.

"I will give serious thought to joining the FBI as the next step. I promise," she said.

"If Gillian was alive, I'd have given her the same advice," Clem added. "She was like you. Intelligent, brave, and resourceful. Exactly the kind of asset the FBI needs." Clem's voice softened as he spoke of his daughter, who'd been killed in a car crash when she was a first-year university student. Stella knew Clem thought of her as his own

3

daughter. His belief in her abilities made her feel more confident about them.

"And don't worry that the law firm hasn't got back to you yet. End of day for them is probably eight p.m., earliest," he added with more than a little humor in his voice.

"Thank you," Stella said, smiling as they ended the call. She gulped down her water and set the empty glass on the kitchen counter.

At that moment, from the lounge, she heard her laptop ping and rushed to it. A new email had arrived. She tensed, leaning closer as she saw it was from the Chicago law firm.

"I don't believe it!" Stella's ice-blue eyes widened. She felt breathless with shock as she read and reread the words. A massive, disbelieving grin spread over her face. How she wished she'd stayed on the line with Clem a few moments longer so that she could share the good news with him immediately.

She had the job!

"Oh, wow," she whispered. Joy flooded through her as she read the wonderful and positive words.

They were impressed by her qualifications and delighted to offer her the position. She could start on the first of May.

"I've landed my dream role!" She danced around the lounge, waving her hands in the air. Returning to her laptop, she stared at the screen again with her heart soaring.

This was everything she'd hoped for. It was a validation of the degree she'd fought so hard to achieve. She'd be employed by one of Chicago's top law firms! She'd be using all her skills and learning many more. Clem would be so proud.

With relief, she realized she'd be able to stay on in the apartment she loved. And it was the best possible outcome for her and Vaughn, too. He'd moved to Chicago from Connecticut to do work experience at a leading finance firm and had mentioned last time they'd seen each other that they'd offered him a full-time job.

Vaughn was taking her out tonight and would be arriving in an hour. She couldn't wait to tell him the good news.

CHAPTER TWO

Vaughn pulled up outside the lobby at seven p.m. on the dot. Stella liked that he was always early or punctual, and never late. It gave her a sense of security.

As always, she'd made sure to look her best for him. Her hair was glossily blow dried and her make-up flawlessly applied. Tonight, she was bubbling inside with the amazing news she couldn't wait to share. She knew he'd be proud of her for landing her dream job and be as thrilled as she was that she could now afford to stay in her lovely apartment.

"Hello, babes!" he greeted her as she opened the BMW's door.

"Hello, handsome!" Climbing inside, scissoring her legs into the low-slung car, she stowed her bags in front of her and turned to kiss him.

Staring into his warm, hazel-green eyes, she felt lucky all over again to be with this tall, fit, and gorgeous man. His chestnut-brown hair was tousled casually across his forehead. The way he smiled when he stared at her always made her stomach flip.

"You look stunning," he complimented her. "I love how that gray top brings out the blueness of your eyes."

He stroked his fingers tenderly down her cheek, twining them through a shiny lock of her hair.

Then, rubber burning, he sped away.

"So, there's this new bar, Mojos, that's just opened. It apparently does killer tapas and margaritas. I thought we could go there tonight."

"Sounds great," Stella enthused. She couldn't wait to experience it. Vaughn had a knack for finding fabulous restaurants and clubs. They'd shared so many memorable evenings together at trendy local hotspots. What fun it had been, experiencing what was now their home city, together.

"How was your day?" she asked, watching the lights of downtown shimmer in the distance as the road unrolled ahead of them.

"My last working day with Colston Corporate? Torture!" He made a face.

"What do you mean?" Stella said, staring at him in consternation. His last working day? He'd just been offered a full-time job. What had gone wrong?

"I can't tell you how glad I am to have that behind me. Talk about purgatory. I feel incinerated. I hated every moment I spent with that stupid firm."

Stella felt her mouth fall open with shock, and quickly shut it again.

She'd had no idea that Vaughn hated his job so much. He'd seldom spoken about work, but now it sounded as if he was letting loose all the negativity he must have bottled up over the past few months.

"Was it really so bad?"

"It was tedious. Annoying. Humiliating, in fact. It was a step down for me and I only did it because I was forced to. The only good thing about my time here was meeting you. The rest of it was a waste. But even so, I made myself a promise that I was going to ace it and be the guy they wanted me to be."

Stella felt as if her world was falling apart. Of course, he'd never have accepted a full-time job if this was the way he felt. How could she have assumed so wrongly?

He glanced at her and laughed. "What's up? You're very quiet. Aren't you happy I did well?"

Her heart was pounding. She had no idea what she should say. Wasn't he just as worried about their future as she was?

But, if he wasn't worried, there was surely a reason. Thinking fast, Stella realized what that must be.

Vaughn was from an extremely wealthy family. In fact, he was the eldest son of an ex-senator who lived in Greenwich. She'd been astounded when she found that out. For a while it had made her nervous about taking the next step in their relationship, despite Vaughn's laughing protestations that he hadn't chosen where to be born. Since then, the differences in their approach to money, and to life, had caught her by surprise a few times.

Vaughn could pick and choose where he wanted to work. He wasn't running out of money like she was. He didn't need to accept the first offer he got. Putting herself in his expensive leather shoes gave her a different perspective.

"I'm just surprised how much you hated it," she explained, glad there was no need for panic after all. "And I'm thrilled you aced it."

He glanced at her and grinned. Taking a hand off the wheel, he squeezed her thigh.

"Yeah, I think they'll be pleased with me back home. I know I did my best."

Back home? Stella felt her stomach clench. It sounded like he was going to leave.

Her fragile sense of security felt shattered all over again.

Arriving at the tapas bar, Vaughn swung the car neatly into a parking space that had just opened. Then they hustled inside, where he snagged the last two chairs at the glitzy bar, just as another couple approached.

"Gold Margarita?" Vaughn scanned the menu. "They have a really classy Patron tequila option here."

While he ordered, Stella gazed around, gathering her thoughts for the difficult conversation ahead. The bar was done to the nines in crazily trendy pink and green décor, with paisley decorations, sombreros and floral-embossed skulls patterning the walls. It was an expensive place and she realized that Vaughn had probably ordered the priciest drink on the menu.

Stella would have looked at the prices first. Vaughn never even glanced at them.

Suddenly, the divide between their circumstances felt unbridgeable again.

The barman, sporting a pink waistcoat and spiky hair, brought their drinks. Sure enough, the glasses were topped with a twist of lime, draped in gold leaf.

"Cheers, gorgeous." Vaughn turned to face her.

Stella sipped from the salt-encrusted glass, needing the courage that the drink's lemon-tinged kick would imbue.

"There's something important we need to discuss," she said.

"What's that?" Now he was looking at her quizzically, as if her words, and their serious tone, had surprised him.

"I got the job that I've been hoping for. It's the jury consultancy job with the Chicago law firm. It's a step into my dream career, Vaughn. But it means I'll be staying here, for a while at least. So we need to discuss our future."

If there is a future, Stella thought, feeling suddenly sick with nerves as she took another gulp of the drink. She could see his face was taut with consternation.

"Stella, no!" Vaughn sounded frantic. He pushed his drink aside and it stood, forgotten, as he stared at her. "I thought that job was in New York?"

"No, I said the law firm also had a branch in New York," Stella explained, feeling stressed that he'd misunderstood.

"I'm heading back to Connecticut soon. That was what I wanted to tell you tonight."

"You are?" Uncertainty curdled inside her. Perhaps she could change his mind. "But you were offered a job here. I know the firm wasn't the right fit for you, but you could easily get another. Are you sure you don't want to stay? For a while, at least?"

He had so many options, and she had only one. She was terrified of losing him and felt breathless as she waited for his answer. Would he consider the move? Or would his next words be that he was breaking it off with her?

He shook his head. "I already have a job back home. This stint was the final preparation for it."

She nodded somberly, her heart plummeting as he continued.

"Now that I'm done here, I can start in the role I've been aiming for. I'll be a hedge fund manager for one of the top finance firms in Connecticut. Stella, this is my goal. It's what I've been fighting for, every day I've stuck it out here."

Vaughn's chin jutted and she could tell that he was set on achieving his aims. His ambition and determination were two of the qualities that had first drawn her to him.

"Then we can make it work long distance," she tried. "I'll be earning a good salary. We'll be able to commute to see each other. I might even be able to transfer to their New York branch in a couple of years, if I do well. In the meantime, we can manage."

Even though she forced the hopeful tone into her own voice, she found herself filled with doubt. What if it didn't work? She knew that wouldn't be what he wanted.

Vaughn shook his head.

Stella stared at him, waiting for the hammer-blow to fall, expecting him to say that he was ending it.

"I want to be together with you. Not to battle in a long-distance relationship. We'll lose what we have. I can't afford to lose you. Please, you can't do this to me," he entreated.

"I – I don't know what to say." She gripped her glass, realizing her hands were shaking. She was all out of choices and couldn't think of any other options.

She started saying, "What do you want me to do?" because she felt trapped in this predicament, but he spoke over her.

"Stella, come with me. Come to Connecticut."

"But –" Her mouth felt dry. How could she throw away the opportunity of a lifetime? She'd have to start afresh in a new city, and right now she didn't have the resources to do that.

His hazel eyes were warm, intense, flecked with gold as he stared at her.

"Marry me," he said.

An icy splash of margarita spilled onto her hand. She felt numb with shock as she rattled the glass down onto the bar. What had just happened? Had he really said that? Could he really mean it?

He reached out, his hand trembling ever so slightly as he stroked her hair, cupped her face.

"I mean it, Stella. Please, marry me. I love you. I want us to be together, forever."

Of course she'd dreamed that one day in the future, if things went well, they might take the next step and move in together. But marriage, now?

Fear flooded through her. This would mean giving up her dream job. She'd never get another opportunity this good. And what would the implications be, marrying into such a wealthy family? She wished she'd had more time to get to know and understand his world, because at the moment, it felt unknown and terrifying to her.

It was as if she saw two different pathways for her life, branching in front of her. She had to pick one and when she did, the other would vanish forever.

Think of the positives, Stella implored herself, worried that her shock might prompt her to make a decision she'd regret forever.

She'd be spending the rest of her life with the man she loved. A brand-new life, and she'd become a new person, Stella Marshall. They adored each other. That was a certainty, and she knew both of them felt equally strongly. Of course they could make it work.

There would be other jobs. She could find the perfect workplace, where she'd be able to further her career and skills.

"Will you?" He sounded anxious now and she realized that none of her frantic thoughts showed on her face. They never did. She was used to keeping her feelings hidden.

In a rush, Stella decided to go with her heart.

"I accept," she said breathlessly. "I love you too, Vaughn. Let's make a future together."

As soon as she'd spoken the words, he leaned over and hugged her so tightly she felt as if he was squeezing the breath out of her. Hugging him back, she was uneasily aware that her happiness was already tinged with worry.

Vaughn would be arriving home after four months away, with a brand-new fiancée. She hadn't even met his family yet. How would that go down with them?

Would his wealthy, prestigious parents accept that their eldest son was engaged to a girl from the Midwest, estranged from her own family, who came from a humble background and had no fortune or social standing to offer?

CHAPTER THREE

Staring out of the window as the airplane descended, Stella watched Connecticut appear through the light bank of cloud. She felt a sense of disbelief that she was already on a journey to a different life.

What madness the past week had been. She'd canceled the lease on her apartment, packed up her clothes, and sold her few items of furniture, as she'd be living with Vaughn in his cottage, which he'd said was fully furnished.

She'd spent hours composing the email declining the job offer and had felt bitter disappointment when she'd finally pressed send.

That was to be expected. Of course, making choices would come with regrets. As soon as she was settled, she'd resume her job hunt. New York City was full of law firms and jury consultancies. Hopefully some of them would be looking for keen juniors. She'd even scouted out a few possibilities during the flight.

Despite these positive thoughts, she felt worried things were moving too fast.

A week ago, she'd never have dreamed that she'd be heading to her new home city, wearing an engagement ring.

Glancing down at the ring, she ran her fingertips over the smooth platinum band and the raised setting of the diamond. Its delicate beauty helped to reassure her fears. This ring emphasized the reality of Vaughn's love for her and his commitment to their new life together. It was the most stunning piece of jewelry she'd ever owned. She had promised herself she would never take it off.

Vaughn opened his eyes as the plane touched down.

"We've landed already?" he said in surprise.

"Yes, sleepyhead," Stella teased.

"Sleepyhead?" Vaughn laughed in fake outrage. "I wasn't snoozing. I was planning our weekend. We need to explore your new 'hood. The 'Art to the Avenue' Festival is on this month, so we could take a walk down Greenwich Avenue this afternoon and see the artworks in the store windows. They have musicians and street performers, too. Maybe we can have dinner at a restaurant."

"Sounds good," Stella said, feeling excited about getting to know her new home city.

"Tomorrow we could go see Putnam Cottage – it's a famous landmark in the Putnam Hill Historic District. And take a sunset walk at Greenwich Point Park, which has the most beautiful beach."

"It'll be like a mini vacation," Stella enthused. Then, as her nerves descended again, she remembered that this was no vacation, but the start of a whole new life, and in a short while she would be introduced to his family for the very first time. "Who's meeting us?" she asked.

Vaughn checked his phone. "Rodriguez," he said.

"Rodriguez?" Vaughn hadn't mentioned him before. The name was unfamiliar to her. "Who's he?"

"He's one of our family's drivers. I don't know him. He was hired while I was away, replacing Nelson, who left."

"Oh." Stella felt taken aback by this information. One of the drivers? It sounded like they were full-time personal employees. She'd always thought the drivers Vaughn had occasionally mentioned, belonged to one of the Marshalls' businesses, but realized now she was wrong. "How many are there?" she asked.

"We have three," Vaughn replied. "Two full-time, one weekends only."

For a family of six? That sounded like a lot, Stella thought in surprise. At least being picked up by a driver would give her more time to prepare for when she met the Marshalls. She wanted to plan ahead so that she could be ready to field any questions, as well as correct any wrong assumptions they might have made about her.

She quickly gathered her possessions together. They stood up from their front-row seat and headed into the airport.

*

As Vaughn wheeled the loaded baggage cart to the exit, Stella scanned the waiting faces. There was a man, in a dark green jacket and gray pants, holding a printed card.

"Vaughn Marshall"

He took the cart and they followed him out of the terminal to the parking lot.

"Mom says we must come around as soon as we arrive," Vaughn said, checking his phone.

"I can't wait to meet your family," Stella enthused, even though she felt a flutter of nerves at the prospect.

"They're looking forward to meeting you, too. Nobody thought I'd leave for work experience and meet the love of my life. I think they all assumed I'd marry someone from the neighborhood." He laughed.

"You've never been conventional," Stella said. Coming from her to him, it was praise. But she felt anxious that, to his family, it could be seen as a defiant move.

They might believe she had pressured him into marriage, or even that she was a gold-digger. That was a humiliating thought, but Stella knew she had to confront the possibility, and address it. She needed to make sure that this high-powered family knew what her own goals and ambitions were.

The driver unlocked a massive, jet-black Range Rover. He opened the trunk and stowed the luggage away. Then he opened the rear passenger door for Stella.

She'd been about to open it herself and they almost collided. Stepping hastily back, she let him do his job. Then, feeling self-conscious, she climbed into the plush, leather-scented space.

"Oh, no. I have to go into work tomorrow to prepare," Vaughn said, checking his messages again. "On a Sunday? No rest for the wicked. I'm sorry, babes. We'll have to postpone the trip to the historic district. Hopefully I'll back in time for the sunset beach walk."

"I guess they need you to be ready to go by Monday," Stella agreed, disappointed that their sightseeing day would have to wait.

However, this reminded her that his family clearly had a high work ethic, and she was determined to prove that she possessed the same qualities. That she was driven to succeed, ready to dedicate herself to a career, just as her father had been.

Her father had been a detective, heading up the investigation unit at the local precinct in the small Kansas town where they'd lived. Thinking back to the last time she saw him as he headed out to work, Stella felt a sense of emptiness and loss all over again. She hoped that if he was alive, he would be proud of where she was now, and how far she'd come.

"We're nearly there." Vaughn's words interrupted her thoughts and she focused on her surroundings again.

Staring in fascination, Stella saw the neighborhood they were driving through was immaculate, and clearly very wealthy. Huge gates, magnificent trees, perfectly maintained sidewalks. She noticed a few people at work in the gardens as they passed. And beyond, set far from the road, the houses themselves were architectural showpieces.

The farmhouse that she had grown up in had been small and shabby, with dusty windows looking out over golden-brown fields, and warped wooden floorboards that creaked at night. The dirt driveway was a dustbowl most of the year and then turned into a riverbed when it rained. Town had been a few miles away, but even the fanciest houses there were simple and basic in comparison to these wedding-cake creations.

This view felt unsettling to her, like driving through a weird, showpiece neighborhood where nobody real actually lived.

But they did. And now, so would she.

"Here we are."

As Stella was rubbernecking the astonishing homes they were passing, the Range Rover stopped outside a massive, wrought-iron gate. A moment later it swung open.

The paved driveway was lined with perfectly kept flower beds. At its end, she spied a three-story building that from a distance, looked more like a palace than a family home.

She laughed, hearing a hint of unease in her own voice.

"Come on. Are you joking? This is a mansion. You said you lived in a cottage. Are we meeting your family first, or what?"

"My cottage is on the family's estate," Vaughn explained. "I told you I stayed walking distance from my parents. The cottage is hidden away in the gardens. It's very private," he added anxiously.

"Oh." She'd never realized that. For some reason, living on the same property as Vaughn's parents made her uncomfortable, but she suppressed the feeling. After all, it seemed to be an enormous place with plenty of room for privacy. A cottage on an estate was the same distance as being down the road in a normal suburb, she reassured herself.

As the family home loomed ahead, she took it in. It was magnificent. The porch was lined with tall, bright white pillars and the front door was an enormous, ornately carved slab of wood. Gracious copper beech trees flanked the building.

"Everything looks the same," Vaughn said, sounding surprised. "Greener than when I left, but otherwise the same."

"Did you expect it to be different?" Stella asked.

Vaughn nodded thoughtfully. "Yes. I thought it would have changed. But I think it's me that's changed. I've never been away from home for so long. I feel I've grown as a person now. I'm different than I was when I left. And, of course, you're in my life now. You're such a positive force for good."

"Well, I feel like I'm in a dream. I didn't know what to expect, but it wasn't this level of grandeur. I'm a little out of my comfort zone so I'll need your support," she shared with a nervous laugh.

"You have it, babes. And you deserve to live in luxury, after staying in that ghetto for years."

There was a disparaging note in Vaughn's voice she'd never heard before.

Surprised, she glanced at him, but he was grinning at her teasingly. She felt relieved that she'd just misunderstood his joke, that was all.

"Uh-oh," Vaughn said, as the mansion's front door opened. "Looks like the family is already waiting. We'd better stop and say hi." He raised his voice, addressing the driver. "Can you drop the bags at the cottage? We'll head there afterwards."

Swallowing down her nerves, Stella climbed out. He took her hand and they walked together up the immaculately paved pathway that led into the shade of the stately front porch. She hoped this introduction would go well and they would like her. First impressions counted, so her future relationship with the family could hinge on this moment.

In the doorway stood a slim woman with a smooth halo of platinum-blonde hair. Her skin was ageless, like silk, and it was more her authoritative bearing that clued Stella in that this was, in fact, Vaughn's mother.

"Mom!" A moment later, Vaughn confirmed this, enveloping the petite, stylish woman in a giant embrace.

"It's wonderful to see you again! We've missed you! You need a haircut." After reaching up to give Vaughn's cheek an affectionate pinch, and brushing his unruly bangs aside, Mrs. Marshall turned to Stella.

Stella felt alarmed to see that her attractively smooth face had grown stern, and her blue eyes were icy. She regarded her for a long moment, without saying a word.

Even though Vaughn had reassured her again and again that his family would love her, and that her poor background wouldn't matter at all, Stella felt differently now. She sensed, with a cold certainty, that Vaughn's mother disapproved of her.

CHAPTER FOUR

Desperate to make a good impression, Stella rushed to fill the silence.

"Good morning, Mrs. Marshall. I'm so thrilled to meet you, and to be here in your wonderful home," she said breathlessly.

Finally, Mrs. Marshall's expression warmed.

"It's wonderful to meet you, too, Stella. Please, call me Cecilia. And welcome to our family. We're so pleased to have you here. When Vaughn said he'd met the love of his life in Chicago, we couldn't wait for him to bring you home."

She embraced Stella. Her scent was subtle, evocative of roses and musk. Stella hugged her back, relieved that she'd ended up getting such a warm greeting from this intimidating woman. In her nervousness, she must have misread her initial body language.

"Come in, please. Gordon is on his way. He'll be home any minute, and Howard is here somewhere," Cecilia encouraged.

Following them inside, Stella stopped, staring in astonishment at the home's interior. At the far end of the enormous, open-plan hallway was a wide staircase. Its white stairs and polished brass handrails guided her eyes to the sky-high ceiling where the crystal globes of an ornate chandelier caught the sun that streamed in through the upper windows.

Glancing through the giant archway to her right, Stella saw a formal lounge filled with pale-upholstered furniture. The fireplace at the far end gave the room a hint of warmth.

To the left, another entertainment area led to a huge swimming pool.

This palace was Vaughn's home? It seemed impossible that he'd had a childhood here. Had he actually grown up, played and run around, fallen and scraped his knees, lived his life in this immaculate residence?

Footsteps from behind snapped her attention that way, and she turned around to see a tanned and more rugged version of Vaughn approaching. He had neatly cut dark hair, graying at the temples, and was wearing an air of supreme confidence as easily as he wore his bright white golf shirt. This must be his father, the ex-senator.

"My boy, you're back! Well done for doing your time in Chicago. Your uncle will be pleased to have you at the firm. We had great reports about your performance, but of course it's the box check on your CV for the out-of-state work that's the most important. Aren't you glad it's done? And welcome to our home, Stella."

After hugging his son, he gave Stella a bone-crushing handshake, but she was too distracted by his words to notice. The comment about the box-check had disturbed her.

So had the fact that Vaughn hadn't told her he was working for his uncle. Why hadn't he mentioned that? It wouldn't have made a difference to her, but it was an odd fact to have omitted. Now that she knew, she could see why there hadn't been a choice about him returning to Greenwich.

"Hey, bro!" A man's voice called down from the top of the stairs, distracting Stella from her troubling thoughts.

"Hey, Howard!" Vaughn replied. "Stella, meet my youngest brother."

Howard looked to be in his early twenties. He was a little taller than Vaughn but oozed the same confidence as he ran down the marble steps to punch his older brother on the arm.

There was another brother, Elmer, Stella remembered, wondering where he was.

"Hi, Stella. Nice to meet you," Howard greeted her. Then, turning back to Vaughn, he continued. "I put your name down for the champs at the tennis club, hoping you'd get back in time. I know you haven't been practicing and are fat and unfit and probably useless." He jabbed a finger into Vaughn's stomach. Vaughn grabbed hold of it playfully and twisted until Howard yelled.

"Let go, let go! Back to the tennis, bro. Are you keen? They need fresh meat just for the spectator value," Howard gasped.

Vaughn brightened. "Sure. I'll ask to be blindfolded for the first game if I play you. Then you won't lose by too much."

Howard guffawed. "We need to leave in five. You need to grab your gear. C'mon, I need a chance to thrash your ass."

"In five?" Vaughn repeated, sounding surprised.

Stella felt alarmed. What about exploring downtown Greenwich and seeing the 'Art to the Avenue' Festival? They couldn't move in till tomorrow because Vaughn would be at work.

"I think that's too soon. We have other plans," Vaughn said, glancing at Stella questioningly.

"You're not getting clearance from the ball and chain? It's the club champs! C'mon, bro!"

Vaughn glanced at him and then looked back at Stella again with a worried frown.

Seeing his predicament, Howard laughed even louder.

His mother was looking at her too. She felt trapped by their stares and unsure of what to say. This wasn't what she had expected would happen.

Smoothly, Cecilia Marshall took control of the conversation, addressing Vaughn with a smile.

"I think you should take part. I'm sure your lovely new fiancée would want you to do well in the club championships," she said. Turning to Stella, she continued, smiling warmly. "Besides, we have a ladies' luncheon planned. I included you on the assumption that Vaughn would be off to one or another sporting event. As it turns out, I was correct."

Stella couldn't help feeling disappointed. She'd been looking forward to the outing and seeing the art displays. However, she needed to build good relationships with Vaughn's family, soon to be hers. That was more important than sightseeing. The ladies' lunch would be the perfect chance to get to know everyone.

"Thank you so much," Stella smiled. She turned to Vaughn. "You go ahead. Make sure you win your game," she teased.

"At least I know I'll win if I play Howard. Have fun, babes!" Sounding relieved, Vaughn kissed her cheek and hustled out of the front door with Howard. A moment later he was gone.

She didn't even know where the cottage was yet and felt a wave of insecurity at being left suddenly alone. Memories surfaced of her father's empty armchair, with the threadbare cushion that she looked at day after day, wondering if he would ever return, if he would ever walk in and sit down on it again.

"Come with me," Cecilia said, grasping Stella's hand. "My daughter Grace will be back from the hairdresser any minute, and my sister Kathy and a friend are invited as well. We do this most Saturdays."

She followed Cecilia through the massive entertainment area and out to the back porch. There, under the covered roof, a large table had been set with white linen, silverware, and crystal glasses.

"You sit there," Mrs. Marshall walked to the head of the table, and pointed to the seat on her right.

Stella headed to her chair and, as if from nowhere, a white-uniformed waiter silently materialized. He pulled out her chair for her and placed a starched napkin on her lap.

"Red or white wine?" he asked.

"White, please," Stella said, feeling as if she was at a fancy restaurant, rather than a family lunch. "Can I also have a glass of water," she asked, needing something non-alcoholic to hydrate herself.

As the waiter poured her mineral water, a chorus of voices signaled the arrival of the others. A trio of women dressed in chic designer outfits walked in.

"Viv! Kathy! Welcome. Meet Stella, Vaughn's fiancée," Mrs. Marshall made the introduction with a wave of her French-manicured fingers. "Kathy is my older sister, and Viv is a long-standing family friend. And this is Grace, the youngest of my four children. She'll be celebrating her twenty-first birthday in July."

As Stella stared at the new arrivals wondering who, if any, might be a good future friend, she realized the women in this circle were all slim, blonde, and stylish, as well as remarkably ageless. She felt like an outsider with her long, dark hair that she now realized needed a trim.

Amid a chorus of hellos, Kathy and Viv both gave her a welcoming smile as they sat. The willowy, platinum-blonde Grace, staying more aloof, stared at her with an assessing expression.

"So, when's the wedding?" asked Viv, the family friend, sitting down to Stella's right. She had tawny golden hair that cascaded over her shoulders and piercing green eyes.

Stella turned to her, pasting on a polite smile at the unexpected question.

"I don't know. We're only recently engaged."

"Show me the ring?"

Viv reached over and grabbed her left hand as if she owned it.

"It's a nice little diamond. Very pretty, and the ring looks good on your hand," she said thoughtfully.

"It's a shame Vaughn bought it while he was away," Grace laughed. "I'm sure he would have gotten a better deal from our family jeweler in Greenwich!"

"Let's see?" Kathy asked from across the table. She had identical bone structure to Cecilia, with defined cheekbones in a perfectly oval face. Her blue eyes were accentuated by a flawless blonde bob.

The next thing Stella knew, Viv had actually slipped the ring off her finger and passed it across the table.

19

This was the ring she'd promised herself she'd never take off! Kathy was scrutinizing it from all angles, peering at the diamond.

"Wait!" Stella said, outraged, but Viv was tapping her on the shoulder again.

"Your dress is nice. Is it Shabby Chic?" she asked.

Stella swiveled to stare at her in bemusement.

"Is it what?" she asked.

"Shabby Chic. It's an affordable design house. I thought it looked like it might be from their new collection."

"Nope. Not Shabby Chic. Just shabby, I guess," she said jokingly, even though she couldn't help feeling ashamed that her clothing looked worn and cheap in the eyes of these well-dressed women.

"Not at all. You're lucky to have a figure that allows you to wear an off-the-rack garment and make it look designer," Viv said. Her smile was unexpectedly kind.

From across the table, Kathy passed her ring back to her, and Stella jammed it back on her finger, still feeling shaken by the suddenness of having it removed.

"Please, ladies, eat!" Cecilia Marshall's words rang out, as sharp and clear as a silver spoon on a crystal wineglass.

The banter quieted to a murmur, and the chink of cutlery replaced it.

She had to admit the food was excellent. The smoked salmon salad, in a creamy dressing, was sumptuous and tasty. The caviar on melba toast was salty but enjoyable. It paired well with the fragrantly dry wine.

"You're quite slim," Grace praised her. "Do you work out at all?"

Stella recognized a backhanded compliment when she heard one but decided to ignore it.

"I like to run," she replied with a friendly smile.

"You should go jogging in the afternoons with Howard, then," Cecilia advised. "He loves to run, too and goes out every day. Vaughn's always been more of a gym addict, and he's a top-class tennis player."

Grace leaned across and prodded Stella's forearm. "We have a great personal trainer who comes here two mornings a week and trains in our family gym. You should book a few sessions with him. He's excellent with toning arms."

Everything Grace said seemed to have a subtly insulting undertone. Guessing this must be a relationship issue between Vaughn and his younger sister that was being carried over to her, she decided it would be best to ignore it. She said nothing in return, deciding to ask Vaughn about it when she saw him later.

"The gym's in the west wing, overlooking the rose garden. Next to Vaughn's old bedroom," Cecilia Marshall added helpfully.

"I'll definitely use it. Thank you," Stella said.

Relieved to have handled Grace's taunt without letting it cause an issue, she carried on eating, listening to the conversation about one of Kathy's daughters.

"She's gotten so sensitive to sunlight since she was pregnant. It gives her terrible headaches."

"Does she have good sunglasses? She mustn't wear contact lenses. It could make it worse," Cecilia warned.

"She bought the best ones she could find. And she's staying indoors and even talking about canceling their trip to the Maldives. If she goes out shopping, their driver takes her in the Mercedes. It has the darkest windows. She's been joking she feels like a vampire."

"A very beautiful and slender one," Cecilia added.

"Carrying small, she gets from me. The light sensitivity must be a problem from my husband's side. Greg always struck me as someone who would stare into the sun," Kathy giggled.

A chorus of laughs resonated from around the table.

"Where did you get your nails done? That French ombre is divine. It actually looks pearlescent," Viv said to Cecilia admiringly.

"There's a stunning spa that's opened down the road. Grace and I spend the day there every Thursday." She turned to Stella. "Would you like to join us next time? Or else, you're welcome to use it whenever you like, on our family's account. They do everything. Hair, nails, body treatments, skincare. If I were you, I'd start with some good face treatments and do something with your hair. They'll sort you out," she explained decisively, as the waiters converged on the table and removed the mostly-empty plates.

"Thank you," Stella said. She already felt self-conscious in this company, like a dark-maned intruder in a tribe of sun-kissed blondes. What would they do to her hair? Bleach it up so she looked like one of them?

"Vaughn's always adored blondes," Grace confided in her, as if reading her mind, as the waiter set down a plate of thickly iced petit fours.

"That's true enough," Kathy laughed. "Blonde has definitely been his type."

21

She turned to accept a cup of coffee from the waiter, and Grace continued, pasting on a fake smile as she spoke to Stella in an intimate whisper.

"Wait till you meet his most recent exes. They're both really pretty. And they'd both love to get back together with him again. I wouldn't be surprised if they try to."

Stella stared at her, biting back a furious retort. What did Grace have against her? Why was she being so vicious?

And even more worryingly, was there any truth to her words?

CHAPTER FIVE

Stella fought for control. She wasn't going to let Grace see how much that comment had hurt and unsettled her. Even if Grace ended up being her enemy as a result, she refused to give her that satisfaction.

"I guess people's tastes change as they mature. Vaughn changed a lot in Chicago. He's a very different person now," she commented in a mild tone, smiling benignly back, and watched Grace scowl in disappointment that her sniping hadn't hit home.

Nobody seemed to be touching the petit fours, and Stella was relieved that, a moment later, Viv stood up.

"I'd better get going. I have to attend that charity musical this afternoon," she said.

"Would you mind if I excused myself also? It's been wonderful, but I have to unpack," Stella added, seizing the opportunity to make a polite exit.

"What fun it's been! It was lovely to get to know you better, Stella. The butler will show you to the cottage," Cecilia smiled, before turning back to her other guests.

The uniformed butler at the door nodded politely. "Please follow me, ma'am."

Walking behind him, Stella made her way back through the huge house, and out onto the grounds. There, he took a paved pathway that led into a formal garden with low topiary hedges and a central fountain. Beyond, it wound its way through a scenic grove of cherry trees and then out onto more perfectly mowed lawns.

As she walked, Stella exhaled deeply, feeling relieved the lunch was over. It hadn't gone the way she'd expected. Grace's comments had gotten under her skin, and she'd found it difficult to converse with the others. She'd looked forward to asking everyone what they did for a living, or if they didn't work, what their hobbies, interests, and passions were. But none of that had been discussed, or even mentioned. The conversation had been dominated by their children, their clothes, their beauty regimes.

Although, thinking back, she realized nobody had mentioned the middle brother, Elmer. He hadn't been at the house earlier or invited to tennis. She wondered if he might be the black sheep of the family, and if so, what he'd done.

She was also surprised that, as the stranger in the circle, nobody had asked her about herself. She'd certainly had a lot of unsolicited advice which brought back stinging memories of her mother's critical words.

But they didn't seem interested in her personally at all. Who she was, what she had studied, what she was aiming for, all seemed unimportant. Perhaps that meant they didn't take her seriously yet. That was a challenge she hadn't expected.

"Here is the cottage, ma'am." The butler's voice interrupted her thoughts.

Ahead, flanked by flower beds, was a large and elegant looking home with a pillared front porch and a tiled roof.

The butler unlocked the door and handed her the keys.

"You will need the wi-fi code, too, ma'am. Cell signal is very weak in this area."

He gave her a handwritten card with the details. Taking it, Stella stepped inside, breathing in the unfamiliar scents of polished wood and the aroma of flowers. It was weird to think this was where she lived now. The hallway was enormous, and the gleaming table looked like an expensive antique. To her right was a well-equipped kitchen, and ahead was a large lounge.

She walked down the corridor, treading over polished wooden floorboards, and at the end, discovered the master bedroom. Their bags had been stowed there, with her shabby suitcase in place of pride on the ottoman at the foot of the bed.

Opening the first of the two magnificent mahogany wardrobes, which had an empty rail and a few free shelves, she began to unpack, noticing how shabby and shapeless her garments looked in contrast to the plush fabrics and fine knits of Vaughn's clothing. She added her five pairs of shoes to the rail below, alongside ranks of his burnished leather footwear. Her sneakers were so scuffed and dirty that she moved them all the way to the back, feeling ashamed.

She heard the solid 'thunk' of the front door open and realized to her excitement that Vaughn was back. Abandoning her task, she rushed to the hallway to meet him.

He was still with Howard, she saw, to her surprise.

"Hello, babes!" he greeted her. "I missed you. I wish you'd come with us to the club. I'm sure you would have had more fun than at lunch, but I couldn't disappoint my mother."

Striding over to her, he slung an arm around her. As he kissed her, she inhaled a distinctive whiff of beer.

"How did the tennis go?" Stella asked, feeling amused. Vaughn wasn't a day drinker. Had he been drowning his sorrows or celebrating victory, she wondered.

"We won our games, so we'll be back next week for round two," he grinned.

"Come on," Howard said impatiently.

Vaughn turned back to him.

"Give me a minute, bro. I need to grab a jacket. So will Stella. And a hat, maybe."

"Where are we going?" Stella asked. It sounded like there was another outing planned, and her heart sank. She'd been looking forward to enjoying some time with Vaughn, unpacking together, and perhaps going somewhere local for dinner.

"We're heading out on the yacht this afternoon," Vaughn told her, looking pleased.

"The yacht?" What yacht? Did the family actually own one? Stella felt thrown. Was there no limit to their wealth?

"Our yacht," Vaughn confirmed. "I'm so excited you'll be seeing it at last. Everyone loves the parties we have aboard."

"We need to get down to the harbor now. Dad said three p.m. and you know what he's like. He'll head out without us," Howard urged.

"He will. He's done it before. Come on, Stella, let's go."

Vaughn grabbed a padded jacket from off the coat stand, and Stella rushed back to the bedroom. She would have liked to have changed. A flimsy dress wasn't practical gear for heading out on the ocean, but there was no time now, so she grabbed the newer of her two summer jackets – which didn't match the dress – and a baseball cap which was all she possessed in the way of headgear and also, definitely, didn't pair with the dress.

Hopefully she could manage without the hat, she thought, stuffing it into her purse and hustling back along the corridor.

They piled into the car waiting outside. It was a Maserati SUV which was also driven by a driver, Stella saw, feeling bemused.

Vaughn glanced at her and saw her looking.

"You know what they say about drinking and driving," he said amiably as they piled into the spacious back seat. "Take us to the yacht club," he told the driver, who was a different man from the one who'd picked them up from the airport.

25

"Yeah. What they say. Sometimes different from what they do. Ask Elmer," Howard joked.

Stella listened carefully. Finally, the black sheep was being discussed.

"Absolutely," Vaughn snorted with laughter. "Tree: one point; parked car: zero; BMW: minus one."

"He's never done it again," Howard said.

"Give him another few months and he'll have his nerve back."

"Nah, I reckon once was enough," Howard argued.

"In front of the cops, literally in front of the cops, once was too many times," Vaughn admitted.

So Elmer must be the family's problem child. He'd crashed into another car in the presence of the police while under the influence?

What had happened next, she wondered. She wanted to ask but thought she'd rather get Vaughn to update her in private. Definitely, Elmer would have been in a lot of trouble. Perhaps he was even in jail. What a shock that must have been for this perfect family with their high social standing.

Troubled, Stella stared out of the window, watching as the harbor gates approached. The driver bypassed the parking lot, crammed with luxury cars, and headed to the drop-off zone outside the impressive main entrance.

"We'll send you a message when we're coming in. It may be late," Vaughn told the driver casually as he climbed out.

The fresh sea breeze tugged at Stella's hair and ruffled the hem of her skirt, sending ripples of cold air up her legs. This was definitely the wrong attire, but, as she stared up at the yacht's gleaming white hull in astonishment, she realized that she would be able to sit indoors where it was warmer. This was no basic boat but more like a luxury sea-going hotel.

While she'd had a vague idea that Vaughn's father would skipper the ship, there was in fact a uniformed captain waiting to welcome her aboard and give her a hand up the wide gangplank.

"Come to the side deck. You get a great view of the harbor from there," Vaughn said.

Beyond the gangplank stood a waitress wearing a white pants suit, her blonde hair shielded by a blue and white sailing cap. She was holding a tray of tall champagne flutes.

Looking at her, Stella was transported back to her all-too-recent days of doing student jobs. She could have been this waitress. In fact, serving champagne at the finance company's year-end party had been how she'd met Vaughn, who'd just arrived in town. She wondered if he remembered that, as he grabbed two glasses and headed over to the railing.

"Remember, that was you, back in Chicago. Prettiest waitress ever," Vaughn observed, and Stella felt thrilled he had also been thinking about that magical evening. They'd both agreed afterwards that the attraction, the spark between them, had been instant.

With Vaughn's arm warmly around her, she watched as the yacht sailed majestically out of the harbor. Once they had reached the open ocean, with the boat listing ever so slightly in the swells, they increased the speed.

Stella would have been happy to spend the entire trip on the railing, but she started to feel cold. Shivering, she pressed herself against Vaughn. A moment later, she heard Cecilia's authoritative voice from behind.

"Here are the two lovebirds. The newly engaged couple! Meet Stella."

She turned to see a group of people approaching. Cecilia led the way, followed by Kathy and Grace. Two pretty, young women followed them.

"Stella, come here."

She stepped reluctantly out of Vaughn's arms and crossed the deck to meet them.

"I'd like to introduce some of our good family friends. This is Haydi, who grew up down the road from us and went to school with Vaughn."

The slender caramel-blonde, with diamond earrings sparkling in her ears, gave Stella a friendly nod.

"How lovely to meet you, Stella. Vaughn is such a close friend; he's like family. I'm sure you will be, too," she smiled.

"This is Mary-Ann, who was born on the same day as Elmer. We always used to have to decide in advance whose birthday party would be on which weekend," Cecilia said, laughing. Quietly, she added to Stella, "She's Vaughn's most recent ex-girlfriend. They dated for a short while before he left for Chicago. You'll meet a few of his previous girlfriends, as time goes by, moving in our circles." Cecilia's whisper carried a hint of satisfaction, as if she was pleased to deliver this unwanted information to his new fiancée.

Stella felt a pang. She hadn't expected to bump into any of them so soon, if at all. Mary-Ann was startlingly attractive, with long, gorgeously styled copper curls and brilliant green eyes. She gave Stella a charming smile, even though there wasn't much warmth to it, and then turned to Vaughn for a friendly hug and a kiss on the lips that made Stella's stomach clench.

Cecilia grasped her wrist firmly.

"Come on in and socialize. There are cocktails in the lounge, and then we're heading to the upper deck for a seafood barbecue."

The sumptuously decorated lounge, decked out in wood and brass, was a hubbub of noise, laughter, and music. And at least it was a little warmer than the breezy outdoors.

A waiter offered her a tray containing several glasses with different, colorful cocktails but she shook her head in polite refusal.

"Look who's here! My rebel brother Elmer," Vaughn called from behind her.

Stella glanced around to see Vaughn sling an arm over the shoulder of a leaner, wilder-looking version of him.

"Elmer, meet my beloved. Stella, meet this reprobate!" Vaughn performed the introduction with a laugh.

There was something weird about Elmer, Stella decided, as he moved in to give her a clumsy hug. He looked out of it, and his pupils were dilated. Remembering what Vaughn had said about the drunk driving, Stella wondered uneasily whether he might be high. He definitely didn't look right, but there wasn't any time to observe him further. Not when a shriek from behind caused her to turn hurriedly.

"Stella! You are wearing the same dress you had on at lunch! And that denim jacket is very light. You're going to catch cold. It gets chilly here in the evenings. Have you not been out on a boat before?" Kathy asked, staring at her critically. She'd changed into trendily bejeweled jeans and plush boots and was wearing a cozy and expensive looking jacket, holding a sunset-colored cocktail.

"There wasn't time to change," Stella explained.

"How long does it take to throw on a pair of long pants? A minute?" Kathy stared at her critically. "Vaughn said you're a grad student. That's not very intelligent behavior, is it?"

Stella literally stepped back, shocked by the unexpected sharpness of the words.

She drew an annoyed breath, ready to snap back that insulting someone you'd just met wasn't very polite behavior. But as she was about to speak, Elmer jostled past them. He cannoned forward, bumping against Kathy.

"Mind where you're walking," Kathy snapped in his direction, sounding annoyed as she steadied her cocktail glass. "If you can call it walking. Just get to the bathroom and sort yourself out." She called after him in a louder voice, "Let me know if you need to borrow my credit card for anything, since the bank has frozen yours recently, I hear."

Stella stared at her, horrified. Then she turned to gaze in concern as Elmer headed unsteadily for the discreet, silver-signposted restrooms. Kathy was implying Elmer was actually going to snort a line right there on the boat?

Maybe the sharp-tongued blonde was just joking and Elmer had drunk one cocktail too many, she tried to reassure herself.

But she hadn't sounded as if she was joking at all. What did it mean if Kathy was serious? Did the whole family know about his habit, and were they enabling him, she wondered uneasily?

CHAPTER SIX

Kathy grabbed Stella's hand. "Your fingers are icy," she told her impatiently, as if pointing out a personal failing.

She tapped the shoulder of a passing waiter. "Go to the second guest cabin." As the waiter looked blankly at her, Kathy continued impatiently, "The one at the end of the upper-level corridor. Bring a warm coat for this guest. There are a few spares in the closet there."

The waiter nodded and hurried away.

"Thank you," Stella said, grateful to see Kathy's kind side. Perhaps the earlier snide comment had just been her attempt at humor.

"Come up to the outside deck. It's where we have the seafood barbecue as it has the best view. You need to socialize with the family," Kathy urged. "Vaughn is already out there with my son, Jeff. I don't think you've met him yet. He works with Vaughn at Mike's finance firm."

Climbing the stairs, Stella heard Vaughn's loud guffaws resounding around the noisy upper deck. He was on the far side of the deck with his father and another similar looking man with the same air of supreme confidence who must be the hedge fund-owning uncle. She guessed the younger man standing with them was Jeff, Kathy's son. As she watched, Howard strolled over to join them.

Despite the cold wind which immediately tugged at her hair and skirt, Stella was enraptured by the view. Out here on the open sea there was a panoramic view of the harbor. Now fully dark, the lights were twinkling in every shade of gold. With the music pumping and the sizzle of barbecuing seafood filling the air, she reminded herself that this was meant to be a fun evening. She should enjoy it and must try and stop being so tense and worried.

"Stella! Come here!" Cecilia grasped her sleeve, drawing her into a group of women just as Stella was about to head across the deck toward the men.

Giving her a friendly wave, Vaughn yelled to Elmer, who was emerging from a side staircase.

"Hey, hey, hey, bro! This way!"

Elmer dashed over, swerving to avoid a waiter and jostling his tray in the process. A glass of champagne toppled from the tray and smashed on the hull.

He did look high, Stella thought uncomfortably.

"Breakage will be docked from your wages," Elmer mocked, half-vaulting the rail as he grabbed a pale-colored cocktail from the array on the sideboard. The other men roared with laughter as the waiter put his tray down and rushed to clear the mess.

"Stella! Have you had a seafood skewer? You need to eat. This spread is excellent," Cecilia invited her.

The group she had joined consisted of Grace and two other attractive, ageless, blonde strangers who Cecilia introduced as her cousins Helena and Lucinda. Haydi and Kathy were standing and whispering nearby. A waiter passed her a silver platter piled with steaming, fragrant seafood skewers. She took one and held it, waiting before she ate in case anyone started speaking to her.

"One of the first things you need to do is get a new wardrobe," Cecilia advised her.

"I will," Stella said, trying not to shiver visibly, and thinking guiltily of the steps she'd have to take before having any spare spending money. She wasn't going to let Vaughn finance her basic needs. She was not! In any case, the caliber of clothing these people wore would be way beyond her budget even when she had a job.

"Tell her to use Easton's," Lucinda advised.

"Easton's is my favorite place," Helena agreed.

Cecilia nodded. "That's a good idea. They supply the best variety of top brands. She can go there later in the week."

"Why does she have to go in? Can't you get someone from there to come here?" Helena said, sounding surprised.

"Not with the amount of clothing she'll need," Cecilia explained. Turning to Stella she continued, "They're a private outfitter with an office in town. We have a family account there. Go any time during the week and ask for Danni. Tell her you need a selection of casual and semi-formal clothing and a few gowns for evening wear. You don't have any of those yet, do you?"

Stella shook her head, feeling humiliated.

"And some shoes. You'll need a couple of pairs for every occasion."

"Shoes are so important. You can't wear the same ones out twice in a row. People notice," Helena added.

31

"Danni will know what to set you up with. Tell her to dress you to the value of about fifty thousand. There's no need to go beyond that for now," Cecilia said.

Helena nodded in agreement.

Fifty thousand? Dollars? For a basic starter wardrobe? Stella's mind reeled at the impossibility of this amount. She steeled herself, summoning the courage she needed to refuse this offer.

"That's so kind of you. The thought of all that clothes shopping sounds amazing. And the shoes, of course! But I'd rather wait until I have a job and buy them myself, even if it takes a while. I'd feel better being able to afford my own outfits."

Cecilia stared at her, and Stella couldn't read her expression. She felt a pang of fear that she'd maybe gone too far and offended her future mother-in-law. But then Cecilia spoke again, with a sympathetic smile.

"Vaughn mentioned that you were independent and proud and you're certainly proving to be. Both qualities I admire. However, you need to look the part, or you'll be letting him down. Remember, the functions and parties that you will be attending are not just social events. Business is done there, too. Many of Mike's clients are from our local area."

Cecilia's tone told Stella that she was not to be argued with. In any case, she couldn't oppose this logic. She didn't want to embarrass Vaughn or compromise his business prospects by having an inadequate wardrobe.

Filled with a sense of shame, she realized that she was already being forced to take hand-outs from this family, despite resolving that she would never accept a thing from them.

"Madam," a voice said from behind.

She turned to find the waiter there, holding a warm, padded coat.

Quickly, Stella handed her uneaten food to another hovering waitress, and gratefully took the garment.

"Thank you so much," she smiled at the waiter.

As soon as he'd helped her put it on, he hurried away. Then, she felt the clasp of Kathy's fingers around her wrist.

"Don't thank the staff," Kathy said firmly to Stella in stern tones that sounded like a warning and not at all like the joke she thought for a confused moment this must surely be.

"Sorry, what?" she asked.

Kathy sighed, clearly annoyed by having to repeat herself.

"I said don't thank the staff. It's impossible to get good people these days, and it takes forever to train them to do things the way you want." Noticing Stella's astounded expression, she continued, "They're workers. Not our friends. They're not the caliber of person we'd socialize with. They're here to do a job and, apart from that, stay out of our way. If you start getting friendly with them, they take advantage, demand favors and special treatment, get lazy and slapdash. That's when the trouble starts. We've seen it time and again," she warned.

At some stage in the conversation, Lucinda had started listening in, and now added enthusiastically, "You have no idea what a mission it is to train maids to do things right when you have to fire one. It takes months. In fact, years. You'll see it for yourself soon, when you employ people of your own."

"Remember how angry Helena was when her neighbor poached her housekeeper?" Kathy giggled, and Lucinda snorted with laughter.

"I'm sure that was the main reason she sold up and moved!"

Stella felt thoroughly put off by this barrage of unwanted advice. Thanking someone was basic good manners, surely? It didn't make you anyone's friend, but rather created a pleasant atmosphere. How could you possibly not acknowledge someone for performing a task, even if they were paid for it?

She had to stand up for her beliefs.

"I don't think that's true," she argued, trying to keep her tone polite even though she could see Kathy was already bristling with anger at her comeback. "I've worked so many student jobs and being thanked by my bosses only made me want to try harder for them. So, if it's all right with you, I'll carry on doing it."

Looking enraged, Kathy turned away. She was clearly livid that Stella had dared to defy her.

What could she do to try and understand this family better, she wondered despairingly? Thinking so differently from them didn't help, and she was already rebelling against their rules rather than blindly accepting them. She'd have to watch what she said, keep her mouth shut and pick her battles, even though it went against her nature.

Across the deck, Vaughn downed a large cocktail before turning and waving to her. Relieved that he was heading over to join her at last, Stella waved back. But as he crossed the deck, Mary-Ann, going the other way, called out to him.

"This is our song! Remember?"

Grinning, Vaughn wrapped her in his arms and started dancing drunkenly, his arms snaking around her waist. She squealed in mock-terror as he lifted her into the air, crushing her against him, nuzzling and growling into her neck.

Stella gazed in dismay. This was unacceptable. She'd never known Vaughn to behave this way, and she felt betrayed as she watched him. Although he was very drunk, groping another woman was absolutely out of line. With a flash of anger, she decided to give him a piece of her mind, right now, and tell him to keep his hands to himself.

But, as she marched forward, Kathy's voice cut through the music from behind her, causing her to pause.

"Let him be! It's only play. Or are you too insecure to let your fiancé hug another woman?" She stared at Stella triumphantly, and with challenge in her eyes. The message was clear. If Stella defied her again, she'd be setting herself up for a major feud.

CHAPTER SEVEN

Stella swung around to face Kathy. Her words were even more hurtful than Vaughn's actions. Vaughn was behaving badly during a moment of drunken merriment. But Kathy was deliberately taunting her. What was with this family? They seemed toxic.

Then, from her other side, she heard Cecilia's bell-like voice.

"Stella, you don't yet know what a playful man our Vaughn is. Such a joker and prankster. He's always been the same, and does it in a good spirit," she soothed.

Stella didn't buy that. But at that moment, to her relief, Vaughn let go of Mary-Ann and turned toward her, heading her way at a meandering walk.

As self-realization penetrated his drunken haze, she saw he looked ashamed.

"Sorry, babes," he said, hiccupping slightly. "I'm so sorry. I shouldn't have done that. We have – had – this thing that I always tickle her when that song comes on. I mean, even before we dated, I used to do that. But I can see you're upset. It was just a stupid joke, honestly, and it won't happen again."

The apology dissolved Stella's anger. Better still, Kathy was looking shocked by it, as if she'd been slapped in the face.

"It's okay," she smiled back, even though she still felt unsettled, both by how unlike himself he had acted, and by Kathy's bullying behavior. Was Kathy drunk, too, she wondered? Thinking back, she realized she hadn't seen her without a drink in her hand the whole evening, so that was a real probability.

Nothing like too much alcohol for creating fault lines in family relationships, she decided wryly.

"Shall we go?" Vaughn asked, slinging an arm around her shoulders and drawing her away from the group. "It's getting late, and I'm totaled. What a day. From winning at tennis, which was easy, to winning a drinking game with Jeff which nearly wrecked me, I feel like it's time to turn in. We're back in the harbor now so we can disembark any time."

"Good idea. Let's go," Stella agreed, thankful that the long day had finally ended.

After calling the driver, Vaughn stumbled down the gangplank ahead of her. He wove his way through the yacht club, which was now almost empty, and out to the pickup zone at the front entrance.

The Range Rover was already pulling up smoothly. Vaughn collapsed into the back.

"That was a hectic evening. What a killer. I haven't drunk so much since – since before I left for Chicago," he said.

"You're going to feel terrible tomorrow," Stella said, worried by the reek of alcohol still on his breath.

"Yeah. My own fault. But being back with my dreadful family would drive anyone to drink!" he slurred.

She didn't think he was joking. Stressful as the evening had been for her, she guessed that it had been for him, too. At any rate she was glad he'd also found some of the family's behavior to be out of line.

His words made her hopeful that if they both felt this way, perhaps they could move elsewhere. An image of them, living happily in a small house in an ordinary suburb, flitted into her mind.

Then they could be like a normal couple.

She glanced down at her ring again, remembering how happy she'd been the day he'd put it on her finger.

Now, she was alarmed to see that the diamond looked loose in its setting.

It wasn't just her hands, which were shaky from tiredness. Touching it gently, she realized it felt wobbly.

Had it been because of Kathy's fiddling with it at the ladies' lunch, she wondered angrily. She'd need to take it to a jeweler and get it secured in its setting again.

"Here we are. Home at last."

They were already pulling up outside the cottage. She scrambled out and they went inside. Stella walked straight to the bedroom. Rummaging in the bedside drawer, she found where she'd put the ring's velvet box. She took the box out, put the ring inside, and placed it on the top of the bookcase.

Then she headed eagerly to the bathroom for her long-awaited shower. Turning the water as hot as it would go, she steamed away the last of the chills from the boat, soaping herself with the luxurious gel on the glass shelf.

When she stepped out again to dry herself, she heard the splash of liquid into glass coming from the kitchen.

At least Vaughn was hydrating, which would hopefully help what was likely to be a monster hangover. But, when Stella peeked into the kitchen, she was shocked to see him carrying a glass of whisky to the dining room.

"Vaughn!" she called, hearing the irate sharpness in her voice.

He glanced around guiltily, spilling a splash on the tiles.

Now he, too, sounded annoyed.

"What is it, babes?"

"Have you forgotten you've got to be at work tomorrow?" she asked, hearing the outrage in her own voice. Had he reached that stage of being drunk where he couldn't think clearly at all?

"You want to control me?" Startled, she sensed aggression in his tone. Never before had he sounded that way.

"What's control got to do with it? You have *work* tomorrow!" she shot back angrily.

For a moment, Vaughn glared mutinously at her and then, suddenly, backed down.

"Look, I'm just having a nightcap to de-stress," he continued in a calmer, though still slurred, voice. "I'll be in bed in a minute."

Feeling upset, Stella shrugged and turned away. He was too drunk to reason with, and clearly too drunk to stop drinking. She'd just have to hope he made it into bed and didn't throw up all over the sheets.

Pulling the covers grumpily up as she lay alone in the bed, she was sure that she wouldn't manage to close her eyes until Vaughn joined her. But, feeling exhausted by everything the day had brought, she fell asleep almost immediately.

*

"You want to control me?" The words echoed in her mind, dragging her out of slumber. *"You want to control me?"*

Vaughn was standing over her, his face flushed with anger, his features drawn in a grimace of wrath. Staring up at him in horror, Stella realized how ugly he was, how intimidated she felt as he loomed over her, how club-like his hands were as he reached for her. It reminded her of the time when her own mother had done the same, turned on her in a fit of rage, with the kitchen knife grasped in her hand.

Suddenly Stella felt ten years old again – small, lonely, and terrified.

"Help me!" she cried, but he didn't respond. Instead, she heard Cecilia's bell-like laugh. She was there, peering over his shoulder, her porcelain skin mottled in dull blue, her fingernails sharpened into bloody claws.

"We know where your father is," she taunted. "We took him! We've locked him away and will never let him out again. He's our prisoner now. Just like you!"

"No!" Stella shrieked. "Let him go! Let me out!"

She sat bolt upright in bed, her breath coming in harsh gasps. Then she stared around in confusion as the nightmare's grip loosened, replaced by the gray light of early morning.

The dream had felt so real. Certainly, her terror had been genuine.

Where had those thoughts come from? She guessed it had been from that weird aggressive moment last night. That had been so uncharacteristic of Vaughn, and not like him at all. They'd never exchanged an angry word in Chicago, but now it had happened. She had known it would be inevitable at some stage – no relationship was perfect - but she hated conflict. Hated it! The dream must have been her subconscious processing her feelings.

Fearful that it might happen again, she turned to stare at Vaughn. Snoring beside her, his face was innocent in sleep, and bore no resemblance to the monster in her nightmare.

As she watched, he opened his eyes.

He gave the broad, drowsy smile she was used to seeing, and she felt a huge burden of worry lift off her. This was the man she loved. He was back to normal again, if somewhat hung over.

"What's the time?" Sleepily Vaughn reached for his phone. Scanning the screen, his eyes widened in alarm.

"I told Uncle Mike I'd be in the office at eight. What was I thinking?" He sat up and winced. "My head!"

Stella laughed. "Well, you let off a lot of steam last night," she joked. "Where can I find the Advil?"

"There's a pack in here. Or there was, at any rate." Vaughn opened the bedside drawer. "Yes. Still there."

"I'll get you some water."

Climbing out of bed, Stella trod over the cool, polished tiles to the kitchen. She hadn't explored any of these gleaming wooden cupboards yet. Experimentally, she opened a few. All were well stocked with top-end crockery and equipment. The fourth one she tried was filled with crystal glasses.

Returning on her mercy mission, she watched as Vaughn gulped the tablets down.

"What are you doing today, gorgeous?" he asked. "Is there anywhere you want to explore on your own? Perhaps I can join you later."

"Let's leave sightseeing for next weekend. It'll be more fun with you. Today, I think I'll go and visit Rebecca." Her best friend had moved to New Jersey two years ago after getting a job in New York. Since then, she'd also been married.

"Your school friend? She lives near here?"

Stella nodded. "She got married last year and lives in New Brunswick with her husband. I said I'd come around to see them as soon as I could. I'm going to message her now to make sure."

Quickly, Stella sent a text. Almost immediately, the reply buzzed through, complete with a row of smiley emojis.

"Great. We're on for lunch," Stella said happily. "Do you know where the closest car rental place is?"

Vaughn shook his head. "No, no, babes. You don't need to rent a car. We have, like, five spare cars just standing in the garages. Take one."

Stella felt herself bristle defensively, reminded again of that awkward conversation about her wardrobe last night. Well, nobody should care what car she drove when heading out to visit a friend.

"I can afford to hire a car. I'd rather do that."

Vaughn frowned. "Please, babes. If my mother finds out you hired a car when there are vehicles available she'll be upset. You're part of the family now. These are family vehicles. It's better that you use them." He stared at her worriedly.

With a sigh, Stella decided it would be better to put her pride aside and keep the peace.

"In that case, I'll take one. That's really generous of your family," she said.

"I'll organize it. Let me shower first." Vaughn stood up, grasped his forehead again with a groan, and shambled off in the direction of the bathroom.

While he showered, Stella bathed in the other bathroom that this well-equipped cottage contained. It, too, was fully stocked with high-end products. Shower gel, soap, expensive shampoo and conditioner. There was even a set of facial and body care products. It was like being in a hotel, she thought, drying herself on the oversized fluffy towel and hustling back to the bedroom to change. Hotel life would have to do for now, but it wasn't the way she wanted to live.

"The car will be outside in five minutes." Vaughn said when she walked back into the bathroom. He was dressed and ready to go, looking smart in black pants and a pale blue Ralph Lauren dress shirt.

"Are you sure you don't need breakfast first? There's a Sunday spread set up at the main house from nine a.m."

Stella shook her head. "I'd rather go now and get back earlier. What time do you think you'll be done?"

Vaughn shrugged. "Uncle Mike was talking about the morning, but I guess I can't rule out a couple of hours more."

"Well, if you don't get back in time for the beach walk, we'll see each other in the evening, then," she smiled.

Perhaps they could cook together in this well-equipped kitchen tonight, Stella thought hopefully, deciding to pick up some food on the way back.

Running gelled fingers through his hair, Vaughn completed his transformation to the smartly groomed, preppy looking man she adored.

"I'll go over to the house. Enjoy your day." Slinging an arm around her, Vaughn gave her a quick kiss before striding out of the cottage. Stella felt a rush of delight at the affectionate gesture.

She headed outside, hesitating when she saw a pristine silver Range Rover waiting there. She would so much rather have hired a zippy little Ford as a less risky, and cheaper, option. Having this car for the day was a big responsibility.

After taking a minute to figure out the Range Rover's controls, she programmed the route. Then, finally, she set off.

As she drove, she started to relax and get used to the car. She found to her surprise that she was enjoying herself. It was a perfect spring day, she was heading through a gloriously beautiful part of the world, and she was driving a comfortable vehicle that felt safe and easy to handle. Best of all, she was leaving behind her intimidating surroundings and her new family-to-be with their strange ways and going to see her best friend.

Perhaps Rebecca, who'd been married for a year now, would be able to give her some good relationship advice.

But, as she had that thought, Stella decided she shouldn't talk about some of what had happened. The heavy drinking, Vaughn groping his ex, and that weird moment of aggression he had shown last night – she decided those were better put out of her mind and not discussed.

After all, they were only due to the stress of Vaughn being back with his family after so long. She was sure they'd never happen again.

CHAPTER EIGHT

An hour and a half after leaving Greenwich, Stella pulled up in a quiet backstreet in New Brunswick, New Jersey. These were the surroundings she was used to, she thought with relief. Compact, pretty houses, cars parked in the street, a relaxed and homely feel. The Range Rover felt overly bulky, and Stella frowned in concentration as she wedged it into an available space, with the parking sensors clamoring at her.

By the time she'd gotten it safely into the gap, Rebecca had seen her. The blue-painted door of the tiny house was open, and Rebecca herself was pacing out onto the street. She looked well, Stella thought as she climbed out of the car. Her green eyes were sparkling and her red hair, which had been longer the last time they'd seen each other, was trimmed into a flattering, jaw-length bob.

"You're here! I don't believe it! It's been two years, so how come it feels like yesterday?" she asked, as they hugged each other tightly.

"I know. Where did the time go?" Stella replied.

"You're looking thin and beautiful. We need to feed you up with a good lunch. And these wheels?" Taking a step back, whistling under her breath, Rebecca admired the car. "Where did these come from? Yours? Or did you borrow Vaughn's car for the day?"

Stella sighed, feeling uneasy again as she got her purse out and locked up.

"It's one of his family's cars."

Rebecca's eyebrows rose. "Really? This is, like, a spare?"

"I guess so," she admitted.

"Well! Come on in," Rebecca said. "You'll have to excuse the state of the house. We've both been working flat out. But even so, we've managed to fit in quality time on weekends together, so at least we have a good life balance!"

Her smile and the tone of her voice confirmed her words. Stella could see that her best friend had never been happier.

"Welcome to our humble abode," she laughed, leading the way inside.

Following her, Stella felt a weird sense of disorientation, as if she'd settled back into reality after waking from a dream. This was how a home should be. The tiny house felt friendly. It was cluttered, even though she knew that Rebecca would have tidied up, ready for her arrival. The hall table was crowded with printouts and folders that looked to be social media related, which meant they were from Rebecca's work. Marco had landed a well-paying IT job last year, she remembered.

Through the open kitchen door, she saw the fridge was studded with magnets and photographs and notes. Atop it, a tabby cat stared curiously down at Stella.

There wasn't an inch of spare space in this compact home, and Stella couldn't help comparing it to the oversized rooms in her new abode. She had so much space, high ceilings, pristine finishes. Nothing out of place, nor a speck of dust anywhere.

But no pets, she suddenly realized. No animals. Perhaps the Marshalls didn't like them. She'd always wanted a cat. Now, living on the same property as her future parents-in-law, she was wondering whether owning a pet would be permitted.

"We generally spend our time in the kitchen, as it has a view over our yard. Which, I have to admit, needs some work," Rebecca joked.

Stella sat at one of the four chairs crowded around the kitchen table. The sash window looked out over a tiny, overgrown square of greenery. Herbs and roses sprouted from a medley of pots. A creeper climbed the back wall, providing a colorful splash of blooms among the wooden fence posts.

"Where's Marco?" she asked.

"He went shopping. We've been so busy the past couple of days that there's not a bite of food in the house, apart from Stripe's kibble." She gestured affectionately toward the cat, but it was the mention of Marco that caused her face to light up.

Stella was astonished to feel a pang of envy at her friend's evident happiness.

She caught herself immediately, feeling horrified. There was no reason to be in the least jealous of Rebecca. Not when she'd been swept off her feet by the man of her dreams. It was just that the situation with her and Vaughn, being so different, required more adjustments. That was all. She was sure that in a year, they'd be as happy as Rebecca and Marco.

At that moment the front door opened, and the dark-haired Marco walked in, hefting four heavy looking shopping bags.

"Hey, Stella! How good to see you!"

She and Rebecca stood up and grabbed a bag each, placing them on the table before Marco gave her a big, friendly hug.

"Are there any more bags?" Rebecca asked.

Marco shook his head. "You know the rules, hon. A man can only make one trip between the car and the house to bring in groceries. Not more than that, even if it kills him." He rubbed his fingers regretfully as Stella laughed.

With Marco's warm presence and personality, the kitchen felt crowded, but in a fun, friendly way. Stella hadn't had much of a chance to spend time with Marco. And Rebecca had only met Vaughn during a lightning lunch when she'd been in Chicago for work a month ago.

As they unpacked the shopping bags, Stella was struck by how harmonious the dynamic was between the three of them, and what an easygoing and likeable person Marco was. Rebecca's gentle teasing and banter with her husband was on a totally different level from the acid sarcasm that characterized the Marshalls' interactions.

"Mayonnaise! You bought mayonnaise?" Rebecca asked, surprised, as she took it out of the bag.

"They had it on special," Marco explained apologetically.

"But didn't we promise we were going to give it up, for health and slimness reasons?" Rebecca queried, raising her eyebrows.

"That was before we had a VIP guest. I thought to myself, I'm sure Stella needs mayonnaise. It would have been wrong not to add it to the cart. I mean, there's no call for us to eat the whole jar just because it's in the fridge. We can leave it there."

Rebecca reached out a hand and tickled him mercilessly on his side. Marco swung away, his laughter carrying a hint of panic.

"I hope you like mayo with your pastrami salad roll," Rebecca said.

"Definitely," Stella agreed. "I'm with Marco on this one."

"You got us good coffee, you angel, so we can have a cup now," Rebecca smiled at her husband.

"I was thinking of going for a quick run with Joey and Ben. They're leaving in ten minutes. Would that work for you?" Marco asked.

"Go ahead. It'll give us time to catch up before lunch," Rebecca encouraged.

"See you soon!" Marco headed out. Rebecca put the coffee on, and they sat down again.

"You look so happy," Stella said. Despite the shoebox-sized house and the insane hours they were both obviously working, her friend was literally fizzing with happiness.

"Honestly, life is so full of joy. And insanity, but mostly joy. Despite the fact I'm working so hard and poor Marco is under the gun at his IT firm, we're both in such a supportive mindset that the work just seems to fly by. And we're having such fun together."

Rebecca passed her a cup of coffee.

"Now that you're closer, we'll be able to see each other much more often. In fact, Marco and I are planning a hiking vacation in July. Not staying in a tent, of course. I don't do tents! I was thinking of basing ourselves in a local hotel somewhere gorgeous, or maybe going inn-to-inn, and doing a different route each day. Do you think it sounds fun? Could you and Vaughn join us, even for a night or two?"

Stella made a face. The timing was all wrong. Vaughn would probably be working flat out at his hedge fund. She'd surely have a job by then, but it would be too soon to take any leave.

Firmly, she put out of her mind the thought that this didn't sound like the kind of vacation Vaughn would enjoy. She was sure he'd love it; it was just that they wouldn't be able to get away.

"Things might not be settled by then. I still have to find work, and when I do, I can't really ask for time off immediately," she confessed.

"I'm sure you'll find work easily. Just make sure it's a job you love, and don't settle for second best."

"You sound like Clem!" Stella joked.

"I know you too well," Rebecca warned.

"I guess you're right. After having to turn down my dream job, I'm already panicking I'm unemployable," she admitted.

"You've only just moved. Give it some time. And how's it going with Vaughn?"

Stella smiled, determined to focus on everything that was good and positive about her new life.

"Wonderful. Obviously it's a lot different. He lives on a massive property. We're in the cottage, which is a short walk from the main house, and not really a cottage at all. It's more like a mansion. There are two huge bedrooms, two huge bathrooms, a dining room, two lounges, and an enormous kitchen. I'm hoping it will give me the chance to improve my cookery skills."

"They do need some work. Remember that time you burned the baked beans and we had to spend an hour scouring the pan before your mother came home?" Rebecca laughed.

Stella rolled her eyes at the memory.

"But how do you feel about being so close to his family?" Rebecca continued, sounded dubious.

Stella sighed. "It's okay. I mean, the grounds are enormous. But I'm hoping that once we're married, and I have a job, we can move out and stay on our own. He's the oldest of four and the others all seem to live at home still, so it's not as if the parents will have empty nest syndrome," she said.

Rebecca nodded sympathetically. "You need to make your own life, definitely. Are the others still studying?"

"I'm not sure." Stella sipped her coffee, feeling floored by the question. What *did* they do? "I think Howard might be studying."

"I guess they don't have to do anything, being so rich," Rebecca said. Her tone was joking – almost.

"Well, Vaughn is a workaholic and determined to succeed in his job," Stella said.

"He's very determined," Rebecca agreed.

There was that note in her voice again.

"What?" Stella demanded.

Rebecca sighed. "Nothing. I'm really happy for you and I think Vaughn is a very motivated and driven person."

Bemused, Stella wondered what was wrong. Something was, for sure, the way her friend was speaking. Could she be jealous, she wondered briefly? She hoped it wasn't jealousy. Surely such a thing could never affect their friendship.

Then another idea occurred to her. Perhaps it was the opposite of jealousy.

"Are you worried because they're so wealthy?"

Rebecca grimaced. Then she nodded reluctantly.

"I don't trust his family, Stella."

"How do you mean?" Stella probed.

"I know you and Vaughn have had a whirlwind romance, but every time I think about it, I find myself getting anxious. I start thinking – what will happen to you?"

Stella felt hurt by that statement but suppressed it as she tried to reassure her friend.

"You don't have to worry. Vaughn actually complained about his family to me last night. It reassured me that he will agree to move away."

Rebecca made a doubtful face. "Complaining is one thing. Doing it is another. Especially as he's the oldest son. He has his inheritance to think of, doesn't he? I've seen how families hold their children to ransom in that regard."

"Why should they do that because of me?" Stella asked, feeling uneasy.

"Isn't it obvious? You're bright and intelligent and very independent. You already have different ideas for you and Vaughn than they planned. Not exactly the kind of wife they want in their circles, I'm sure."

"You think?" Stella said.

She could hear the doubt in her own voice. There was truth in what her friend said, especially when she remembered yesterday's conversations, and how the women discussed only their material possessions, their families, how they were spending their money.

Rebecca nodded firmly. "I'm concerned that you won't have an easy ride."

"Well, I'm different. They'll have to accept that," Stella shot back.

She had the disturbing feeling she wasn't only arguing this point for Rebecca's benefit. Her own insecurities and fears were surfacing all over again.

"That's the problem. You're too perceptive. You'll see them for who they are, skeletons and all. See through their superficiality. And they will sense that and won't like it."

"I'm positive this family doesn't have any skeletons," Stella laughed, glad to be back on firmer footing. "That's one thing I don't have to worry about. With Vaughn's father an ex-senator and all."

Rebecca sighed.

"You've never been naïve. Don't let them fool you. And more importantly, don't let your loyalty to Vaughn make you fool yourself, because I think that's what's happening right now. You know people who have influence can get away with more. Power corrupts, right?"

"Why are you being so negative?" Stella glared at her friend.

The warning frown was wasted on Rebecca, who'd never been scared to speak her mind, from the very first moment Stella had set eyes on her as a lanky, flame-headed twelve-year-old. She'd received a detention on the first day at her new school, she remembered.

"In the social media marketing company where I work, a lot of the staff are ex-journalists. You must hear the stories they tell about what they couldn't print about rich, powerful folk who used their position and status to protect themselves. The threats the journos received. The lawsuits. Things like case files disappearing. Evidence of bribery and corruption. They do what they please and money smoothes the way. I guarantee you that Mr. Marshall is the same, ex-senator or not."

Her voice was filled with contempt.

Stella thought uneasily of Elmer. There were circumstances surrounding his situation that she wasn't sure about. It was possible that he might recently have been in trouble with the law. What had happened?

For some reason, that uncertainty plunged her into denial. She found herself leaping to the Marshalls' defense.

"I like to think that I'm marrying into an honorable family," she retorted.

"Well, you're not," Rebecca shot back.

Stella clenched her hands. She wanted to yell at her friend for daring to voice these scathing and insulting views, that were making her feel so deeply uncomfortable.

In fact, she decided, she'd had enough of this disturbing conversation and didn't need to take any more insults. After giving Rebecca a piece of her mind, she was going to stand up, walk out, and head back home.

CHAPTER NINE

As she squared her feet on the floor, ready to jump to her feet, Stella realized with a shock how idiotic she was being.

She must be more stressed than she'd thought, if an argument with her best friend was making her overreact this way. How had things degenerated so fast, she wondered. They were about to actually fight. Over what, exactly?

She let out a deep breath and shifted in her seat, stretching her legs out, forcing the cramps in her shoulders to ease.

"Perhaps we should change the subject," she suggested, hearing the tension in her own voice.

Rebecca nodded apologetically. "I'm sorry, Stella. I didn't mean for this to escalate. I wish I'd never said anything."

"But you like Vaughn, don't you?" Stella asked, feeling anxious for her friend's agreement on this point at least.

"I've only met him once for a couple of hours," Rebecca said.

"Isn't that enough time to form an opinion?" Worry knotted her stomach.

Rebecca sighed. "I admit, I'm suspicious of who he is."

"So you don't like him?" Stella pressed.

Evading the question, Rebecca shook her head. "I don't dislike him, Stella. He just wasn't someone I connected with instantly. I would also like to think that his family are good people, but I suspect they are not."

"Why?" Stella probed.

"Okay, please don't get mad if I tell you this."

"I promise I won't." Finally, Stella hoped, she was getting to the real reason for Rebecca's mistrust.

"When I heard you were marrying Vaughn, I got one of my colleagues to check out his father. And they did find some irregular stuff."

"What?" Stella asked, alarmed. "Was it to do with his son, Elmer's, car crash?"

Rebecca shrugged. "Yes. There was a car incident I believe. You need to ask Vaughn the details. He'll be able to tell you more about it."

"I will," Stella sighed. She felt deeply uneasy that Vaughn's dad had been involved in anything shady. "Thanks for the heads-up on it, and sorry for being so defensive. You were right and I was wrong. It's another good reason for us to move out."

"Remember, powerful people can be very manipulative. When I was at lunch with you and Vaughn back in Chicago, I was wondering what would happen if his parents decided you weren't right for him. What if they gave him an ultimatum – his inheritance, or you? Which would he choose? It was going through my mind, and really freaking me out."

"He'd choose me, of course," Stella reassured her, but she couldn't prevent a flicker of doubt. Really? Would Vaughn really be able to turn his back on the massive wealth, the entitlement, the automatic ownership of so many good things that he'd grown up with?

She told herself to stop worrying, because his parents would never put him in such a situation.

In any case, it was time to change the subject. Thinking this way was stressing her out. She felt worried by how close she and her best friend had come to actually fighting.

What had gotten into her? She wasn't that kind of person at all.

*

As Stella drove back into Greenwich, she did her best to enjoy the spectacular sunset, but she was too distracted, still fretting over the conversation they'd had.

It was worrying in so many ways. Firstly, that Vaughn's father had some sort of shady history with the police, probably involving Elmer, the extent of which she didn't yet know. Secondly, that she hadn't picked this up herself. It had taken a near-fight with Rebecca for her to acknowledge it. Was she in denial, or turning a blind eye to things she'd usually notice?

Stella sighed. From now on she'd have to keep her eyes open and be honest with herself. She'd ask Vaughn about it at the right time and make sure she learned the truth.

In the meantime, she had a more practical challenge – preparing dinner. She wasn't a good cook. Her lack of skill in this area frustrated her. How could she pay so much attention to detail when writing a paper or doing research, but end up being hopelessly disorganized with timing in the kitchen? She didn't want to end up testing the cottage's smoke alarms, and knew she'd have to focus carefully if the pasta, shrimp, and sauce was to be a success, or even edible at all. This would be their first meal together in their new place, so the pressure was on.

She parked the car outside the house and let herself into the cottage.

From the silence that greeted her, Stella realized to her surprise that it was empty. Even so, she called out, "Vaughn? You home?"

Just more silence.

Feeling confused, she put the shopping bags in the kitchen, noticing the cottage had been tidied since they'd left. Heading through to the bedroom, she saw the bed had been immaculately made. Had Vaughn come home and gone over to the main house?

Rummaging in her purse, Stella found her phone and called him.

The phone rang and rang. She thought that it was going to go through to voicemail, but just before it did, Vaughn answered.

"Hey, babes! What's up?"

To her surprise, she heard loud music in the background. It didn't sound as if he was driving. Where was he?

"Just checking when you'll be home," she said.

He laughed. "Not for a while. We're out having drinks with clients. I'm sorry I didn't call you earlier. I thought we'd be leaving after one round but then Mike bought another. I'll be home as soon as possible. Love you!"

The call cut off abruptly. With a twist of her stomach, Stella realized that Vaughn had sounded drunk. And even though he'd said he loved her, he hadn't given her a time when he'd be home.

She bit her lip with frustration as she put her phone back in her purse.

So much for a romantic evening together. It would have to wait. There was no point in preparing dinner, as she wasn't hungry enough to cook for herself. Feeling sad as she packed the ingredients away, she decided to turn in early.

After showering and climbing into bed, she read for a while but couldn't focus on her book. Not when her gaze was being drawn again and again to the gold-framed clock that hung on the bedroom's side wall near the door.

The far wall was dominated by a massive, flat-screen television. Stella turned it on and surfed a few channels, hoping to distract herself from the clock-watching. But she couldn't stop worrying where Vaughn was, and whether anything had gone wrong.

At least he'd be using a driver and wouldn't have to find his own way back after a few drinks too many. That was one positive, she tried to console herself.

Eventually, with worry giving way to dull resignation, she turned off the TV and slipped into an uneasy doze.

It seemed like only a minute later that the smashing of glass startled her out of sleep. She sat up in bed, eyes wide in the darkness, hearing the sound of heavy, uneven footsteps.

What had happened? Was there an intruder? Her heart accelerated as she listened for any clues, while silently reaching for her phone.

Then she heard a dull but familiar sounding voice, letting out a slurred curse.

Stella exhaled slowly. Vaughn was home and must have dropped a glass. She should help clear it up, she thought, but then decided against it. He'd come home drunk. He'd broken it. Let him deal with his own mess.

Angrily, she turned onto her side and pulled the covers over her, while staying instinctively aware of every sound and movement he made.

He filled a new glass and drank deeply. Then he put the glass down with a sigh and stumbled to the bedroom.

Pressing her eyes tightly closed, Stella pretended to be asleep as he sunk heavily between the covers. The alcohol on his breath smelled raw and strong. She lay as still as possible so that he wouldn't think she was awake. She didn't want to speak to him. How she wished the evening had gone differently.

Then her sadness solidified into resolve.

First thing tomorrow, she was going to confront him about his behavior and set boundaries. She was going to tell him exactly what she thought about him getting falling-down-drunk while out with clients, and that if his uncle thought this was okay, he was nothing more than a damned enabler.

Then, she was going to have a serious talk about them moving out.

She was sure that his family's influence was a big part of the problem. She had to get him away from it.

CHAPTER TEN

The next morning, Stella woke up feeling nervous about the confrontation ahead.

Her stomach growled uneasily, and she realized this was more than nerves. Instead, she was feeling a low-grade nausea. Her head was pounding. She wondered if she'd picked up a bug from somewhere. It surely couldn't have been from the fresh, tasty cold meats and salad that she'd enjoyed yesterday at Rebecca's.

Staring at Vaughn, conflicting emotion surged through her as she saw his handsome features, his eyes closed in slumber, his wayward hair which he hadn't yet cut, tousled over his forehead.

Then, her stomach flip-flopped and she sat hastily upright.

The movement pulled Vaughn out of his uneasy sleep. He opened his eyes, which were swollen and bloodshot, and stared at her for a few moments in silence.

Despite feeling as if she was about to throw up, Stella got ready to steam ahead with what she had to say. But as she took a breath, another wave of nausea made her shut her mouth hastily. In the meantime, Vaughn spoke.

"Babes," he groaned. "Jeez, I'm sorry. I am so, so sorry. Last night was hectic. Mike and I visited one of our biggest clients' premises – it's a hotel and casino complex. We had to wait ages for him to be available and then he insisted on taking us for drinks and dinner. And then more drinks. I had no idea this was all going to happen and before I knew it, we were all ordering doubles. That casino owner is a borderline alcoholic, and I was stupid enough to keep pace with him."

Stella didn't know what to say. It felt unfair to lash out at him after his apology, but she needed him to know how she felt.

"I was upset when you didn't come home. This was going to be our first dinner in our new place, and I was looking forward to spending time with you. I didn't expect to go to bed alone and worried," she complained.

"I know. I was looking forward to being with you, too. I didn't expect this either. But work's work. What can I do? I have to go along with things. I don't have a choice at this stage."

"You do have a choice about how much to drink. Being that drunk is only going to cause trouble. Especially with work clients," she said.

He nodded, looking abashed. "You're absolutely right. I need to do things differently. If this happens again, I'll have one drink for politeness, and then switch to soda."

"Can I get you an Advil?" Despite herself, she made the offer.

"I need two. In fact, three. But don't go into the kitchen, babes. I dropped a tumbler last night in my drunken search for hydration," he snorted regretfully. "Fetch me water from the bathroom rather."

He hadn't cleaned it up?

"I'll sweep up the glass now," she said.

"No, no, there's no need. The maid will do it. Our staff have a whole technique for dealing with glass. They'll vacuum and so on, and make sure there are no splinters. Don't worry about it. You need to go to breakfast. I'll join you as soon as the meds have kicked in. I'm in too much pain to face my family now."

"Go to breakfast?" Stella was appalled. Now that she was sitting up, she felt seriously sick, and not at all like eating. Surely they could just make a cup of tea here? But it didn't sound like it, as his next words confirmed.

"It's at the main house. It's served from seven-thirty onwards during the week, and it's nearly eight already. Please tell them I'll be there soon."

Stella scrambled out of bed, grabbed some clothes, and headed to the bathroom to get ready. She felt terrible, and her face looked pale and drawn. As she slathered on make-up, hoping to fake a semblance of health, she wondered why it was necessary to go to the main house for breakfast on a Monday morning of all times. Weren't they going to have any private life?

Heading out of the cottage and following the paved path to the mansion, she then realized that Mondays were probably not different from any other day for the women of this elite family.

The front door was open. She stood in the hallway, listening for any sounds that could guide her where to go. There weren't any, because the damned place was so large. As she hesitated, a maid walked out of the lounge.

She gave Stella a quick nod without really looking at her and then turned her gaze away. That was something she'd noticed the staff did, as if they wanted to remain unobtrusive, or even invisible.

"Excuse me," she called.

The housemaid stopped and turned. She looked apprehensive. Stella noticed she was young and pretty, although her white-blonde hair was scraped back into a tight ponytail and her face was free of make-up.

"The family. Where are they? I'm supposed to join them for breakfast."

As she spoke, she felt guilty that she hadn't asked this young woman her name. If she was going to defy Kathy by being nice to the staff, she needed to be friendly at all times.

The maid nodded politely. "The breakfast room is in the east wing. Shall I show you there?"

"Yes, please," she said. "What's your name, by the way?"

"Anya."

Her accent was definitely foreign, Stella decided. She must be from Eastern Europe or even Russia.

"I'm Stella." Fighting down a wave of nausea, she smiled.

Then she followed Anya to the archway beyond the staircase and down a long, wide corridor until they reached a room decorated in white, green, and gold. With its large windows looking out onto the tended lawns, it reminded her of an old-fashioned conservatory.

There, the family was gathered. A long table had been set with a starched white cloth, and silver salvers were placed on the sideboard.

Everyone turned to look at her when she walked in. Cecilia Marshall was serving herself a mini croissant with cream cheese. Grace and Howard were huddled together at a corner of the table whispering something. Vaughn's father was pacing up and down at the far end of the room, talking on his cellphone.

Kathy, standing near the far window, turned to stare at her and then looked deliberately away.

"Good morning," Stella said, summoning up a confidence she didn't feel. She walked into the room and inhaled a whiff of scrambled egg from one of the salvers. It was never her favorite smell. Now, it made her stomach lurch.

"Morning. Where's your drunkard fiancé?" Howard asked.

His tone was playful, but the words cut through her. Not only were they insulting but they were also worryingly accurate.

"He'll be here in a minute," Stella said.

Cecilia put down her plate and walked over to kiss Stella on her cheek. Her lips were warm, but her blue eyes cool and frosty.

"Breakfast in this home is an informal affair. We all have things to do and lives to lead. On weekdays it's self-service. Our staff try to cater for all tastes, but if there's anything you want that is not prepared, just call through to the kitchen and they will bring it."

She pointed to the intercom, discreetly mounted on a wall bracket near the far door.

The amount of food on display was mind-boggling to Stella, even for a large family. There was toast, croissants, Danish pastries, eggs, bacon, salmon, cream cheese, fruit salad, as well as a selection of cereals. Food-wise, she noticed the divide instantly. The men were piling their plates as if preparing for a famine, while the women doled out minimalistic portions of everything, as if the calories might attack them.

That suited Stella fine. She took a bowl and spooned some fruit salad into it, hoping she'd be able to push most of it aside uneaten.

At that moment, Lucinda walked in, followed by Elmer. Elmer looked pale, and as nauseous as Stella felt.

"Morning," Lucinda said. "Are we on for the bridge game, ladies?"

"We should be. Or did you say you were heading out?" Kathy asked Cecilia.

"No. We'll need to start later than usual as I've got someone coming in to do some redecoration. I want to go through the plans with them as we weren't happy with the last interior design firm."

Kathy looked put out. "If you'd used Carstens, the one I recommended, that wouldn't have happened."

"My wife can use who she wants. She doesn't answer to you, Kathy," Gordon Marshall said, sounding combative as he pocketed his phone.

"And I can speak for myself, thanks, Gordon," Cecilia spat at him.

Stella found her stomach clenching at the prospect of conflict. Kathy seemed to hate everyone, not only her. Her mind flashed back to the easy partnership between Rebecca and Marco that she'd admired so jealously yesterday. Why couldn't this family, who had every privilege, live in better harmony?

It was amazing that Vaughn had turned out to be so polite and considerate, if this acid repartee characterized his everyday life.

Howard let out a bark of laughter. "Aunt Kathy, if Carstens are the ones who did your house, they're best avoided."

"Thank you for your opinion. Coming from the boy who flunked art and math in tenth grade, it's very valuable," Kathy shot back. "If only you could buy some intelligence the same way you bought a place in college."

Clearly, this struck home because Howard glowered. So did Gordon, but Kathy turned away wearing an inscrutable half-smile.

Grace sat down beside Stella. Her plate contained a bird-sized portion of salmon and cucumber.

"Where's your ring?" she asked, sounding surprised.

"The diamond was loose. I've put it away until I can get it fixed," Stella explained.

"Oh. For a moment I thought you'd changed your mind!" Grace laughed. Overhearing her, Kathy laughed even louder.

"But talking of weddings, do you have a date organized yet? The summer venues will all be booked out soon. We reserved a place months ahead for my twenty-first. Or are you going to wait a whole year?" Grace continued.

"We haven't really discussed it," Stella said, feeling rattled by the question. It was something that they should have talked about but hadn't, and she sensed Grace was testing her defenses and looking for weak points.

Kathy weighed in on the conversation. "You also need a good prenuptial agreement. Do you have a lawyer?"

Stella stared at her in confusion. Did she mean Stella personally? Or her and Vaughn as a couple? She sensed there was an agenda to the question but couldn't work out what it might be.

"We're definitely going to discuss the wedding soon," she said.

"It's not only your responsibility. We must sit down together and sketch out some details," Cecilia said in tones that allowed for no argument. "You're going to need a wedding planner to organize everything. We have a very high-profile firm that we use. I will give you their details just now. You can make first contact, as the bride-to-be, and then I'll handle the rest."

Clearly, there was going to be no choice in this matter. If this was how something as important as a wedding was done, she'd have to go along with it.

This conversation was making her feel even more nauseous. Luckily, she was saved by Vaughn walking in.

"Morning, all."

He'd done a magnificent job of overcoming his hangover. His hair was slicked back and there was color in his cheeks. He wore a cream-colored dress shirt, a dark blue tie, and charcoal pants. He looked every inch the successful young hedge fund manager.

"Are you running late? What time are you heading into work?" Cecilia asked.

"I've got to be there in half an hour."

Vaughn was already working his way methodically down the line of salvers, piling his plate high.

"Are you taking a driver?"

Vaughn popped a mushroom in his mouth while considering the question.

"Yes, I'll take a driver."

"I'll ask Rodriguez to wait outside for you." Cecilia took out her phone and tapped keys.

Vaughn sat down next to Stella, enveloping her in the familiar cloud of his aftershave and shower gel.

"Got to take part in the speed eating champs this morning," he said. "That's what sleeping in does for you."

"You can expect to have many more late nights," Cecilia said, sounding approving. "Mike is hosting a lot of after-hours functions. High-caliber clients need to be treated well."

She glanced at Stella, who had a strong suspicion she was being baited, and that Cecilia was waiting for her to complain about this.

Well, she wasn't going to. Instead, she stole another glance at Elmer. He was clearly trying to act normal and had dished himself a plate of scrambled eggs. As she watched, a piece of egg fell from his trembling fork as it reached his mouth and dropped back down to the table.

This triggered a surge of nausea in her. Her mouth flooded with saliva, and she felt pinpricks of sweat break out on her forehead. She swallowed hard, pushing her bowl away. There was no way she dared eat another bite.

"I'd better get going." While she was battling with her churning stomach, Vaughn had devoured the entire contents of his plate. He leaned over and gave her a quick kiss on the lips. "See you later, gorgeous," he said.

Stella stood up, deciding to take the opportunity and leave with him. She was feeling so ill that she couldn't spend a minute more in the breakfast room.

"Thank you for the food," she said, following him out.

Vaughn peeled off, heading for the waiting car. Stella sprinted back to the cottage, doubling over with nausea.

A housemaid was heading the other way, carrying a trash bag and Vaughn's work jacket that he'd slung over the chair the previous night. Stella recognized her. It was Anya, who'd directed her to the breakfast room earlier. She glanced at Stella curiously and then looked down, clearly choosing to mind her own business.

She was relieved that Anya had already left the cottage, because she burst through the door at a run, and only just made it to the bathroom before she threw up.

Hanging over the toilet bowl, panting and retching as another wave of sickness overwhelmed her, Stella had a sudden thought that made everything seem even worse.

What if she was pregnant?

With sweat trickling down her face, she considered the possibility from every angle.

They'd been careful, of course, but not that careful. There had been that one time, when it could have happened. Should her period have arrived by now? She thought so, but the past week had been so crazy she'd completely lost track.

Breathing deeply, she stood up on shaking legs, wiped her face, and rinsed out her mouth.

She'd always believed that being pregnant would be a joyous occasion. Now, all she could think was that this was the worst possible time. Worse still, she couldn't call Vaughn to share her fears, as she didn't dare to interrupt his working day.

Instead, she decided to take a test immediately.

CHAPTER ELEVEN

On the drive from the airport, Stella had noticed a local shopping center a few blocks away. She decided to go there straight away.

Grabbing her purse, she headed out, feeling exposed and vaguely guilty as she walked up the long driveway. At any minute, she expected to hear the clatter of wheels on paving and for one of the family to pull up next to her and demand to know where she was going.

They didn't, and she got through the gate without seeing anyone except a gardener toiling over a flower bed on the far side of the lawn. Breathing in the fresh air as she walked made her start to feel better, even though nausea still roiled inside her.

She passed a couple of people jogging, and a dog walker who looked to be a professional hired for the job, as she was wearing a branded top and efficiently walking five different dogs of various breeds.

The wealthy elite didn't seem to do anything for themselves. Wedding planners, dog walkers, chefs, gardeners, and housemaids. How would she ever be ready for this world?

To her relief, there was a pharmacy in the small center, which also housed a chic looking coffee shop, a hairdresser, an antiques store, and a fashion boutique. She headed into the pharmacy where the attendant bustled over immediately.

"Morning, dear. How can I help?" she said in a friendly way.

Staring at the ropy gold chain around her neck, and her well styled steel gray hair, Stella suspected this might actually be the owner. She wished she'd been served by a disinterested employee, and not by someone who might be connected to customers and their families.

"I'd like a pregnancy test, please. And something for nausea," she said in a low voice.

"Of course."

Efficiently, the woman collected the items, while Stella prayed that she wouldn't pursue any further conversation with her, or ask her where she was from.

She didn't, but at the till, she said, "Will this be on an account?"

"I'll pay cash," Stella said, getting her wallet out of her purse.

As she handed over the notes, the old-fashioned bell at the door pinged as someone else walked in.

"Well, hey!" The greeting startled Stella and she jumped.

Turning, she saw to her dismay that the arrival was Haydi, the family friend who'd been on the yacht outing.

She was staring at Stella with a curious, piercing gaze.

Sliding an arm protectively across the counter in an attempt to hide what she was buying, Stella stammered out a greeting.

"How nice to see you," she managed.

"I was on my way to the hairdresser and thought I recognized you. Did you enjoy the rest of the night on the boat?"

"It was fun."

Stella glanced around to see that the store owner had packaged up her goods in a semi-transparent plastic bag. Haydi glanced curiously at it, and she felt her stomach lurch. She knew she should immediately deflect the other woman's attention away, but in that moment, with nausea and fear warring inside her, her psychological skills deserted her. The most she could do was to grab the package as quickly as she could, and stash it in her purse.

"I must say, I was a little too drunk that night. Your family's hospitality is always so good," Haydi continued as if she hadn't noticed. "We always say it isn't a Marshall party if you don't have a headache the next day. I remember Vaughn's cottage-warming. That was such a blast it carried on till noon on Sunday," she laughed.

"That sounds fun," Stella agreed, trying to muster up enough fake enthusiasm to pass as genuine.

"I'm living in my own place now so I can't do things on the same scale, but I have fabulous dinner parties and girls' nights. Of course, you're invited. The next one is in two weekends' time. Here, take my card." She handed over what looked like a business card, but which Stella saw was just a personal card with her name, number and address.

"I can't wait! Thank you," Stella gushed, even though her nausea was worse than ever, and she was desperate to take the meds. Also, she was starting to feel frantic about getting any time alone with Vaughn. She'd never expected to be drawn into such a social merry-go-round.

"How are you, Gaby?" Haydi said to the store attendant, and Stella's heart sank even further. She knew her by name. Now, all it would take was an innocent question and Haydi would know what she'd bought.

"I'm well, honey. What do you need?"

"You delivered to us yesterday. I only came in to say hi, so I'd better get to my appointment. Can't wait to see you at dinner, Stella, if not sooner."

Swishing her hair back, with another confident smile, Haydi headed out.

Once she was sure Haydi really was safely in the hairdresser, Stella detoured to the coffee shop and bought a bottle of water.

As she walked home, she swallowed two of the nausea tablets, hoping that they'd settle her stomach by the time she arrived back. As she walked, she realized they were working. Her nausea was being replaced by fear.

*

Arriving home, Stella planned to go straight to the cottage and take the test, but, as she passed the house, Cecilia called her name.

Guiltily, Stella spun around to see her standing in the doorway.

"There you are. Where did you go?"

She was flanked by a retinue – Lucinda on her left, Kathy on her right.

"I went out to get some air. I wasn't feeling well," Stella lied, not wanting to admit she'd been to the shops.

"Hope you're not pregnant," Lucinda said jokingly, and Stella had to stop herself from flinching at the uncomfortable accuracy of that guess.

"I'm so sorry you were unwell. I noticed you didn't eat more than a bite at breakfast," Cecilia sympathized. "But if you're feeling better now, I need you for a minute." Her voice was sweet, but it held a note of command.

Stella didn't want to join her. She wanted to slink away to the cottage and take the test. She was so anxious about it that she couldn't think of anything else.

Reluctantly she turned toward the house.

"Danni is here," Cecilia told her, looking pleased.

The name didn't ring a bell, but Stella hadn't been able to keep track of the sheer numbers of family, extended family, and friends she'd been introduced to since arriving.

"She is?" she asked cautiously, hoping more information would be forthcoming.

"Our personal outfitter from Easton's. She came to drop off a few garments for Grace, which I'd forgotten about. While she's here, she can measure you up. That'll allow her to make a start on your wardrobe. She might even be able to deliver some items this afternoon."

Stella gazed at her in alarm. This was not a good time. Her nausea was barely under control, and she had no idea when it might surge again. Every bone in her body felt exhausted and she needed to lie down.

But she didn't have a choice, since Danni was now waiting.

"Sure," she said, and headed into the house. Lucinda and Kathy peeled off into the formal lounge, leaving Stella to walk down the corridor with Cecilia.

In an undertone, Cecilia murmured to her, "It may not be my place to criticize, but I hope you will be pleasant to Danni, and appreciate that she is giving her time and expertise to measure you today. Rather than showing your customary bad attitude which I've noticed far too often since you've been here."

The words lashed Stella, so unexpected that she literally stopped dead.

Bad attitude? Was Cecilia being serious? Had she been silently judging her from the moment they'd met? And now, finding her wanting, was reprimanding her like a naughty schoolgirl?

How, and where, had she inadvertently displayed this attitude? She'd been trying her best to be polite, while every other family member seemed to have leeway to be blatantly rude and sarcastic to each other.

The unfair criticism burned her, making her feel inferior and not good enough.

"When did this happen?" Stella stammered out.

But Cecilia wasn't listening. Without missing a beat, she strode purposefully down the passageway leaving Stella to hurry after her.

Was that what her future mother-in-law thought of her?

Feeling thoroughly shaken, she tried to think back over the whirlwind of the past days. There had been the moment she'd stood up for herself and told Kathy she would continue to thank the staff. Was that what this was about?

As Cecilia reached a doorway to the right, her voice changed, ringing out as clear and sweet as a bell.

"Oh, Danni, I'm so excited to introduce Stella, our future daughter-in-law. Stella, this wonderful woman is our outfitter and a good family friend."

Stella blinked at the glowing introduction. Why had Cecilia snapped out such a nasty warning, but was now being so nice to her again? Had the earlier words been a joke? They'd sounded deadly serious.

The room was a spare bedroom, splendidly decorated in cream and gold. Danni, a forty-something curvaceous blonde, was sitting in an armchair. A pile of clothes was strewn over the bed. Grace was twirling in front of a full-length mirror, wearing a turquoise ball gown.

"How lovely to meet you," Danni declared, standing up from the seat to clasp Stella's hand. "Grace told me we'll be organizing a new wardrobe for you. Aren't you excited?"

Her smile was wide, even though Stella could see it was plastic and fake. Her mascaraed brown eyes were calculating as she ran her gaze over Stella's clothes. She felt ashamed that her current outfit was among the shabbiest in her meager collection.

"I'm very excited," she said, forcing enthusiasm into her voice.

Cecilia turned to Grace.

"That gown is the perfect color for you. Perfect!"

"It's the ideal match," Danni enthused. "And you'll find it still complements you, dear, even with a summer tan. It's an incredibly versatile shade. Those darts we added on the side have tightened the waist just enough. I don't think it needs further work."

"Great. Thanks, Danni."

Grace gathered up the colorful heap of clothes and hurried out.

Danni was rummaging in her large tog-bag. She pulled out a tape measure.

"Let's have a look at you," she said, staring at Stella expectantly.

"What do you want me to do?" Stella asked politely, self-consciously aware that Cecilia had settled into another armchair.

"Off with your clothes," Danni said briskly.

Stella gaped at her. This was seriously not a good time. She felt frayed and vulnerable and had never thought, when choosing her underwear, that anyone apart from Vaughn would see her in it. Plus, after that lashing comment, Cecilia's presence in the room seemed like a deliberate taunt.

She had to strip off, in front of her and the outfitter?

This wasn't just a routine fitting. This felt more like humiliation, and Stella knew she couldn't do it.

CHAPTER TWELVE

Stella turned to Danni. Seeing her expression, Danni laughed. "You're only going down to your underwear, honey. I just need to get an idea of the body shape under that baggy clothing." She regarded Stella's outfit dubiously.

She turned to Cecilia, wondering if she would listen if she asked her to leave, but felt confused when she saw she was smiling supportively. No trace of her earlier viciousness remained.

"In summer on the yacht, when it's bikini time, you'll be wearing even less," Cecilia explained with a sympathetic smile. "But I can see you feel awkward. There's no reason to be, but would you like me to step outside?"

That unexpected comment disarmed Stella. It felt even ruder to say yes, when Cecilia was now showing empathy.

"I'm okay, thank you," she said reluctantly, deciding to meet her halfway.

Cecilia's smile broadened and she sat back in her chair.

Stella had a sudden, strong feeling that she'd been outplayed. She might be a psychology student, but she realized Cecilia was a master. Effortlessly, she'd just manipulated Stella. Accusing her of having a bad attitude had been guilt-tripping, designed to throw her off balance and make her doubt herself. Then, she'd followed it up with the subtle use of reverse psychology to ensure Stella agreed she should stay and watch.

The end result, which she was sure Cecilia had intended, was that she felt small and inferior and very much under Cecilia's control.

Stella's hands were shaking as she undid her top and pulled it over her head, placing it on the bed. She unbuckled her jeans, kicked off her scuffed sneakers, and removed them, too.

She felt embarrassed beyond words to be standing there, as their gazes scoured her, staring mercilessly at her old panties and her favorite bra which was cheap, plain and beige.

"We have shoes and footwear on the list, do we?" Danni asked Cecilia, stepping forward with the tape measure. "And a few items of underwear, I think, also. Correct underwear really improves the line of clothing."

"Underwear, definitely," Cecilia said firmly.

Stella's cheeks flamed scarlet.

"What an athletic build you have." Danni moved inexorably to her with the tape measure and Stella felt its chilly touch on her skin. "Very well-proportioned figure, and slim, too. More boyish than curvaceous, with those broad shoulders and slender hips. We'll look for scoop necks and V-necks, and you can carry off flared skirts and A-line dresses, which gives us a lot of options with gowns as well. Wide hips are so much more difficult to fit. How tall are you?"

"Five feet seven," Stella replied.

Danni nodded approvingly. "An easy height. Nothing usually needs shortening or lengthening. How tall is Vaughn?" she asked Cecilia.

Stella knew the answer to that, too, but waited politely for Cecilia to reply.

"He's six-foot."

"So we can include any heel height, apart from the very highest, then.

Because in this society it would be unseemly for her to be taller than her partner? Stella's mind reeled.

"They make a lovely couple," Cecilia said, and Stella was suspicious of how approving she sounded. What was Cecilia planning next? Was she going to try and manipulate her in some other way?

"You two will have beautiful children." Danni slid the measuring tape around her waist.

Her comment dragged Stella back to harsh reality. She hoped she wasn't pregnant. Imagine if the Marshalls splashed out on a costly wardrobe of clothing that she wouldn't be able to wear for a year, if ever again.

"You're slightly bloated, honey. Are you premenstrual?" Danni asked the shockingly personal question as if it was routine.

Confusion filled her and she had no idea what to say.

"Yes. I think so," she stammered out, hoping it was the truth.

"Always need to keep an eye on that, when we're looking at how the waistline fits," Danni chattered, moving down to measure her hips. "Some garments are so close fitting; they can only be worn certain times if your monthly cycle causes issues. I think we'll steer away from those for now. Of course, diet also plays a role. Have you been tested for wheat intolerance? That can cause terrible bloat."

"No, not yet. I've never noticed a problem."

Maybe she should have said she had, Stella agonized. She didn't want anyone guessing that there was even a chance she could be pregnant. Was the bloated belly a sign, so soon? She had no idea.

"How old are you?"

"Twenty-six."

Danni laughed. "Youth gives you such a free pass! It's only when time goes by that these things start becoming major headaches."

"Grace doesn't touch wheat. She barely eats carbs at all," Cecilia said proudly.

"And it shows in her figure. She'll look the same when she's thirty. Fifty, even," Danni cooed.

Abruptly, Stella felt another wave of nausea clench at her insides. Her stomach gurgled and she tensed her muscles, knowing how audible the sound must be to Danni, who was now measuring her inner thigh.

Luckily, at that moment Cecilia spoke again.

"We need to get you on a sun bed. Get some color into those lovely legs. You did say you'd be available on Thursday for our spa session? Grace and I are so looking forward to you joining us."

Gritting her teeth, Stella gave the only acceptable answer in the circumstances.

"I really can't wait," she enthused. "It will be such a treat."

The hell that Thursday would be was something that at this stage she didn't dare to think about. At least there was some time to come up with an excuse for canceling.

She hoped that this fitting was not going to continue too much longer, because she was starting to feel like she needed to throw up again. Breathing deeply, she forced oxygen in without making it seem obvious. Her forehead was damp with sudden cold sweat, and she hoped they hadn't noticed that either.

"Right. All done."

To Stella's extreme relief, Danni put her tape measure away.

"I have a few suitable garments on hand. I can have them delivered tomorrow," she said.

"How wonderful. You're a miracle worker!" Now it was Cecilia's turn to gush.

"Well, I'd better get on. I have to pass by the Polo store and pick up a few samples for my next client."

"I know how hectic you are, especially this time of year with everyone needing a summer wardrobe," Cecilia agreed.

Quickly, Stella pulled on her clothes, feeling thankful that she was no longer under the two women's scrutiny.

"Thank you for your time, Danni. I can't wait to see the clothing," she said.

"It's wonderful that you appreciate this so much, Stella," Cecilia smiled. "It makes it even more special. You're a real beauty and once you have a new wardrobe, you're going to look like a model."

Once again, she sounded genuinely kind and friendly, and hearing this tone, Stella's mistrust of her deepened.

She followed the two women out of the ornate bedroom and down the long corridor, in the direction of the front door. Her stomach was now cramping painfully, and she couldn't wait to go back to the cottage and take the test. The uncertainty was gnawing at her, as unpleasant as the waves of sickness.

With any luck, the results would set her mind at ease, and she could lie down and sleep off this stomach flu.

On the way to the front door, she heard voices from one of the sun-filled lounges, and saw that Grace and Kathy were both there, talking to Lucinda.

Stella hoped that she could use this moment to make her escape, but Cecilia's cool fingers closed around her wrist, making her think for a moment of a handcuff's cold clasp.

The grip was irritating her. It implied ownership. She wanted to pull free but knew she couldn't even twitch her hand, because Cecilia would pick up on the small act of rebellion. In fact, she might even be waiting for it.

"Now, Stella, I need you here a little longer. We must make a start on organizing the wedding. In any case, you can't go back to the cottage yet, as I sent a crew over to measure for up-grades I want done. They won't be long. Come with me to my office, and I'll get the planner's number," Cecilia said briskly.

Stella bit her lip. Setting the wheels in motion now felt as if things were being rushed. She had no idea what timeframe Vaughn was thinking of, and if she was pregnant, it would drastically affect everything.

"I'll be back in a moment," Cecilia called to the other women, before turning around and propelling Stella down another spacious corridor.

Stella felt an increasing sense of panic as she walked. This wasn't right. Surely she and Vaughn should check with each other what they wanted, before the family took charge?

They entered the elegant, sun-filled office.

"Sit down, sit down." Cecilia gestured to a floral wingback chair as she headed to the desk.

Stella perched on the chair, fidgeting unhappily with the strap of her purse.

Despite the consequences, it was time to put a stop to this. Stripping off and being measured was bad enough. But going ahead with wedding plans before she'd even spoken about it with her fiancé was taking the family's control way too far.

"I think it would be better for me to discuss this with Vaughn first," she said, summoning up all her bravery.

"Discuss what?"

Stella was alarmed that, once again, the saccharine sweetness had vanished from Cecilia's voice. There was a vicious tinge to her words.

"The wedding plans. As I don't know what Vaughn wants in terms of timing, or any of the other details. We could talk about it tonight, and then call the planner tomorrow, if that works for you?"

Stella felt suddenly as if she was in the presence of an enemy. Cecilia drew in a sharp, angry breath and her face hardened, the charming half-smile slipping away in an instant.

"Gordon and I are paying for this wedding, in more ways than one." Staring at her through narrowed eyes, Cecilia lashed out the words. "I'm not going to allow my son to make any more irresponsible decisions. He had his moment. He didn't want to work out of state and so he made his revenge move by bringing you home. Now we'll all live with the consequences. But the one thing I will insist on is that this gets done right."

She turned away and opened a leather-covered notebook on the large, ivory-white desk, but Stella barely noticed her actions. She felt stunned by the viciousness Cecilia had shown, and by what her words had revealed.

She was insinuating that Vaughn's proposal was nothing more than an act of defiance, because of being banished to Chicago. That was gaslighting, and Cecilia was doing it in the most deliberately hurtful way.

It hadn't been like that. Not at all, Stella told herself, shaken by the terrible insinuation. They'd fallen in love, so deeply and intensely that they'd both agreed they'd never felt this way before. There was no revenge move involved.

At any rate, she now knew for sure that her future mother-in-law disliked and disrespected her. She had earned no place in this family and would not ever be welcome.

"Here are the wedding planner's details. Let's make the call in the lounge."

Turning away, Cecilia strode out of the office. After an astounded pause, Stella scrambled up and hurried after her.

They arrived in the lounge, where tea had just been served on a silver tray. Kathy was transferring the filled cups to the nearby card table.

"Shall we start now?" Lucinda asked. "Are you going to join us, Stella?" She glanced around. "No, you can't be. We're four already."

"Stella will be with us for a few minutes, while I call the wedding planners," Cecilia smiled, and Stella was astounded that the saccharine tone had returned to her voice. "This will be a big moment, welcoming her into our family. We want to make sure the day is as special as it can be."

With her stomach aching and her nerves shredded, Stella couldn't control herself a moment longer.

"That's not what you said a minute ago," she snapped.

"What?" Cecilia whirled around and she saw real fury in her eyes.

It was too late to take back her words, so Stella decided to press forward. Shaking with anger, she continued.

"In your office, you said differently, Cecilia. You insulted me and told me I was your son's revenge move. Now you're acting like I'm the best thing ever. So, which is it? What do you really think of me? Is it what you say to me when nobody else is around? Or is it what you say when others are around? Because whichever is the truth, I think it's best that you stay consistent. It will make things easier for us all if I know where I stand with you."

There was a stunned silence in the room.

Cecilia stared at Stella, and she saw a flash of genuine hatred in the other woman's eyes. For a moment, Stella had forced her mask to slip. But then she regained control.

"I am shocked that you would think that way," Cecilia said, and her voice shook with genuine emotion. "I don't know what you are implying. You've received nothing but hospitality and welcome here. We have tried, from the moment you arrived, to include you and make you feel part of the family even though you are from a very different background. Now, in front of my daughter, my sister, and my closest cousin, you are accusing me of being false and a liar? This has shaken me to my core."

"That's unacceptable." Kathy sounded furious. "Let me tell you right now, I know who's the one making up stories here."

"Cecilia, I'm so sorry." Lucinda moved forward to squeeze Cecilia's arm while glaring daggers at Stella.

"You're such a hypocrite," Grace spat at her. "Accusing my mother of being two-faced? Just look at your own behavior."

"Perhaps the wedding planning can wait till tomorrow. Or some other day." There was ice in Cecilia's voice.

Stella felt so far on the back foot she had no idea what to do. With smooth cunning, Cecilia had countered her outburst by effectively positioning herself as the victim. If the others hadn't already hated her, they did now. Her life was shattering around her. How had everything gone so bad, so fast?

Turning, she stumbled out of the room, trying to keep control even though sobs were threatening to burst out of her. She managed not to cry the whole way down the long, tiled passage. It was only when she reached the hallway that she allowed a wail of grief to escape. Her shoulders shook as she stumbled through the hall.

Through her tears, she noticed one of the housemaids, polishing the floor near the entrance to the lounge. The woman glanced at her and then hastily resumed her task.

She didn't come over to comfort Stella or ask what was wrong.

In this house, the help clearly tried to remain invisible, and Stella could see why. Remembering the evil gleam in Cecilia Marshall's eyes as she'd stared at her, she could see it was safer that way.

As she reached the cottage, with a lurch of her stomach, she realized the most terrible fact of all.

She'd forgotten her purse. She'd put it down in Cecilia's office and then, distracted by her shocking accusations, hadn't picked it up again.

Her purse, with the pregnancy test inside.

CHAPTER THIRTEEN

Stella never wanted to set foot in the Marshalls' house, ever again, after what had played out, but she had no choice. She had to go and fetch her purse. What if Cecilia saw it there and looked inside? It would be exactly the kind of thing she would do. She'd seen Cecilia's total disrespect for her privacy.

How could she have forgotten it there? Why had she been so careless, Stella berated herself, feeling dismayed that she now had to head back again.

Pushing open the main home's elegant front door felt like entering enemy territory. Listening, she could hear faint conversation from the nearby lounge. She hoped they were all immersed in their game.

She walked quietly in the direction of the office, keeping her head down, just like the servants did. Like them, she wanted to be invisible now.

The office door was closed.

Should she knock? There couldn't possibly be anyone inside, not when Cecilia was playing bridge. Stella turned the handle quietly, and then, feeling alarmed, tried it harder.

Her heart crash landed as she realized the office was locked.

Who had locked it and when? Had Cecilia gone back and done that? What on earth could the reason be?

Most importantly – was her purse still in there? If not, she didn't want to think where it was. She couldn't interrupt the bridge game, so she'd have to wait until Vaughn got home and ask him to go in and fetch it. Now she was stuck. She couldn't take the test, and she couldn't go out to buy another, since her wallet was in there too.

Stella headed out of the house, feeling prickly with anxiety as she hurried past the lounge.

As she left the house, her anxiety changed to anger.

How dare Cecilia treat her this way! She refused to be dominated by a controlling matriarch who hated Stella because she didn't fit into the right box. If she'd known what hell living with the family would be, she would never have agreed to move in with Vaughn.

Stepping into the spacious dining room, she glared resentfully at the no-doubt-expensive, but, in her opinion, hideous paintings on the walls.

This wasn't even Vaughn's taste – she knew what art he loved, and this was nothing like it. Being in this cottage was living proof of the oppressive control that the Marshalls had over them.

Well, she wasn't going to take any more of it. It was time to put her foot down and insist that they move out and find their own place. Living on the family's estate was toxic in every possible way. She'd noticed how it was changing Vaughn, and how different he was from when he'd been in Chicago, and now she'd seen what Cecilia truly thought of her.

On impulse, she called Vaughn, hoping that he might answer. Even though he was so busy, this wasn't a minor interruption but an urgent problem. He needed to know what had happened and how she felt. But, as she'd feared, he didn't pick up.

Trying to put Cecilia's stinging words out of her mind, Stella hunkered down with her laptop and began looking for jobs. There was nothing suitable in the local area, and the closest opportunities were mainly in New York.

But why should she restrict herself to jobs that were driving distance from the Marshalls, she decided. The further away they were from his family, the better.

Widening her search, Stella began to explore opportunities in other states. Places she'd always wanted to visit. California. Louisiana. Oregon. Possibilities beckoned to her, exciting and full of promise. Vaughn didn't need to work for his uncle's firm. There were finance companies statewide, ones which wouldn't expect their hedge fund managers to go out and get blind drunk with clients every night.

Whatever it took, she was going to save them from this situation, and she and Vaughn were going to reclaim the life they'd had in Chicago.

*

Just after seven, she heard a car door slam outside. It was time for the discussion she'd been steeling herself for all day. She didn't know how to start explaining what had played out. How could she describe, to her own fiancé, that his mother had called his proposal a 'revenge move?' Would Vaughn accept that Cecilia had actually said that?

From the way the front door banged shut, Stella realized with a jolt that Vaughn must already know what had happened. Leaping to her feet, she rushed out of the study and met him in the corridor.

He'd taken off his jacket, which was slung over his shoulder, and yet again she smelled alcohol on his breath. He wasn't coming home straight from the office. He'd been out 'entertaining' again.

His face was like thunder.

"We need to have a serious talk," she began, trying to set a calm tone for the conversation, but Vaughn was beyond reason.

"What the hell is going on?" he shouted. "Mom called this morning and she said you upset her so badly that she doesn't want anything to do with you anymore. I've been freaking out about it all day."

Stella gritted her teeth. She'd tried to get hold of Vaughn too and he hadn't picked up. But when his mother called to bitch about her, he answered immediately.

"We had a fight. She was treating me one way when it was just the two of us, and another way when there were other people there. I called her out on it. She was being an absolute bully, Vaughn. What she said was way out of line."

In his eyes, she hoped to see the sympathy that he'd shown in the past, when she'd shared her problems and inner thoughts. But there was no sympathy to be seen, only furious panic.

"That's not what Mom said. She said you insulted her, out of nowhere, while she was trying to help you. Now she thinks you're vindictive and selfish."

"Me? Vindictive? Have you lost your mind that you think I'd behave that way?" Stella yelled back.

She was shocked to see Vaughn raise his hand, his handsome mouth twisted into a snarl.

"Don't shout at me!" he shouted.

He was going to hit her, she realized with a surge of adrenaline. He looked enraged.

But he didn't hit her. He punched the air angrily. She realized he looked close to tears as well.

"I'm only human! You have no idea how much trouble this has caused!" he cried out, sounding on the edge of losing control.

Stella felt horrified. This entire scenario was giving her flashbacks to all the times when she was younger, during her mother's fits of rage. Memories surged – of her mother screaming at the top of her voice, her face so close to twelve-year-old Stella that her spittle showered over her cheeks. Of the times she'd smacked her and slapped her and, once, thrown a heavy chopping board that had glanced painfully off her shoulder.

73

And something else, also. A darker memory lurked that her mind shied away from.

She was terrified of this conflict that was ripping open old, forgotten scars. It had to be resolved, and fast.

Even though her heart was racing, and she was so keyed up she wanted to scream back at him, she forced herself to take a deep breath. Given that Vaughn was now completely overemotional, she would have to be the one to defuse it.

"Your mother's version is wrong," she said as calmly as she could, even though her voice sounded high and wobbly. "Don't you want to hear my side?"

"It's a bit late for that." Vaughn swiped the back of his hand across his eyes. "She's furious with me, too, and she and Dad have given me an ultimatum. You must apologize and promise that it never happens again. Or I get disinherited."

Stella literally gasped as she absorbed this body blow.

"What?" she spat out the word.

"Yes. I feel like I'm in a total living nightmare. I can't believe my own family is about to disown me. I have no idea what to do now."

Stella was aghast by how accurately Rebecca had predicted this would happen. The big guns were out, and Vaughn was in their sights.

He was clearly shattered by the ultimatum. His entire identity, his ego, his set of beliefs and expectations, were all based on being the eldest son and heir. Now they'd threatened him with taking all of that away. This was who he was. Apart from his time in Chicago, this was all he knew, and this scenario was destroying him.

She hated his parents for having done this. It was an evil, manipulative move. How Stella wished he'd stand up to them. She knew he could do it if he found the inner strength. He just hadn't recognized it was there.

"It's just money," she said, spreading her hands expressively. "You're a clever guy. You know how to trade. You can earn your own. You don't need your family's. Especially not when it comes with all those terms and conditions."

"Just money," Vaughn muttered. "And the property portfolio which I receive, as the eldest son. And my trust fund payments. Plus the shame of everyone knowing. But yes, just money."

He stumbled over to a couch and slumped down.

"This is totally unfair," she said. "They have absolutely no right to force you into doing what they want by threatening to disinherit you."

"It's more than that," Vaughn stared at her with defeat in his eyes. "Mom called Uncle Mike. Now he's also worked up about this, and he won't allow me to stay with the firm unless I apologize. He said that a family feud will bring the company's name into disrepute. A lot of his clients are good friends with my parents."

"You can find another firm," she began, but he shook his head.

"He's a powerful man, Stella. I don't want to be on his bad side. He's said that if I don't make things right, I won't work in finance anywhere in the country again. He'll make sure of it."

He jerked angrily at his tie, loosening it, and snapped his collar button open.

Stella sat down beside him. She closed her eyes and buried her face in her hands, feeling frustrated beyond words. The family had effectively checkmated them.

After a pause, Vaughn started rubbing her back. From the gentle touch, she knew he'd calmed down and wanted to apologize for his flare-up of temper. Meanwhile, Stella thought furiously. How could she solve the situation? There didn't seem to be a way because they were being blocked in every direction.

But then, the solution came to her, and she sat upright, shaking her hair back.

"I'm going to give you an ultimatum too," she said firmly.

"You are?" Now Vaughn's voice was high with anxiety as if he simply couldn't take any more. Well, too bad. At this point, there wasn't a choice.

"I'll apologize. I don't want to and feel it's totally unfair, but to mend the situation for now, I will do it. But my conditions are that we move out."

"Move out?" Vaughn repeated, sounding startled.

Thinking quickly, Stella added a timeframe. "Within a month. I don't want it put off until it never happens. We move into our own place, which we pay for. Not in the same neighborhood but somewhere else. We need to live our own lives! It's unhealthy being on the same property as your folks. We have no proper time together, and I doubt we ever will. It feels like they own us. I'm sure they think they do."

She saw emotions chase across Vaughn's face. A flash of anger, followed by uncertainty, and then resigned acceptance.

"I see your point, babes. I really do. It's not working out here, and we do need time on our own. I've also been thinking that, but I've had no idea how to approach my folks about it."

Again, Stella felt incredulous that he even needed to, as a twenty-eight-year-old adult. Why was the parental nod necessary for him to live where he wanted?

"Now, I can see a way forward," Vaughn continued. "If I say you'll apologize, then it'll give me the chance to push my side. I'll say we should move out so that there's less chance of it happening again. How does that sound?" He looked at her anxiously.

"It sounds good. Imagine what fun we'll have, setting up our own place the way we want it. I was looking at the art in this cottage earlier today. It's not even what you like."

"Tell me about it," Vaughn agreed. "My mother can be very stubborn. I asked if we could have a different cleaner for the cottage and she flat-out refused."

"You see?" Stella said, encouraged he was speaking out, even though she had no idea why he didn't like the cleaner. The cottage had always looked immaculate to her.

"I know I'll have to be assertive about this," he agreed.

"Shall we do it now? I also need to get my purse. I left it in your mother's office, and when I went back, the door was locked."

At least, that way, she'd have one less worry hanging over her head. With any luck, the test would be negative. Stella fervently hoped so, given these other complications.

Vaughn grimaced, looking frustrated. "We can't do it now. She and my dad have gone out for dinner. They'll probably be back late."

"Well, first thing tomorrow, then?" Stella said.

Vaughn looked uneasy.

"There was something else, as well, that my mother wanted you to do. To keep the peace, I promised her you would."

Stella stared at him in alarm. Where was this going?

"You need to talk to someone. That's what Mom is insisting on."

"Well, to whom?" Who could give her any advice in this situation? She thought longingly of Clem's calm logic. He could help, but she'd had a message from him to say he would be out of the country for a week, visiting friends in Brazil.

"We have a family shrink, Dr. Lloyd. He's very good. My mother wants you to have a session with him. She said she'd book it for tomorrow morning."

"A shrink?" She stared at him incredulously. Agreeing to this without asking her first wasn't like Vaughn at all. This wasn't the same defiant man who had muttered that he needed to drink because of his dreadful family. This Vaughn was fearful and insecure and was buckling to his family's pressure.

Stella felt a sudden flash of fear. What if he didn't have the strength of will to resist his mother's cunning manipulation? She'd seen for herself how effective Cecilia's tactics were.

There was no way she wanted to see a psychiatrist just because his mother had ordered her to. But on the other hand, saying yes would briefly appease Cecilia and that meant they could hopefully get away.

And perhaps it would be a good thing, she thought suddenly. After all, psychology was her chosen subject, but she'd never had a proper consult as a patient. It would be interesting, and might be enlightening, too. If Dr. Lloyd knew the family well, he might share some insight on how to cope with them.

In fact, she thought, feeling more positive, Dr. Lloyd might be able to advise her how to get Vaughn out of their clutches. He could suggest a workable plan, and Stella needed one. She was beginning to realize the tough choice that lay ahead. Either it happened, or she would have to leave Vaughn, because she couldn't carry on this way.

"All right," she agreed. "I'll go and see Dr. Lloyd tomorrow."

CHAPTER FOURTEEN

At quarter to eight the next morning, Stella headed outside. She'd slept badly and felt worried and unsure about the session ahead. Her stress wasn't helped by the low-grade nausea bubbling inside her as she headed to the waiting car – a steel-gray BMW with a driver she didn't know at the wheel.

The sickness was probably just nerves, she told herself. At least the early appointment had been a good excuse to miss breakfast and head straight out.

Vaughn had gone to the house to get her purse. Anxiously, she peered down the path, hoping he'd come back with it before she left.

Would it still be there, and would he find it? Would he get distracted and start talking to one of the family, and tip the purse so that the test fell out? It made her uneasy to think that she didn't fully trust Vaughn to take proper care of this important possession.

There he was. Relief filled her as she saw he was carrying it.

"Here you go." He handed it to her, and she clutched it gratefully.

"Thank you."

"I'm sorry about last night. I behaved terribly to you. All the more reason to go ahead with our plans," he said with meaning.

"It's no problem. Apology accepted. I know how stressed you must have been," Stella said.

"Good luck with the shrink," he added with a grin. "It'll be an experience, I'm sure. And I'm going to ask my mother if we can meet with her this evening. Then we can discuss moving out."

"That's great. I'll come with you to the meeting and apologize to her while you're there. That way, we can sort everything out." Vaughn's smile encouraged her, and she felt filled with hope that he was taking this seriously.

She climbed into the car and greeted the driver, who responded with a polite nod. Glancing down at her purse, she noticed the zipper was halfway undone. Had she left it that way?

She'd been so distracted yesterday that she couldn't remember how far she'd closed the fastening. Quickly she rummaged inside, checking that the test was still there. It was, and so were the tablets. Unobtrusively, she dry-swallowed one. She didn't want to throw up during her appointment. Then she fastened her purse tightly closed again and tried her best to put the worry out of her mind.

Instead, while the car wound through the scenic suburban roads, Stella tried to get her thoughts together. This would be such an important session. She needed to explain all the complexities of her situation and do so in a balanced and respectful way.

So, what were the priorities?

Firstly, her relationship with Vaughn. How could she get him away from his family's influence? What would be the best way to approach this?

Secondly, how should she handle the manipulation and gaslighting from Cecilia, or any other of the more toxic family members? Perhaps Dr. Lloyd could give some insight.

"We are here, ma'am," the driver interrupted her thoughts.

Stella looked curiously at the palatial home where he'd stopped to ring the outside buzzer. That meant the doctor was one of them. He was part of the super-wealthy, which made her feel nervous.

The gate swung open, and they headed down the drive.

The main house was more modern than the Marshalls', with silver-gray walls and sweeping, curved lines. To the right was a separate and smaller building and it was here that the driver stopped.

"The rooms are through the side gate, ma'am."

Feeling nervous, Stella climbed out of the car and opened the side gate that led into a small, walled garden featuring gravel paths, lavender bushes, and a trickling fountain.

The door ahead was partway open, and she stepped inside. Her mouth felt dry, and her heart was racing.

Behind a reception desk that looked like a spaceship console, a pretty, young woman with short, wavy hair was typing notes on a computer.

She smiled when she saw Stella.

"Good morning. Miss Fall?"

"That's right," Stella said.

"Dr. Lloyd will be with you in a minute, and you can go through to the consulting room in the meantime. It's the door on the right. Can I get you any tea, coffee? A glass of water?"

Stella knew she couldn't stomach coffee, not with the nausea that still lurked.

"I'm fine, thank you."

She headed to the consulting room, which was furnished with a desk and a chair, and two sumptuous leather couches upholstered in gray. Bright modern art screamed from the walls.

She perched on one of the couches, wondering how the session would play out. How far back would he go in her history? There were issues she didn't feel ready to talk about.

At that moment, the door opened, and she jumped to her feet, anxiety surging inside her.

The suave man who strode inside looked to be in his sixties. He had immaculately groomed silver-gray hair and was wearing a glossy taupe leather jacket that exactly matched his shiny shoes. He gave her a brisk, professional smile and a firm handshake.

"Morning, Stella Fall?"

"Dr. Lloyd. Thank you for seeing me."

"It's my pleasure to help out in an emergency. When Cecilia called, I was able to move another patient to accommodate you. Please, sit down." He gestured briskly to the couch she'd just vacated. Taking a leather-covered notebook and gold pen from his briefcase, he sat down on the one opposite.

"So, you're Vaughn's fiancée?"

"Yes, I am."

"How long have you been in Greenwich?" he asked conversationally.

"Three days," Stella said, feeling astounded all over again by the shortness of the timeframe. It hadn't taken long for things to go wrong.

"Before that?"

"I lived in Evanston, in Chicago. I studied at Northwestern."

She liked that he was opening the conversation with simple and easy questions, as she felt she needed to relax. She hoped the doctor might ask her what she'd studied, but he didn't.

"And before that?" he asked.

Surprised, Stella replied. "Well, before that I lived in Kansas. That was where I grew up and went to school. On a farm, near a small town in the middle of nowhere. At least that's what it felt like."

"And you've known Vaughn for how long?"

"Just over four months," Stella said. "We met at a year-end function. He'd recently arrived in Chicago to do work experience, and it was his first event with the firm. I was waitressing, and we got to talking," she smiled, remembering that happy night.

Dr. Lloyd tapped his pen on the plush cover of his notebook and stared at her thoughtfully.

Taking this as an invitation that she should explain her circumstances, Stella gathered the courage to open up.

"When I first got here, I realized how different this family was from what I was used to. That was the one thing that worried me when I met Vaughn," she explained.

"Please explain more," he said, sounding sympathetic.

Stella took a deep breath.

"I feel like an outsider here. They haven't accepted me and never will. Things reached a head yesterday when I got into an argument with Cecilia. She was being sweet and kind when there were other people around, and vicious to me when we were alone together. I called her out on it and then it all exploded."

"Is that so?" Dr. Lloyd asked with a frown.

"I don't know how to handle behavior like this, or if there even is a way. I feel that living so close to the family is completely unhealthy, and I don't think it's good for Vaughn. He's not the same person he was in Chicago. I want to negotiate for us to move out. Vaughn doesn't assert himself with his family and it's impacting on our relationship."

Dr. Lloyd nodded, jotting a note on his pad as she continued.

"In the meantime, I need to know how I can cope better with his family's behavior. To me, it's toxic. They are rude and sarcastic to everyone, and awful to the staff. But maybe you can give me a different perspective," she added doubtfully, wanting to show that she was a reasonable person.

Stella felt relieved that she had gotten to the gist of the matter, but to her surprise, the doctor raised a hand.

"Wait. Just wait a moment, please, Stella. We're moving too fast here."

Surprised, she lapsed into silence.

He leaned forward and looked at her intently.

"Let's get more detail on your background before we go any further. Tell me, when did you move to Chicago?"

Surprised by the question, Stella thought back.

"When I was eighteen. I applied to Northwestern University and luckily was offered a partial scholarship. I paid my way with part time jobs. I then went on to complete a master's degree, so I still have some student debt I'll be paying off for a while," she said, with a nervous laugh, thinking of the urgency of her job applications.

She was worried that he might pry further into her family history. She didn't want to spill all of it out or mention her broken relationship with her mother. Surely that couldn't be relevant here?

"How many relationships have you had in the past, before you met Vaughn?"

How was that relevant either?

"Five, not counting him." She felt herself redden. Was that too many for someone her age?

"Tell me about the first," he encouraged her.

"He was a housemate in the place I stayed after I moved out of home."

That had been at seventeen, following yet another bitter fight with her mother. She'd packed her bags and moved in with a group of students staying in a ramshackle house in town. Odd jobs had paid her way for her lodgings and the final year of school. Of course, she'd fallen for the guy in the room next door; a twenty-year-old hitch-hiking his way across the States. He was also escaping a fractured family background and, as she'd discovered, fleeing addiction issues, too.

They'd had an intense few weeks together before he'd moved on. She'd thought she was in love, and had dreamed of following him one day, but a few weeks later his number didn't work anymore. She eventually learned via a friend of a friend, that he'd reached San Francisco and then checked into rehab.

All this was going to provide a lot of fuel for discussion, Stella thought resignedly, waiting for the doctor to ask about her troubled first lover.

"So he was the home owner? Was he much wealthier than you?"

That was a weird question. Was he serious? She looked more closely at him. He seemed serious.

"No. He wasn't the home-owner. He was just a lodger, and he was broke, like we all were."

Dr. Lloyd nodded wisely.

"Now tell me about your most recent relationship. The one before you met Vaughn."

"Adam was a soldier. He was twenty-nine, and he'd served a couple years overseas. We were together for six months," Stella said. They'd met when she was working shifts at a local bar. She'd been instantly drawn to the handsome, softly spoken man. Later she'd realized that he was suffering from post-traumatic stress disorder.

She'd longed to help him and had held him through the screaming nightmares.

In October, he'd started a job with a construction company in Canada. They'd discussed her moving too, but Stella had reluctantly decided that her career and studies had to come first. They'd ended it, with tears on both sides.

She was sure that the doctor would have questions about why she'd dated an ex-soldier, and how she'd felt compelled to help him heal.

But, instead of exploring those motives, Dr. Lloyd cut to the financial chase again.

"His family? Wealthy?"

"No. Not at all."

He nodded, and then bent his head to scribble more notes.

Stella felt confused. Why was he asking these things? How was this going to help with her new family dynamic? She felt anxious that time was ticking by, and that she might leave without the insight she so desperately needed.

The doctor finished his notes and nodded decisively.

"I've been practicing in this area for my entire career, Stella," he said. "During this time, I have seen a few people like you, coming in from poor backgrounds, and being introduced to the world of the very wealthy."

She nodded eagerly. Finally, the doctor was getting to the salient point of her problems. How could she understand these people? Why were they so discontented, despite their easy, pampered lifestyle?

"It's a shock for you, seeing what they have, and realizing the disparity in your backgrounds and everything you lacked."

"No, not really," Stella corrected him, frowning. That wasn't the reason for the problems she was having. She didn't feel inadequate. She was put off, in fact repelled, by how this family misused their money and status, and how they felt entitled to treat others badly. That was a completely different problem.

"I've seen it before," he said firmly. "It's affecting you more than you realize. Probably, it will take a few months for you to adjust and when you do, the problems you've mentioned won't seem serious anymore. You'll understand your in-laws better and have more empathy for the stresses and responsibilities they face – because their life is not easy, even though it might seem so at first glance."

He gazed at her with a hint of a smile.

Stella was starting to lose what little faith she'd had in this professional. These were huge issues she'd described. How could they disappear without being addressed? And why did she feel as if he was belittling them?

"Until then, I am going to prescribe medication for you."

"Medication?" Stella repeated, shocked.

"Yes. You, my dear, are suffering from depression. You might not know it, but it's very obvious to me. We need to put you to rights immediately, before you cause even more damage to your family relationships."

Stella stared at him in utter disbelief.

"It will have been triggered by your recent change in circumstances. Most probably, it's been underlying for a while. I am certain that it's caused you to act overemotionally and irrationally. Think about it," his words were a challenge.

"I don't –" Stella began, feeling outraged. She hadn't been the irrational one!

"Wouldn't you rather repair a relationship than damage it more badly?" he interrupted her.

"What about threatening to disinherit your son?" Stella snapped back. "That's damaging in my opinion."

Dr. Lloyd laughed. "Cecilia has a terrible temper. I counsel her for this regularly. She says things in anger that she doesn't mean. Most times, she apologizes afterwards."

Stella didn't know what to say to that. He seemed to be describing a different person from the one she knew.

"A course of antidepressants is essential for your well-being right now and you must start them immediately," the doctor continued. "I'm going to give you two different antidepressants to take long term, and a shorter course of tablets that will have a calming effect. Also sleeping pills to ensure you rest well at night. Take all of these medications twice a day, apart from the sleeping pills, which you can take at bedtime. In a month, we'll book you in for a second session, and I'm certain we will have a different conversation next time."

He gave her a confident, professional smile.

Was he trying to bamboozle her? That was what it felt like, even though his argument appeared logical.

He placed the pen on the notepad decisively and glanced at the clock.

"I see our time is up. It's been good to meet you, Stella. I wish you the very best in your journey with this wonderful family."

"Thank you," Stella said.

As she walked out of his rooms and back to the waiting car, she decided that her gut feeling was right.

This doctor was not legit. He hadn't asked relevant questions. He hadn't even checked with her about any potential side effects the meds might have. She didn't trust him and didn't believe his diagnosis. She wasn't going to take the meds.

And, if Vaughn didn't agree to move away, she was going to do it on her own. With or without him, she needed to live independently again.

Of course, that all hinged on the fact she wasn't pregnant.

Fear clenched inside her as she remembered she had to take the test as soon as she got home.

CHAPTER FIFTEEN

As soon as Stella got back to the cottage, she decided to take the test. Now that it was finally time, she was feeling extremely scared. The weird session with the shrink had only reinforced to her how far-reaching this family's influence was.

A pregnancy now would complicate things horribly. She was sure that if Cecilia were to find out, she would use it as another means to exert control.

Clutching her purse, she headed into the second bathroom. Her hands were shaking, and butterflies filled her stomach at the scariness of what she was about to do.

She did the test and sat, staring nervously at the door while she waited. It was sure to be a negative, she thought. She didn't feel pregnant, and her nausea had subsided. Surely she would feel more different if she actually was?

It was time. She focused on the lines of the test.

There were two lines there. Two lines meant a positive.

Two lines. Positive. She was pregnant.

"Oh, no! No!" she whispered.

She dropped the test onto the floor. Her fingers felt numb.

Pregnant. She was pregnant.

At the worst possible moment, she'd been precipitated into this huge life shift.

"It can't be," she muttered to herself, while staring down at the test results with the cold knowledge that it could be and was.

Hurrying out of the bathroom, she agonized over what this meant for her future. The timing was as wrong as it could be. Would this jeopardize their chances of independence? Would Cecilia disapprove of this happening so early on? She felt cold with worry at that possibility.

She needed to tell Vaughn straight away. Perhaps he could come back from work, and they could discuss this together. At any rate, she didn't want to bottle this bombshell up another moment.

Quickly, she grabbed her phone off the bedside table and dialed his number.

It rang and rang, and then went through to voicemail. He must be on another call, but hopefully he'd call her back as soon as he could.

She wished she could speak to him immediately. Why was it that he never answered her calls in working hours?

"Oh, hell."

As the reality of her situation pummeled her again, she sank down onto the bed and buried her face in her hands.

She fervently wished this hadn't happened and that she could somehow turn back time and change things. The only problem was that at that moment, she didn't know how far back she wanted to go, or how many decisions she would end up choosing to reverse.

Gathering herself together, she stood up. She opened the bedroom door and froze in shock.

A housemaid was walking into the second bathroom.

The room where she'd just left her positive pregnancy test, discarded on the floor.

"Hey! Wait!" Stella shouted in a panic, exploding out of the bedroom.

The housemaid looked equally shocked to see her. It was Anya, the pretty blonde with the scraped back hair. She spun away from the bathroom door and faced Stella, looking horrified and guilty.

"What are you doing?" Stella asked, her voice shrill with tension.

She remembered Vaughn had said he wanted a different cleaner. Now she wished she'd asked why. Did Vaughn not trust her? Would this woman run straight to Cecilia and tell her what she'd seen?

Fear flitted over the other woman's face.

"I – I'm sorry," she stammered. "I didn't know you were here. I thought you'd gone out in the car. I was tidying up and taking out the trash."

"I came back!" Stella said, frantically stating the obvious. She didn't care what she gabbled out, as long as it stopped Anya from walking back into the bathroom. "I'm in a hurry now. Please clean up later. In – in an hour," she said, trying to sound firm despite being in a complete panic.

"Yes, ma'am. I will do. I'm so sorry for disturbing you."

Anya backed away from the door and practically ran down the corridor. A moment later, the front door closed with a quiet and respectful click.

Stella stepped up to the bathroom entrance. She drew her breath in with a horrified hiss.

The pregnancy test was immediately visible, lying on the tiles near the toilet where she'd dropped it. She bitterly regretted that she'd been too shocked to throw it away in the trash can where it would at least have been out of sight.

Gathering up the test and the packaging, she fretted over what to do with it. Servants were in and out on a whim; she couldn't stop them. Eventually she wrapped the test up in its original box and pharmacy bag and stashed it all the way at the back of a kitchen drawer that was crammed with tea towels. Tugging towels over the bag, she hoped that it would be safe there for a while.

As she slammed the drawer shut, she heard the front door open.

Was Anya back already?

Whirling guiltily around, Stella peered through the kitchen archway, her heart sinking as she heard footsteps come in. Hissing in a breath, she recognized the clip-clop of Cecilia's fancy shoes. She was talking to someone. Stella darted out of sight, pressing herself into the corner. Don't come into the kitchen, she prayed. Please, not now. She couldn't handle Cecilia now.

"... so as we discussed, a large amount of work must be done in the master bedroom. You need to install under-floor heating as my son feels the cold, and it's a very chilly room in winter. I looked at what you sent through after your site visit yesterday, and I decided we should add an actual fireplace. Let me show you where I want it."

Three sets of footsteps headed down the corridor.

Stella had to avoid them. She felt totally uncertain about what her future held. Vaughn had said he was going to insist on moving out, but at this very moment Cecilia was doing major renovations to make the bedroom warmer for him. She could see that it wouldn't be easy for him to get out of her clutches and might not be possible at all.

As soon as they disappeared into the bedroom, Stella tiptoed outside and hustled along the path. She didn't know where she could go. Her purse was beside the bed, and she couldn't retrieve it now, so hiding out in a coffee shop was out of the question. She'd just have to lurk nearby until Cecilia had left.

At least she had her phone in her jacket pocket. Taking it out, and sidling behind a tree for cover, she tried calling Vaughn again.

Yet again it rang through to voicemail and she glowered in frustration.

Then a voice from behind her caused her to spin around in shock.

"Well, hello, Stella!"

Her heart sank as she saw Haydi approaching, her arm linked through Howard's in a friendly way. They were both wearing sneakers and shorts and looked dressed for tennis.

"How nice to see you again! Did you get what you needed from the pharmacy the other day?"

Feeling prickly with dread, Stella gave a fake smile. "Yes, I did, thanks."

"I've just been having coffee with Cecilia. I told her I'd seen you in there and she was horrified. She said with so many staff standing idle, you shouldn't be shopping for yourself, but either send someone out or get a delivery."

Ice traveled down Stella's spine. What else had Haydi seen and what else had she told Cecilia?

"She mentioned there were meds arriving for you this morning – antidepressants and tranquilizers. Good stuff, I believe," she said, winking at Stella. "You've been to see their shrink, she said?"

Now Stella felt appalled. Clearly, the session had not been privileged. First thing after she'd left, Dr. Lloyd and Cecilia had been merrily chatting on the phone and discussing what he'd prescribed. That was unethical, surely?

To her astonishment, Howard echoed her thoughts.

"Isn't that stuff supposed to be private? Don't know what my mother's doing gossiping about it," he remarked. "Makes me think that if I ever go see anyone, I'll choose someone different than Dr. Lloyd."

Haydi giggled. "You're so funny, Howard. Oh, there's Kathy with the new rackets. We can go up to the court now and test them out."

Stella glanced over her shoulder, tensing as Kathy marched out of the front door. She was also dressed in whites and carrying three tennis rackets and a gym bag.

This wasn't what she had wanted. She'd hoped to disappear into the grounds and avoid the family. At any moment Cecilia might emerge from the cottage.

"Stella," Kathy snapped, giving her a dagger-like stare. "Your meds have arrived. They're on the hall table. Please fetch them and take the first dose immediately."

So now Kathy was her medical adviser?

"Thank you," Stella replied coolly. At least it gave her the chance to leave the group. She headed for the main house and walked in. There, on the hallway table, was a pharmacy bag. Suspiciously, Stella picked it up and hurried out. She turned the other way, hoping she could now stay out of sight in the grounds. The tennis court was beyond the cottage so she couldn't go too far that way. Instead, she walked the other way, past an ornamental pond, and eventually found herself in a fruit orchard.

One of the maids was picking fruit from an apricot tree. As soon as she saw Stella, she turned and walked quickly away. Was she worried about being in trouble, Stella wondered? At least the orchard was an out-of-the-way spot. She sat down on a bench and tried to call Vaughn again, feeling bludgeoned with shock all over again as she thought about the results of that test.

"Please call me back," she texted him when he didn't pick up. "It's very urgent."

Then, with frantic worry about her pregnancy consuming her thoughts, she opened the pharmacy bag and took out the containers. What had this doctor given her? On principle she didn't want to take them. Being pregnant, and with her future now feeling so uncertain, made everything even more complicated.

Would she keep the baby if she had to leave Vaughn?

She didn't want to think about that decision, and what the implications would be. She didn't feel ready to consider this subject. Never, ever, when Vaughn had proposed, had she dreamed she'd end up in this situation.

But for now, at least she could research whether the tablets were contraindicated at this time. Carefully, she typed in the names on her phone.

As she researched, Stella grew angrier and angrier. The class of drugs this doctor had prescribed was definitely not what would usually be indicated for a patient who'd never taken antidepressants before. Reading furiously as she took a crash course on antidepressants courtesy of Google, Stella discovered that doctors usually prescribed selective serotonin reuptake inhibitors as a first option. Only if those were ineffective did they then move on to other classes of drug. But Dr. Lloyd had picked two much stronger drugs that had a long list of side effects and were most definitely not indicated during pregnancy.

And over and above this – double dipping in Stella's now irate opinion – he'd prescribed powerful sedatives to be taken twice daily. Those were not indicated during pregnancy either. The only one of the four medications that was pregnancy-safe was the sleeping pills.

This cocktail would turn her into little more than a zombie! Seething, she guessed that was the whole idea. She'd be too out of it, and battling with problems from the side effects, to show any more defiance to Cecilia.

She couldn't imagine job hunting while under the tranquilizing influence of all these meds.

"How unethical!" Stella hissed to herself. Fuming, she jumped to her feet, unable to stay seated a moment longer. Cecilia and the doctor were in on this together, she was sure. Cecilia had given him her wish list of desired behavior and he'd complied.

Hoping that the contractors had finished their measuring by now, she walked back to the cottage. Sure enough, it was all shut up and empty. Well, as empty as an unlocked place that was treated as public property by the family, could be.

"We have to get out of here," she repeated to herself, pulling out a chair at the dining room table and opening her laptop to hunt for affordable apartments. "Or else, I have to," she added, staring again at the list of unreturned phone calls and her message which Vaughn still hadn't replied to.

Whenever she thought about their relationship, she felt filled with a sense of doom. The only ray of hope was that Vaughn had promised that they would meet with his mother tonight to discuss moving out.

Everything now hinged on this outcome.

CHAPTER SIXTEEN

Sitting in the cottage, Stella watched the time tick by. She'd expected Vaughn would be home by eight at the latest to meet with his mother, but eight had passed by, and nine, too. Now it was nearly ten and she'd given up any hope of this discussion ever happening, now or in the future.

She'd tried to call him twice more, but he hadn't called her back. She felt frustrated beyond words that he'd broken his promise. Also, she felt intensely emotional about being ignored, because that was what it amounted to. Vaughn was stonewalling her. He could have found a minute to call, or text. He couldn't be that busy, especially not after office hours, when he'd be out 'entertaining' with Uncle Mike.

Was that a car outside? Stella sprang to her feet as she heard the front door open.

"Hey babes!" The slurred words rang out as he stumbled inside.

Storming into the hallway, she couldn't hold back her frustration.

"Vaughn, what is going on? Why didn't you call me back? And what happened to the meeting this evening?"

"I've been busy," he replied irritably. "I've had a lot to deal with today. I had to fix things with Uncle Mike. I told you how angry he was about this."

"So you fixed things over, like, ten whiskies?" Stella flashed back. How come his uncle didn't mind that Vaughn got falling-down drunk when 'out with clients,' but wasn't willing to forgive Stella for standing up to Cecilia?

She was sick of the double standards, and not in the mood for excuses.

She'd expected Vaughn would back down when he realized how angry she was. But he didn't.

"I didn't fix anything because my mother called me to say that she hasn't had an apology from you yet. So now everything is worse than it was. My uncle's furious with you. What's your answer to that, Stella?"

"I said I would apologize when we met with her this evening. I didn't realize there was an earlier deadline in place," Stella said sarcastically.

Vaughn wasn't listening. His gaze fell on the pharmacy bag that she'd placed on the hall table. "Are those your meds? Have you taken them?"

Stella walked over to the hall table. She opened each of the containers and shook a tablet out of each. Then she turned back to Vaughn.

"No I haven't."

"Why not?"

"I'll tell you if you explain why you answer your mother's calls but not mine. That's unacceptable. I needed to speak to you urgently, and you didn't pick up or call back or answer my message. But you speak to her. It makes me realize that you'll never be out of her control."

"That's unfair!" Vaughn raged. "I'm not being controlled by her. You're the one trying to control me and refusing to do what will help you!"

Angrily, he walked into the dining room, grabbed a glass from the sideboard, and poured whisky in. He was drunk beyond reason. Drunk to the stage where all he could do was drink more. She felt a surge of fright.

Suppressing it, she decided enough was enough.

"I'm not taking these tablets." She turned to the window, wrenched it open, and flung the handful of pills out, ignoring Vaughn's now-horrified cry. "They weren't responsibly prescribed. I researched them and apart from the sleeping pills, they all have bad side effects which were not explained to me. They're way too tranquilizing for me to function normally. They're meant to control me, nothing more."

"They're not!" Vaughn insisted, his anger now tinged with desperation. "Stella, please. I couldn't call you back until I knew things were right between you and Mom. And now you won't even take the damned meds! There's nothing wrong with antidepressants. Mom said they'd help you a lot. How can I persuade her to let us move out if you don't do your part?"

Stella lowered her voice, fighting for calmness. "You are twenty-eight years old. You shouldn't have to persuade your mother to let you move out. But in any case, there's another reason I'm not taking the meds."

"What's that?" Vaughn asked suspiciously.

"Because I'm pregnant." Stella steeled herself as she delivered the bombshell. Facing Vaughn across the spacious dining room, she felt scared and frantic and utterly alone. This wasn't how it should have been. They should have been holding hands.

"What?" Vaughn bellowed. "You can't be serious! Pregnant? You're joking, right?"

"I took a test this morning," Stella said. The quiver in her voice was audible. She couldn't believe the awfulness of how this was playing out.

"Oh, hell! I don't believe this. I do not believe this is happening. Do you have any idea how much trouble this will cause?" He sounded frantic. Grasping his whisky glass, he headed past her and into the kitchen. Ice clattered loudly into the glass.

Now Stella couldn't control herself another moment. She raged in behind him.

"I can't believe you just said what you did! This is your child we're talking about. We discussed this! You told me you wanted kids and we agreed on it. Now you're making out like it's the worst disaster ever. This is your reaction and what you choose to say? This is what you want us both to remember when we look back on this moment?"

"It is my reaction! It's too early and everyone's going to freak out about it! Stella, you don't understand. We're not an ordinary family. With my dad being an ex-senator and all."

"Do you have any idea how arrogant that sounds?"

"It's the truth! It might be strange to you, but it's what I've lived all my life with," Vaughn shot back.

Stella clenched her teeth. "Well, it's happened. And we have to handle it. That's if you're with me on this. Otherwise I'll make decisions myself, on my own. And they might not be ones you like," she added threateningly.

"You won't decide anything on your own!" He thumped his glass down onto the counter and stormed over to stand face to face with her. Sensing his furious energy she recoiled from him, fearing that his anger could flip over into violence at any moment. She'd never, ever seen this side of him. Never dreamed it existed. He was drunk and enraged and could easily do something he'd regret.

"You will do exactly what I say," he thundered. "I'm not getting disowned by my family because of you."

"I don't care about your rotten family. And I've made up my mind. I'm not putting up with this! I'm leaving you, Vaughn."

"You are not!"

Stella blinked. There had been a fuzzy moment, and now there was a knife in his hand, the kitchen light flashing off its steel.

It was her mother all over again, that awful evening when she'd turned on her, that soul-destroying moment when she'd feared for her life.

Happening again.

She heard her own screams of terror, and his furious roar.

"Stop it! Stop it! Please, stop. What are you doing? What are you doing?" her voice was high and breathy. She sagged back, feeling dark circles obscure her vision.

"What am I doing?" Vaughn stared curiously at the knife. Then he dropped it. It clattered to the floor.

Stella picked the knife up with trembling hands and placed it on the archway, out of his reach. Then she turned and ran to the safety of the bedroom. She slammed the door and locked it. Her hands were shaking so badly she could hardly turn the key.

She collapsed onto the bed. Her shoulders heaved with sobs.

From down the corridor she heard Vaughn shout again and jumped at the sound of his voice. But he wasn't speaking to her. He was calling out to someone else.

"Who's there? What are you doing?"

Then his footsteps hurried to the bedroom. The door handle turned.

"Stella, please. Open up. Please, babes. I'm sorry." His voice was low, shaking. All the anger had gone.

"No," she said, scrubbing furiously at her eyes. She wanted to face plant on the bed and cry buckets but forced herself to swallow down her sobs.

Outside, Vaughn knocked forlornly. "I am so, so sorry. I can't believe how I acted. I'm drunk and should never have said what I did. Please open up so I can apologize face to face."

"Who was that you were calling to?" she called warily.

"I don't know. I was closing the window and saw one of the maids heading past. I don't know who it was. They sometimes come back from the shops late at night." He paused.

An expectant silence followed.

Stella stood up and wrenched the door open.

With open arms, Vaughn lurched toward her, but Stella sidestepped.

"I am not discussing this now. In the morning, when you're sober, we will have a serious talk. But I'm warning you now that I've pretty much decided what I'm going to do."

"I understand," Vaughn sounded on the brink of tears. "I'm going to turn in before I mess up any more badly than I already have." He

95

glanced toward the door. "Did you say one of those meds you got were sleeping pills? Can I have one?"

Stella had no idea what the effects on top of so much alcohol would be but that was his problem, not hers.

"If you like," she said. Then, on impulse, she added, "I'll take one, too." Those were safe for her to take, and she didn't think she'd be able to sleep otherwise. She was far too wound up. The morning would bring tough decisions and she needed to be rested.

Vaughn gave her the haggard ghost of a smile.

"I'll bring us some water. We can do this together. Couple's activity, right?"

Stella didn't smile at that pathetic joke. Too little, too late. By the time Vaughn was back, she was in her nightshirt and in bed.

"Here's yours." He handed her the tablet and water.

"Thanks." Stella had seldom felt so relieved to take a pill, knowing that in a minute, the unbearable stress of the evening would be over.

She turned her back to Vaughn, pushing her head into the soft feather pillow as she waited for sleep to take her.

Although she was sure his apology was genuine and that he was appalled at his own behavior, the fact remained he had behaved that way. She'd seen hints of it recently, and tonight it had come out. It was a dark, ugly side. For a moment she'd been genuinely terrified. And it would happen again. Of course it would. In fact, Stella realized in a moment of enlightenment, her being with him was making it happen, because she was the one pushing for different choices than what his family wanted.

For her own well-being, she needed to put a stop to this destructive cycle. Tomorrow she was going to leave him for good. No negotiation. No second chances. She'd make a clean break and start afresh.

The thought flitted into her mind, shocking in its resolve. She needed to do what she'd always done to save herself.

Leave.

With that thought in mind, the tranquilizer took hold, pulling her down into a fitful and troubled slumber.

*

She woke with difficulty, dragging herself out of a dark pit of sleep. Opening her eyes, she glanced at the curtains, just starting to brighten with the early dawn beyond. This was going to be a tough day. She'd need every inch of her determination and mental strength to get through it. This was going to be the day she changed her life and left Vaughn.

Fractured memories of nightmares lurked, dissolving as she eased into wakefulness.

But there was something that had flavored her dreams that didn't disappear; the odd, metallic odor that she could clearly smell.

And the sheets felt wet. Cold, wet, and heavy.

With panic surging inside her, Stella threw back the covers and reached for the bedside lamp. As she snapped it on, her heart jumped into her throat.

Blood. There was cooled blood on the sheets, deep crimson stains that had oozed onto her nightshirt. Her left arm was smeared with it.

"No! What happened!"

In panic, she turned to Vaughn, a motionless weight on the bed by her side.

He lay face up. His mouth and eyes were half open. His chest and stomach were a raw, bloody mess.

From out of his chest jutted the hilt of a knife.

CHAPTER SEVENTEEN

"Oh, no! No!"

Stella jumped out of bed, hyperventilating with shock.

She backed away toward the door, tearing off her bloodstained nightshirt and flinging it onto the floor. More black spots flashed in front of her eyes, and she grabbed at the wall for support. This was a nightmare. It must be. It was a crazy, vivid dream.

But as she huddled by the doorway, her skin prickling with goose bumps, the truth sank in. This was no joke and no dream.

While she had slept, Vaughn had been murdered.

Bile surged inside her, and she retched. Then she ran out of the room, heading blindly to the second bathroom. She threw up in the toilet, heaving and coughing until her stomach was sore and her throat raw. She was shaking all over. Now there were smears of blood on the toilet bowl, too.

Climbing up from the toilet, Stella knew she needed to call the police immediately.

Returning to the bedroom on cotton-wool legs, she felt the black shapes loom at the edge of her vision again. She fought them off as she picked her way around the bed to grab her phone.

She stumbled down the passage. Standing in the hallway, she called 911.

"There's been a murder. Please, come quick. My boyfriend's been attacked."

"Are you in any danger, ma'am?" the operator asked.

"I don't think so. I'm alone here," Stella gasped. The routine question about her safety was causing her to dissolve in tears.

"What is your address?"

Stella gave the road name, but realized with a shock that she didn't know the house number? What was it? She couldn't remember.

Then, with a rush of relief, she recalled what it was, and that she'd used it on her job applications.

"Ma'am. Are you there?" the operator asked.

"Yes, I'm here. Number fourteen. The cottage. There's a main house and then a cottage nearby."

"The police will be there in a few minutes, ma'am."

Stella put down the phone on the dining room table, next to her laptop. Her hands were shaking so badly she almost knocked it off the table but managed to fumble it back to safety in time.

Why was it all still there? She'd assumed there'd been a break-in. But everything was as it had been the previous night, and nothing seemed to be missing. Her phone, the laptop. The front door was closed. Nothing looked disturbed or broken.

But one thing was out of place and as her gaze swiveled to the kitchen counter, she realized with a gasp what it was.

The sharp, heavy kitchen knife Vaughn had picked up so threateningly yesterday was missing. It was no longer in its place, and she let out an anguished cry as she realized where it was.

The knife that she had been the last person in the house to touch, was the one now jutting out of her dead fiancé's chest.

She already knew she was in trouble. But only at that moment did Stella realize how bad it was.

*

Footsteps approached from outside, and the crackle of a walkie-talkie brought Stella a sudden, vivid memory of her father. After a perfunctory rap of the knocker, the door swung open even as she stammered, "Come in."

Stella found herself staring at a stocky, tough-looking man with neatly trimmed brown hair. He was wearing a shirt and tie. He looked at her inquiringly, his dark eyes piercing and intelligent. She saw his gaze intensify as he took in the bloodstains on her nightshirt and skin.

"Morning. Are you Stella Fall, who made the call earlier?"

"I am," she whispered.

"I'm Detective Bradshaw."

Behind him, she saw others standing. Two cops were waiting, and the clatter of wheels on paving told her a stretcher was being unloaded. Another wave of dizzy sickness swept her, and she bent forward, leaning on the dining room table, breathing hard, grateful for its solid support.

"Can you tell me where the deceased person is?" Detective Bradshaw asked her gently.

"He's in the bedroom," she pointed. "At the end of the corridor." She was shaking violently, and the sight of the detective had caused her to start sobbing again. She fought to control herself, biting her lip so hard she tasted blood.

At that moment, from the front door, a shout rang out.

"What are you doing here? What's going on?"

It was Gordon. He must have seen the cars outside the cottage and had stormed down to find out what was going on.

Stella stepped back, feeling horrified. She didn't want to confront any of the family now, while she was covered in blood and feeling close to hysterics with shock.

One of the police, on his way in, turned to block the doorway.

"Sir, there's been a suspicious death. Please stand back,"

"A death? What the hell?" Gordon's voice was a roar. "This is my house. I demand to be allowed inside."

"Please keep away from the entrance," the policeman said again, louder this time. "You may not enter until we have examined the scene. A crime has been reported. Wait outside."

From further away, another voice resonated, loud and shrill.

"Gordon, what's going on? Why won't they let you in?" It was Cecilia, clearly on the warpath.

"I don't know. They're being obstructive," Gordon snapped.

"Make them let us in. Can't you explain who you are?"

"Officer, I am an ex-senator," Gordon said authoritatively, but his deep voice sounded bullying, rather than the commanding tone she guessed he was hoping for.

"Nobody is allowed in the house," the policeman repeated. "Please wait outside."

The police had finished donning their gear. They trooped inside. Detective Bradshaw led the way. Behind him, a cameraman and another uniformed officer followed. The two stretcher-bearers brought up the rear.

Detective Bradshaw turned and instructed the other cop. "Stay by the door. Nobody goes in or out."

The officer closed the front door and the police headed down the corridor to the bedroom where Vaughn's body lay. From down the corridor she heard raised voices, as the police viewed the crime scene.

Stella felt filled with despair. She closed her eyes, wishing that she could open them and find this had all been a terrible dream.

How had it happened? Who had killed him? Why hadn't they taken anything and why hadn't she died, too?

"Ma'am? Ms. Fall?"

She looked up.

Detective Bradshaw stood opposite her, watching her with an expression that was stern, but not condemning. His body language seemed open. She was confused by how calm he was after having been in that hideous charnel house of the bedroom. Obviously he was used to seeing these horrors.

"I need to ask you some questions. Do you feel capable to answer?"

She must look as shredded as she felt. Stella felt a flash of fear that for once, her true feelings and emotions were visible.

"I – I'm covered in blood. I don't want to answer questions like this. I want to take a shower. Please can I?"

The detective frowned thoughtfully before making a decision.

"We need to photograph you. Wait a moment. We'll get that done and take swabs of the stains. Then you can shower."

He went to the door and called out to the cameraman who hurried back to the dining room. Numbly, she obeyed the instructions to stand straight, turn, hold out her arms, as he photographed.

"All right. You can go and shower." The detective paused, staring at her. "I'll ask one of our officers to leave you a change of clothes in the bathroom."

Stella headed to the second bathroom. There, she stripped off her stained nightshirt and got into the shower. She turned the water on full blast and scrubbed the blood from her skin so violently it felt as if she was scraping herself raw. Sobbing under the blast of water as if she would never stop, she washed her hair again and again, still feeling that the taint lingered in her nostrils, despite the fragrant, floral shampoo.

Eventually, she climbed out of the shower, seeing to her relief that her bloodied clothes had been removed and someone had set an outfit on the chair – fresh underwear, jeans, T-shirt, socks, and shoes. Stella felt unreasonably grateful for this and began to sob all over again.

She pulled on the clothes and brushed her wet hair before walking out. The second bathroom was further up the corridor so thankfully she didn't have to pass the scene. She fixed her eyes firmly ahead on the dining room, where Detective Bradshaw was waiting.

"Feel better now? Are you ready to answer some questions?"

"Yes, I am."

The detective pulled out a chair and helped her into it. Stella collapsed onto the seat.

He sat down opposite. "We'll record this, of course."

Even though he said so, and she assumed he was recording it somehow, he wasn't shoving a recorder in her face, and she was grateful for that.

"Tell me in your own words what happened."

She stared at him, blindsided by the sheer scope of the question.

"How far back should I go?" she asked in a wobbly voice.

A slight frown creased his forehead. "Start with the immediate circumstances leading up to this incident. From yesterday evening up until the time you made the call."

Stella shuddered as she recalled their loud, noisy fight. Describing this would make her look guilty. It might be better to downplay what had happened and to say it had been a normal evening.

But could she lie? It wouldn't be wise. Even to save herself in incriminating circumstances, even knowing she wasn't guilty, it would still be wrong. As her father's daughter, Stella realized she couldn't do it. However hard it was, she'd have to tell the truth and admit to the fight.

"Vaughn is my fiancé," she explained. "He got back home late last night after work. He had been drinking. We had an argument and ended up shouting at each other. I'd been trying to persuade him to move out. I criticized his family. That was mainly what the fight was about."

The memory of it felt seared in her mind – the emotions as vivid as the words. She couldn't tell the cops about the pregnancy test, she decided. She didn't want to tell anyone.

"Anything else?" Clearly, Detective Bradshaw was perceptive and had noticed her hesitation.

"He picked up a knife at one stage. He was very drunk and not thinking clearly about what he was doing. I screamed at him, and he dropped it. I then put it on the archway. That was the knife that was used on him. I know how that looks."

Fear filled her as she thought about how guilty the circumstances made her appear. Would there be a way out for her?

Detective Bradshaw's frown deepened.

"Just tell me your version. The more honest and detailed, the better. What happened after you put the knife on the archway?"

"I was shaken up by the fight. I ran into the bedroom and locked myself inside."

At that moment, Stella remembered with a jolt that there had been a witness. Vaughn had called out to one of the housemaids, when he saw her passing by. It was lucky she'd admitted to the fight, because through the open window, their shouts would easily have been heard from outside. But what exactly had this maid overheard? Her stomach twisted as she wondered how far from the window she had been.

"Vaughn begged me to open up, and started apologizing," she continued. "Eventually I let him in. He apologized some more. Then he brought us two of the sleeping tablets that his family shrink had prescribed for me. We both wanted to calm down and get to sleep, but by that stage I'd also decided that this wasn't going to work out and that we needed to split up. I planned to tell him so in the morning but when I woke, I found – I saw..." Her voice tailed off.

"Those tablets?" the detective asked, seeing the direction of her gaze. "Are all those medications yours?"

"They were prescribed for me, but I didn't take the others. I wasn't happy about doing that. Vaughn and I each took a sleeping tablet last night."

Even as she spoke, Stella realized that if the police counted the tablets, they would find one missing from the other bottles, because she'd thrown them away.

"I threw one of each out of the window while we were arguing," she added hurriedly, not wanting to be made out as a liar.

Bradshaw stood up and photographed the labels carefully before turning back to her.

"Tell me about this morning, when you woke."

"It was barely light. I felt very tired and disoriented. The sleeping tablet was stronger than I'd thought. I smelled blood and realized the sheets were wet. I saw Vaughn and realized it came from him." Stella closed her eyes, feeling sick as she relived that moment. The awful, metallic reek surged in her memory again and she wondered if she'd ever forget it.

"I panicked. I jumped out of bed. I was sick. I wasn't thinking straight." Stella felt ashamed. She'd always thought that in such a situation, she would be calm. "Then I called you."

"It's alright. You didn't do too badly, under the circumstances," Detective Bradshaw said, and she stared at him in surprise. It sounded as if he did have at least a shred of sympathy for her.

"You've been with Vaughn Marshall for how long?"

"Just over four months. We met in Chicago. He proposed to me when his work experience contract was up, and we moved here a few days ago."

"And was anyone else supposed to visit last night? Anyone invited to socialize?"

Stella shook his head. "Vaughn got home at about ten. There was nobody with him and he didn't mention anyone arriving."

"I'm going to go outside and speak to the family now. Stay in here. Just keep away from the bedroom while the team works down the passage. Make yourself a cup of sweet tea," he invited her.

Detective Bradshaw strode to the front door and opened it. Immediately, a chorus of raised voices erupted.

"Detective, it was a mistake," Cecilia Marshall urged.

Stella felt confused. They were speaking in her defense? That was impossible. Had she misheard?

"That woman, his fiancée, was unstable. She'd recently been to see our family psychiatrist. Most likely she was suicidal," Gordon agreed.

"She was a clumsy little thing, too. Forever tripping and falling," Cecilia mused.

Stella felt icy with shock. They automatically assumed that she was the deceased, and that Vaughn was now under suspicion, and were already trying everything they could to clear their son's name. Without even knowing the facts!

She felt horrified by their behavior.

The sound of low voices followed, and she knew, tension filling her, that Detective Bradshaw was explaining the true story. He was telling them that their son was dead.

Even though he had invited her to make a hot drink, there was no way she could climb to her feet. She cowered down on the chair, huddled over the table, waiting for the moment when she'd hear their reaction.

Cecilia let out a horrified scream.

"My son! It can't be! He can't be dead. I must see him! Let me see him now!"

"It's that woman!" Gordon's voice bellowed out. "It's her fault. She killed him. I knew she was trouble from the very first moment she stepped in here!"

Cecilia's screams rose. Her cries sounded feral in their grief and rage, and Stella felt a sickening sense of self-blame. She feared her arrival had set off this chain of events. If she hadn't returned to Greenwich with Vaughn, would he be alive and well and living his life?

His parents had lost their eldest son and the pain she heard in their cries was raw and real.

Stella knew she was going to be in deep trouble. She had no alibi apart from being asleep. She'd heard nobody else come in. They'd had a screaming fight which had been overheard by someone passing by.

The evidence was incriminating, and it pointed toward her. How could she convince the police that she was innocent when this powerful, influential family would be doing everything they could to make sure she was accused of the crime?

CHAPTER EIGHTEEN

In another half-hour, Detective Bradshaw walked back into the cottage. He looked stressed as he closed the door firmly behind him.

"We're not bringing you into the station. Yet," he added, cutting short Stella's surge of premature relief. "There are still other angles to investigate, with so many staff and family members residing on the property. However, the Marshalls want you gone. They want you to leave, now."

"That's fine. I'll go." At least she could get out of this place, she thought. Whatever happened, she wouldn't have to see any of the family again.

But the detective's next comment told her otherwise.

"There's one problem. You are officially, a murder suspect, so we need you to stay in the local area and not leave Greenwich. We have to know your whereabouts at all times, and you must stay contactable as we may need to interview you again. Do you have alternative accommodation?"

In Greenwich? She didn't know a soul apart from the Marshalls and their circle of friends. And a guesthouse in this area would be way beyond her budget. Her bank account was bled out. A few hundred dollars were all that remained between her and the streets.

"I don't have any other place to go here," she admitted.

Or anywhere, she realized, with a sense of fear.

The cop nodded. "I already told the family that you have to stay close by during the investigation. In the absence of any alternatives, I'll tell them you'll have to remain on the premises."

Horror filled her. Stay? Here? In the same place where Vaughn had been murdered?

She couldn't bear to spend another night in this place. It felt saturated with terrible memories. The only alternative was the main house, which would be even worse.

Drawing in a sharp breath, Stella realized another truth. Unless a stranger had somehow come and gone without stealing anything, then somebody within the fractured, conflicted circle of family and friends must have done this deed.

What if they decided to kill her as well?

Staying in this cottage, she knew full well that she could be next.

"I don't feel safe here," she stammered out to the detective.

He grimaced. "I understand. I sympathize. We're out of options at this time. I can ask the family to change the locks on the front door." As he looked at her face, Stella could tell they shared the same thoughts. "Okay, they might not agree to do that but there is a safety chain on the inside of the door which you can use."

Stella glanced at its flimsy gold links. She had no idea why it was there at all. The door itself was finely crafted from oak, but security was not its main function. The lock and chain were mostly for show.

"And I see there's a furnished second bedroom and a second bathroom?" the detective continued. "We'll move all your clothing into the other room for you straight away, so there will be no need for you to ever walk into the master bedroom again. We'll keep the master bedroom sealed until we can get a clean-up crew to do a deep clean later today," he reassured her.

That would have to do, Stella thought. Unsafe as it was, at least she wouldn't have to go into the room where it had happened again.

"Are there any other details on the crime?" she asked, anxiety surging. "What time did it happen?"

At least she'd know when to be careful, and listen out, she thought.

"Coroner thinks between midnight and two a.m., but that's only an estimate until the postmortem is completed. Do you have any input on that?"

"No. I was in bed and asleep before eleven," she said regretfully.

A shout from down the passageway alerted Bradshaw and he looked around.

"They're nearly ready to wheel the stretcher out," he told her. "If you want to go outside and get some air for an hour or so, that's fine, just keep your phone with you and stay close by in case we need to speak to you again." He paused. "You're already a suspect, Ms. Fall. Don't do anything that will make things worse for you."

"I promise I'll stay," she said.

She wasn't going to go out the front door. The family would descend on her like a pack of wolves.

Taking the bunch of keys, Stella opened the kitchen door. She stepped out into a well-tended garden. It was a haven of tranquility, with climbing creepers and a few flowering shrubs, and a wooden bench beyond.

Feeling nervous to walk any further in case she encountered one of the family, Stella sat down. She placed her hands on the varnished wood. The touch reminded her of the work bench in her father's shed, behind the farmhouse, where he used to go on his occasional time off. That place had been a refuge from her mother's constant anger and bitter criticism. He'd done some woodwork, repairs to furniture. He'd fixed a chair that her mother had smashed during a fight. He'd even made a few toys for Stella.

If her father had been alive and working in this area, he'd have taken on the case. What would he have done, Stella wondered? How would he have begun the hunt for Vaughn's killer?

Her thoughts went again to the detective in charge. He seemed stern but fair – but was he? What if he was corrupt or somehow under the family's influence?

How could she help him, she wondered, and felt breathless with surprise at the audacity of her own thoughts. *Could* she help him?

Someone here must know something. If she could find the killer, she could clear her name and avoid being wrongfully arrested. It would be the first step to getting her life back again.

Feeling a spark of hope, Stella got up from her bench. She'd been sitting there for longer than she'd realized, processing the horrors that she'd seen, and then immersed in thought. Now she felt cold and decided to walk to warm up. Keeping to the back of the cottage she set off along the path.

A police car and an unmarked vehicle were parked outside the main house. The ordinary sedans looked out of place next to its splendid frontage. She guessed the police were interviewing the family inside and asking for their whereabouts last night. Avoiding the front of the house, she headed around the back. There, she stopped, staring in concern.

Under a wrought-iron gazebo in the garden, the police were interviewing some of the household staff. A gardener and two of the housemaids were talking to one of the policemen, while the other housemaid was being interviewed separately. She was seated at the table facing Stella, opposite a detective she hadn't seen before.

Looking more carefully, Stella saw it was Anya seated at the table. Had she been the one who passed by last night and overheard the fight between her and Vaughn? Why else would they be speaking to her first? Turning, Stella headed hastily back the way she'd come. She didn't want the police to see her standing there and watching. It might appear guilty.

Feeling worried, she returned to the kitchen garden. The back door was open. Through it, she saw to her dismay that Kathy was standing in the kitchen.

"What do you mean, this murderess has to stay here?"

Shocked, Stella shrank away as Kathy continued her tirade to Detective Bradshaw in a hoarse, choked voice.

"We don't want her here. The poisonous little gold-digger should be in jail. All of us regret the day she arrived. It was clear from the beginning she was only after my nephew's money and would go to any lengths to achieve it. That's why this has happened. It's completely obvious."

Stella twined her fingers with anxiety as she thought about the positive test. That wouldn't look good for her now, in light of these words. She had to keep her pregnancy a secret. If that was still possible, she thought miserably.

"Ms. Fall has nowhere else to stay while we investigate. If she stays here, it may allow us to conclude the case faster," Bradshaw's voice was calm and unemotional.

Kathy sighed, clearly frustrated.

"We don't trust her. In our eyes, she's a criminal. We will not feel safe with her on our property and will have to organize additional security."

"If you have any concerns, we are a phone call away. As a suspect in this case, I'm sure she will abide by any rules you set. This is a top priority case, and we certainly hope to make an arrest soon," Bradshaw reassured her in respectful tones. "We have allocated a team of detectives who will be working around the clock."

Kathy seemed mollified by this.

"I'll run it past Cecilia and see if she agrees. Obviously, she's in immense grief."

"I sympathize with your loss," Bradshaw agreed quietly.

They walked out, closing the front door, and Stella sneaked in and closed the back.

The family was organizing extra security. She didn't know what form that would take, but she hoped that it might protect her as well.

The cottage felt like a trap. How could she stay here with these toxic people, who she bitterly hated for having corrupted Vaughn from what he could have been into one of them? Worse still, they believed – or wanted to believe – that she was guilty. They had the money and influence to get their way. What if they were able to convince, or pressure, the police into arresting her?

She had to fight back.

Letting out a deep breath, Stella decided to look at her situation from a different perspective. Staying here gave her an opportunity she would otherwise never have had – the chance to save herself and clear her name.

As soon as the police had finished up, and the deep cleaning crew had done their work, she was going to start prying into this family's secrets.

One of them had hated Vaughn enough to murder him. She was going to find out who it was.

CHAPTER NINETEEN

Stella was woken by the drumming of rain on her window. It was a cold, gray dawn, so dark that she felt briefly disoriented.

Then reality came rushing back and she sat up with a gasp, snapping the light on.

The spare bedroom looked just as it had when she'd fallen asleep. It was furnished elegantly and impersonally in cream and beige, like a hotel room. The antique wooden desk chair was in the place she'd left it, wedged against the door handle. Nothing looked disturbed, and the plush curtains were still tightly drawn.

She'd locked up and gone to bed last night at about eight p.m., after the police and clean-up crew had finally left. At least she had survived the night.

Now she could start with her investigation. The day lay ahead of her, filled with promise and threat.

Checking her phone, Stella realized that no emails or messages had downloaded since yesterday afternoon. She refreshed her mails but was met with the terse message, 'No Signal.'

The rain must have knocked the wi-fi out, and she remembered now that the cell signal on the property was very weak. That was more than an inconvenience. What if she needed to make a call urgently because she was in danger?

She hoped that it would be up and running again soon.

A rap on the front door made her jump. Who was knocking so early in the morning?

With anxiety surging inside her, she quickly pulled on the clothes she'd left folded at the bottom of the bed. She tugged a brush through her hair and slipped on shoes. Then she hurried down the corridor just as another knock resounded through the house.

"Who's there?" she asked.

She grasped the door handle. It felt cold in her hands.

There was no peephole. She guessed the family never thought they'd have need of one.

Taking a deep breath, she unlocked the door and swung it open.

She stared out at the empty porch. Beyond, cold rain streamed down. There was nobody in sight, but she heard the distant sound of a golf cart.

Shivering, Stella closed the door again. Who had done this?

Deciding to start her day early, she headed for the guest bathroom. She turned on the shower and waited for the water to warm up. Usually it took only a few seconds.

Today, the relentless stream of water remained icy cold.

Puzzled, Stella turned it off. She tried the water in the basin with the same result. There, too, was no hot water.

Had the rain damaged the water heater also? Surely not. It would be safely hidden away in the roof somewhere, and there was no sign of leaking or any power outage.

Another, and more valid, suspicion was starting to occur to Stella.

The family was responsible for all of this. They'd turned off the hot water. They'd cut off signal to the cottage, either by disabling it or changing the password. And they were knocking on her door in the early morning to scare her.

She thought of Kathy, rubbing her hands in satisfied glee.

It was clear that they were going to make her life hell. This was just the start. This was what they'd managed to do in one short day, while in shock over the death of their eldest son. She had no doubt that they'd come up with other malicious ideas, and it filled her with fear.

They were so powerful, so influential. In what other ways, outside of these four walls, were they working to make sure they would win and she would lose?

Right now, on this chilly morning, she couldn't face a cold shower. There was electricity – for now, at any rate. Probably they hadn't figured out a way to disable it. But she was sure they would be working on it.

She boiled a kettle and, after making a few trips, had enough hot water in the bottom of the enormous bath that she could have a sketchy wash.

After that, she pulled on her rain jacket and a pair of boots, and then she left the cottage, tugging the hood up over her head.

It was time to start digging.

Splashing her way across the mushy, rain-soaked lawn, she headed for the small access gate near the main gate, where she had seen the household staff come in. It was still early, before seven, and she hoped that she might find a few people arriving to start their morning's work.

The best place to start getting background on the family would be to question the people who worked with them. Or so she hoped.

She reached the gate and waited, huddling out of sight near a tree and feeling nervous. They would think she was one of the family and would have no reason to trust her.

There was someone. She straightened up expectantly as the door unlocked and the woman stepped inside and closed it again, pocketing her keys. She was wrapped up in a gray raincoat, and rain spattered off her umbrella. Stella didn't recognize her, but she hadn't expected to. She hadn't spent much time in the main house and in any case, the staff did their best to stay invisible and out of sight.

"Good morning," she said, stepping forward and giving her most genuine smile. The expression felt strange on her face. It had been a long time since she'd used it.

The woman turned, looking stressed. She was dark haired and probably in her thirties, Stella thought.

"Morning, ma'am," she muttered.

"Do you have a moment to talk to me?" Stella asked.

The woman tilted her head, wiping rain off her forehead.

Casually, Stella mirrored the action. Doing this could build a feeling of greater trust. She'd been fascinated by body language in her psychology classes.

A host of emotions flitted across the woman's face. Looking stressed, she nodded. "I suppose so," she said warily.

"Oops!" Stella dropped her keys and bent to pick them up. "My hands are so cold! This rain feels like a real winter downpour."

Showing vulnerability, through a silly moment, was another way to help someone relate to you. And it worked. She saw the woman's expression relax slightly.

"What's your name?" Stella asked.

"Marta,"

"Marta, I'm Stella. I'm sure you know what happened yesterday. To Vaughn, my fiancé?"

Marta nodded. "Yes, ma'am. I'm very sorry."

Turning, Stella walked with her, heading down the driveway toward the house.

"I'm feeling very scared now. I was wondering, if the killer was someone who knew Vaughn but who didn't live here, how they could have gotten in? Because the property is secure and that's an automatic gate."

Marta nodded. "We are issued keys for the side gate and have to sign for them."

"And the main gate? Do people always ring for entrance?"

"A few people have buzzers. Friends and family. I often see them driving in and opening the gate themselves."

Stella felt disappointed as this widened the pool of suspects. It would have been much easier if all visitors had to ring at the gate.

Her next question to Marta would be an important one. She was going to ask if there had been any family fights within the house recently.

But at that moment, she heard the rattle of a golf cart, approaching from behind them and a man shouted something. Marta's face changed. The expression of openness was replaced by fear. She glanced around, then veered off and headed to the house at a half-run.

Stella turned to scrutinize the man in the golf cart. He had short, blonde, buzz-cut hair and wore a black bomber jacket. He had a handgun on his hip. Stella didn't know enough about guns to know its type.

He stared at her suspiciously. So this was the hired security, who'd probably knocked on her door early in the morning to frighten her? She guessed he knew who she was, but he didn't speak to her directly. His role was clearly more to intimidate.

Seething with anger at these bullying tactics, Stella decided to head back inside, but as she neared the house, a thought occurred to her. Not all the staff would be live-out. There must be some who lived in.

After all, the drivers had to be available at all hours, and the family entertained nonstop, and Anya had been walking back toward the house late at night.

So, where did the servants who stayed overnight, sleep?

Feeling impatient with herself at her sketchy knowledge of this enormous house, Stella decided to find out. It was crazy that nobody had given her a guided tour. Not once had she had the chance to wander all the way through its elegant halls and actually familiarize herself with every room.

Where would the servants' accommodation be located, she wondered, hoping that logic and deduction would provide the answer.

Once the guard had driven away, she followed the route that Marta had taken and found herself on a narrow, paved path that hugged the perimeter of the garden. Probably, treading over the pristine grass was forbidden territory for servants.

The path snaked its way around the lawn and then skirted the formal garden, leading to the back of the house. She guessed that it might end up near the main kitchen, and she was right. It led into a walled courtyard. Through the archway she saw a kitchen door, closed against the weather. The courtyard was filled with herb beds and pots, and a washing line on the far wall that was currently folded down.

She guessed the door led into the scullery. Perhaps there was a cloakroom or changing room where they dressed for the day.

Her eye was drawn downward, and it was then that she saw where the staff must live.

Beyond the kitchen door, a narrow staircase, half hidden by a bushy hedge, led steeply down.

Intrigued and unsure, she followed it.

CHAPTER TWENTY

The paved steps led Stella to a lower level that was concealed from view by another sheer wall. Between the walls ran an alleyway. Here, the paving was not as well cared for as it was in the rest of the house. It was uneven and she noticed a few of the tiles were broken.

On the right of the alleyway were five doors, spaced just a few yards apart. Again, she was surprised by how ordinary they looked. These modest doors, scratched and scuffed, wouldn't have been out of place in a tenement building. What were they doing at the back of this showpiece home? She felt disoriented all over again, that another small world existed within this house that she'd never dreamed could be there.

Her foot squelched into a puddle, and she stepped hurriedly around it, approaching the first weathered-looking door.

Feeling nervous, she knocked, wondering if anyone would answer. She felt as if she was imposing horribly on whoever was inside.

Nobody answered, so after a minute she moved onto the second door.

A grumpy voice muttered something in sleepy tones. A few moments later the door was wrenched open. Standing there, blinking tiredly and with his dark hair mussed, was Rodriguez.

She felt pleased to see someone she recognized, but he looked horrified to see her.

"Rodriguez. I'm so sorry to disturb you."

"What is it?" he replied. His tone was not quite hostile. She sensed resentment and an unwillingness to speak.

"Could you do me a favor? I want to ask you something important."

As her eyes adjusted to the darkened room beyond, Stella saw that it was tiny. Smaller than a prison cell. Just big enough to house a single bed, a rack for clothes, and a tiny chest of drawers. The walls were whitewashed and there wasn't even a window, just a ventilation grille set into the concrete above the door.

"What is so important?" he asked warily.

He'd hung a photo on the wall next to the bed, of a smiling, dark haired woman. Was she his girlfriend or his wife, Stella wondered?

Was she the reason he endured the unforgiving hours and cramped accommodation?

"You know Vaughn, my fiancé, was killed yesterday?"

Rodriguez nodded. "I heard, yes. I am sorry." He didn't sound sorry, though. His voice was toneless.

"I need to know what happened," Stella said in a low, pleading voice. She felt worried that she wasn't getting through to him. She sensed no sympathetic response and felt he'd walled himself off emotionally. "Please, I need your help. The police suspect me, but I didn't do it. I'm desperate to find out who did."

"I can tell you nothing," Rodriguez replied.

"Someone must have walked in and done that terrible thing. So I'm wondering if it could have been one of the people close to him. Possibly even one of the family."

Rodriguez shrugged expressively. His action spoke louder than words.

Stella decided to level up. "I know the family treats you appallingly. I've seen how they speak to you and also how they speak over you, as if you're not there at all. You might have heard something while you were driving. Perhaps Vaughn fought with someone at work or had an angry conversation on the phone. Anything would help me."

She spread her arms in appeal.

Rodriguez shook his head. "I cannot answer. I will not be able to. This is my job."

She heard resignation in his voice and, finally, the note of sympathy she'd expected at the start.

"Please, there must be something," Stella entreated, but he shook his head again.

"I must rest now. My shift starts at lunch time," he said.

Rodriguez closed the door – softly and politely, but very decisively. She was getting no more information from him.

He must be afraid of losing his job. This couldn't be misplaced loyalty. She hadn't sensed the entitled zeal of a faithful retainer and in any case, he had been hired while Vaughn was in Chicago, so he hadn't been there long enough for that. Rather, Rodriguez wanted to stay out of things, earn his money, and endure his daily tasks.

To her shock, Stella realized she hadn't even seen a bathroom door in that narrow, spartan room. Did the live-in staff all share a bathroom? That would mean going out in the rain or cold at all hours. That was horrific.

How could the servants' quarters be so different from the house? It seemed like they were designed to be shabby and poky, with comfort and dignity deliberately withheld.

There was no answer when she tried each of the two following doors. The second to last one was half open and, peeking in, Stella saw it was in fact a bathroom, with a small basin, a tiny shower, and a toilet door beyond.

A few paces ahead was the final door in the row, and she smelled a familiar aroma as she approached it. Toast.

Peering around, Stella saw that this room was a kitchenette. There was a hot plate, toaster, and kettle on the counter, which also contained a few cupboards below. Beyond, on the back wall, a washing machine churned vigorously.

The woman who was making toast spun around on seeing Stella, looking appalled. She was wearing a pair of old jeans, slippers, and a worn knit top. The lines on her face made her look tired and defeated.

Then she realized who Stella was, and her expression changed to suspicion.

"Hi, I'm Stella," she began softly. "I'm really sorry for interrupting. I need to speak to you quickly and I'd so appreciate if you could help me. What's your name?"

"Juana," the woman said reluctantly.

"Where are you originally from?" She detected a hint of an accent but couldn't identify it further.

"From Mexico," Juana said.

"How long have you been working for the family?" Stella tried for a conversational tone. She didn't think there was any way of easily breaking the ice here because Juana was surprised and on the defensive. Therefore, Stella decided to start with easy questions that didn't jolt her out of her comfort zone. Once she had gained the confidence to answer, she might relax.

Juana paused. "Six years," she said.

"Have you lived in for all the six years?" Stella asked, surprised. Inwardly she felt a flare of excitement. Six years meant Juana would know the family well.

"I worked part time for a year. Since then, I have lived in, yes."

It was time to cut to the chase, Stella decided.

"Juana, I really need your help. Please. As you know, my fiancé Vaughn was murdered. I need to find out who did it. It must have been someone who knew him."

"And you are asking me?" Juana queried, with a note of incredulity.

"I need some background. I don't know the family well, and there are things going on I don't understand."

Juana stared at her for a thoughtful moment.

"Yes. You are right. There is a lot going on that you don't understand."

Feeling hopeful, Stella edged forward.

From behind Juana, the pop of the toaster made them both jump. Stella saw the shift in her eyes. The sound had broken the moment, and the connection between them was gone.

"I can't tell you," she said.

Stella bit her lip in frustration. Forcing herself to keep calm, she continued.

"Why not? Are you worried they will threaten you?"

There was silence for a little while longer, the only sound the pattering of the rain outside.

Then Juana said something else, almost inaudibly.

She turned away and started rummaging in the cupboard. The conversation was clearly over.

Stella felt deflated as she headed out into the rain again. Her interviews with the staff had been an absolute dead end. Nobody would talk. The atmosphere of fear and distrust was palpable. They were terrified of losing their jobs and getting fired on a whim, she thought dispiritedly. All the family's secrets, the important nuances that she needed to know, were being kept from her.

It was only as she climbed the steep stairs that Stella finally figured out, with a shock, what Juana's words had been in response to her question about whether the family would threaten her.

The muttered phrase had been, "They already have."

CHAPTER TWENTY ONE

Stella climbed the uneven stairs leading out of the servants' quarters, feeling deflated. She'd held high hopes for what the staff might know and did know – she was sure of it. But they wouldn't tell her and had shut down. It was frustrating beyond belief that she couldn't get the information she needed, and it meant she would have to find another way.

As she neared the cottage, she saw with apprehension that the door was standing open.

Who was inside?

She stepped cautiously inside and jumped as she saw Kathy coming out of the kitchen. She looked less perfectly groomed than usual. Her make-up was smudged, and her hair mussed and full of static.

"Where were you?" she snapped out in a hoarse voice.

"I was taking a walk," Stella replied.

"Looking for a way out?" Kathy laughed bitterly. "There's no way out for you, honey, after what you've done. The next place you're going is jail."

"What do you want?" Stella retorted. She understood Kathy was grieving and looking for someone to blame, but she was sick of these accusations.

"Gordon wants to see you in the main house. He has some news for you." Kathy sounded harshly satisfied.

What did Vaughn's father want and why was he summoning her to the house? This directive filled her with dread. Gordon was hugely influential. What if he'd persuaded the police to arrest her, and when she headed over to the house they would be waiting?

"He's busy today so I suggest you go over immediately. He'll be in the breakfast room now," Kathy told her before walking out.

This was going to be bad, Stella knew. The triumphant glance Kathy gave her as she reached the doorway confirmed it.

Kathy climbed into a silver BMW and sped off, wheels splashing.

Wanting to get this confrontation over with as soon as possible, Stella headed straight up to the main house. Entering the hallway, she peeled off her drenched rain jacket. It hadn't done a good job of keeping her dry. The rain had seeped through her neckline, making huge, damp stains on her shirt, and her jeans were spattered with drops. Her hair hung in rat's tails, and even in the well-insulated house she was still shivering.

She barely noticed how cold she was. The horror of having to confront Gordon Marshall in his home, after what had happened, pushed everything else to the back of her mind.

Her mouth felt dry, and her heart was hammering as she walked into the breakfast room. Howard was sitting next to his father. He glowered at Stella as she walked in. Of everyone in the room, his resentment was the most palpable and she felt herself cringe away.

Who else was there? She glanced around. Grace, looking pale and shaken, was glaring daggers at her. Lucinda marched out angrily as she entered. Viv, standing near the sideboard, had her back turned and didn't look around.

Despite the atmosphere of hatred in the room, Stella forced herself to stay strong. She had to act the way she felt she should, and not be forced into becoming the version of herself that they wanted to see.

Giving her sympathies would certainly be in order. She didn't care if they were going to accuse her of the crime. She couldn't let that stop her from doing what was right. She walked directly up to Gordon.

"I'm so sorry about what has happened," she said in a low voice. "I'm heartbroken to have lost Vaughn and can only imagine how you must be feeling."

He stared at her angrily.

"Are you apologizing? If so, too little, too late," he said, with heavy sarcasm. "Obviously, it's a question of time until you are arrested. We know you're guilty. I brought you here today to tell you that we are assisting the police from our side."

"You are?" Stella asked cautiously. This didn't sound good.

"I have hired a private investigator to look into your background. It's the least we can do. We consider it our duty. Our obligation to our eldest son. Whatever the investigator finds out, we will share with the police. Is there anything you want to say?"

He stared at her challengingly. Stella felt herself shrink at this bombshell.

If he dug into her background, what would he find?

It hadn't been a typical hardscrabble Midwest upbringing, apart from the setting. She had a father who'd disappeared and torn her world apart. A mother who'd reveled in the role of helpless victim, while doling out vicious psychological abuse.

There would be a lot to keep the investigator busy.

She imagined him flying out to Kansas, driving out of town. Taking the long dirt road that wound its way past the sunflower farm. Arriving at the shabby house and knocking on the peeling door.

And then, confronting her bitter, manipulative mother.

How would Rhonda Fall react? What information would she spit out? There was no guarantee she'd tell the truth, or that she even knew what it was anymore.

Additionally, Stella worried that one of the events in her unusual past could be twisted to make her seem guiltier now.

"You're looking scared," Gordon said, sounding satisfied.

"I'm sorry you're doing this," Stella replied.

"Not as sorry as you're going to be." Gordon's voice rose. Color flooded his face. He was livid, Stella realized, already on a knife edge. "You murderess. Why did you do it? What got into you?"

"I didn't do it," Stella flashed back. "You have no right to accuse me of anything. I could also have been killed, and don't know why I wasn't."

"Clearly an oversight," Gordon snapped back, his voice as sharp as a whiplash.

"You tell her, Dad. She's the reason why our bro is dead today," Howard encouraged.

But then, from across the breakfast room, a woman's voice cut in.

"Gordon, Howard. Leave her be. Let the police do their work."

Stella turned in surprise to see who this unlikely ally was.

It was Viv.

"This is not your business," Gordon roared, but Viv stood her ground.

"I am Grace's godmother. I've always tried to do my best for your kids, even though it hasn't always been easy, especially during my divorce. I'm warning you, if you interfere you will end up making things more difficult. Just let her alone and stop bullying."

"How can you speak to me this way, after what I've been through?" Now there was an unpleasant note of self-pity in Gordon's overbearing tones.

"Stella has been through a lot too. I've seen it for myself since she's been here."

"What do you mean by that?" Gordon snarled.

Clearly unwilling to argue further, Viv shrugged, and walked out.

"It's a question of time before the police have you behind bars," Gordon threatened her. "The best thing you could do would be to turn yourself in."

"If I get arrested, then it means you've helped a killer to walk free," she said, fighting for calmness even though she felt scared and outnumbered now that her only supporter had left.

Gordon drew an angry breath, ready to come back at her fighting. But at that moment his phone rang. With a grimace, he answered it, and Stella took the moment to leave.

She urgently wanted to speak to Viv. She seemed to be on her side, even if temporarily, and might be willing to share some insights into the family.

Accelerating down the corridor, she saw Viv hurrying toward the front door, and raced to catch up. As Viv reached the front door, a butler materialized, carrying an umbrella. He held it over Viv's head as she walked out in the direction of the visitor's parking area.

Rushing after her, Stella tugged her jacket over her head as she jogged through the rain. She arrived at the low-slung Mercedes sports car at the same time as Viv and the butler.

"Please, may I speak to you for a moment?" she asked.

Viv looked surprised.

"What is it?" she asked.

"I need to ask you something in private," Stella pleaded.

"Why's that?" Viv asked, staring at her sternly. "Thanks. You can go," she told the butler, taking the umbrella from him before he headed back to the house.

"I don't want to be wrongfully arrested. I'm trying to find out who killed my fiancé," Stella confessed.

"Isn't that a job for the police?" Viv asked.

Stella shrugged. "My input can only help them," she said in diplomatic tones.

Viv smiled slightly, as if pleased with her answer.

"So how come you want to talk to me? I'm no detective."

Again, Stella felt the blonde woman was testing her.

"There's so much I don't know about the family. Knowing more about people's relationships, and their past history, would help me understand if anyone had a motive."

"And why should I tell you any of that?" Viv asked.

Stella thought back to that weird snippet of conversation that had taken place in the breakfast room.

"Because I'm guessing you've also been on their wrong side. During your divorce?" She stared at Viv appealingly, hoping that she'd relent. After a pause, she did.

"Get in," she said decisively.

CHAPTER TWENTY TWO

Stella opened the Mercedes' passenger door and climbed inside, breathing in the smell of new leather and the undertone of perfume. She didn't know how much time she'd have, as Viv seemed in a hurry, and in fact, she was.

"I've got a meeting with a charity at a hotel nearby. We can talk while I drive," she said.

She started the car and reversed impatiently out of the bay.

"Thank you," Stella said in heartfelt tones, relieved that Viv wasn't going outside of town, because the police had warned her to remain in the local area.

As Viv drove out of the property – opening the gate with a remote in the car console, Stella noticed – she felt more positive, as if she was leaving behind the Marshalls' toxic influence.

"What happened during your divorce?" Stella asked. She was sure Viv must be battling with divided loyalties. Perhaps talking about this would help her open up.

"The Marshalls treated me horrendously," she shared after a pause. "I became the outsider who broke their precious cousin's heart and damaged the family's name. I should have shut up and allowed him to do what he pleased, and not gotten upset about the affairs and the heavy drinking."

Stella could hear the anger in her words.

"But you're friends with them now?" she probed.

Viv nodded. "My ex was killed in a car wreck while driving drunk. He died on the scene, reeking of the whisky he'd been drinking at the moment he lost control. There was no opportunity for anyone to 'manage' the situation. Police and witnesses made it impossible. They had to publicly condemn his behavior so – well, you know how it goes? The enemy of my enemy is my friend? That's how it went. I think it helped that I inherited his estate. Ironic, because he was trying every tactic to make sure I didn't get a penny in the divorce settlement but hadn't bothered to change his will," she laughed.

Stella wondered if that was why she was so involved in charity. Perhaps it gave her satisfaction to donate her late husband's fortune to worthy causes.

"I'm surprised you stayed friends with them," Stella said, feeling she should be honest.

Viv nodded as she turned onto a side road that ran alongside a park. "I am Grace's godmother. If not for that, I'd have told them to go to hell. But I take that responsibility seriously. We also have a lot of mutual friends, which made it easier. As time goes by, one forgets the details of the past."

Grateful for this fascinating glimpse into the family's history, Stella honed in on the phrase that had stuck in her mind.

"You mentioned 'managing' the situation. That's something I'm worried about now. I know they must be pressuring the police to do what they want. Has anything like that happened before?" she asked anxiously.

Viv sighed. "There were a couple of incidents. I'll tell you, but if anyone asks, say Vaughn explained them to you."

"I will," Stella said gratefully.

Viv swung the car down a long gravel driveway. At the end of it, Stella saw a large hotel.

"This is the Putnam Hill Historic District, by the way," Viv said conversationally. "It's the town's old government center. You'll notice the historic homes with their Victorian architecture when you walk back, which should take you less than an hour. The Second Congregational Church is down the road – it's a lovely stone building if you want to take a look."

She sounded a lot happier to be speaking about the area's architecture and history, than about the family. Stella didn't blame her. She remembered this was where Vaughn had wanted to spend their first Sunday here, before everything had started to go wrong.

"Thank you. I will," Stella said.

Viv eased the car into a parking spot outside the hotel, which Stella now saw was another magnificent Victorian building.

"Anyway, back to the family history. The Marshalls' main gate never used to be locked. Gordon tightened up security a couple of years ago after an intruder got into the house one night and stole valuable paintings and antiques."

"How were the police pressured through that?" Stella asked.

"Well, the family made a massive fuss. Had to be a high priority case, wanted it solved yesterday, this was unacceptable. Until they realized the thief must have been a connection of Elmer's. One who supplied him with certain 'recreational substances.'"

"I see," Stella said.

"After that they told the police to drop the case, because they knew that if an arrest was made, their son's habits would become very public. They've protected him a few times since then, most recently when he caused a car crash while high."

"Wow." Stella felt alarmed by their ability to start or stop an investigation on a whim.

"Anyway, since then the Marshalls installed an automatic gate. Friends and family get remotes, but not if you're Elmer's friends. Unspoken rule. Then he has to let you in. And he has his own suite now, with a separate entrance, so his friends don't go through the house."

"I see." Thoughtfully, Stella took in these interesting tidbits of information. "Are those all the incidents?"

"No. There was one other very puzzling one involving Vaughn."

"What happened there?" Stella felt a sense of dread.

"You probably don't know about it. A year ago, Howard got engaged to a local woman from a very wealthy family. Everyone approved of her. Not like you." She gave Stella a sidelong glance.

"And?" Stella asked. She felt a sinking sensation as she considered what might have happened next.

"Vaughn seduced her. It happened the day after the engagement party, the day before they were supposed to move in together. She and Howard were going to occupy the cottage that you now reside in, by the way."

"What?" Stella gasped. She felt shocked to her core. Even if he'd been drunk out of his mind, such a thing didn't happen by accident. It was deeply cruel and completely immoral.

Up until yesterday she'd never have believed Vaughn capable of it. But after that vicious fight, and that moment when he'd brandished the knife, she realized there was a different side to him, one she'd never known or even suspected.

Vaughn had been hiding who he really was. Perhaps he'd wanted to become a better person while away from his family in Chicago, but when he got back home, it had no longer been possible.

"He and Howard have always been 'frenemies,' if you can call it that," Viv said thoughtfully. "Cecilia and Gordon used to pit them against each other competitively. Elmer, of course, being a lost cause," she laughed. "It created a lot of jealousy. But anyway, a short while later, Vaughn started dating a new girlfriend, Mary-Ann."

"I've met her. Did something go wrong?"

126

"It was all good until they were about to head off on vacation. They went to a fancy restaurant in Greenwich. While they were eating, someone torched his car."

"What?" Stella said, shocked.

"It was his beloved vintage Mustang. Whoever it was poured gasoline over it and lit it. It burned right down to a charred wreck. Damaged a couple of neighboring vehicles and of course, all Mary-Ann's clothes and bags were inside. They canceled the vacation and after that, the relationship petered out. He didn't date again until he met you."

"So Howard did that?"

Viv shrugged. "He denied it, of course. Got extremely angry and defensive. But they found an empty gasoline can in the Marshalls' garage, so Gordon put a stop to the police investigation."

"He did?" Stella asked incredulously.

"He paid for the repairs to the other cars and to a damaged store front. The 'camera footage' from a nearby business that would have allowed them to trace who did it, disappeared. The whole thing was brushed under the carpet to protect Howard because Gordon didn't want him to have any kind of record. And that's about all I can tell you," Viv said.

She sounded quietly satisfied. Stella thought she'd gotten a perverse pleasure out of gossiping about the Marshalls' misdoings.

"Thank you so much for the information," Stella said. "I heard it all from Vaughn."

"Of course you did. But, one last thing." Viv held up a warning finger.

"What's that?"

"From my own personal viewpoint, I don't see how any of the kids could have done this. I've known them since they were babies. I've never had much time for Gordon, and I know all of them have their problems, but for them to kill a sibling? I just can't get my head around it." She shook her head. "However, human nature is a strange thing. I could be wrong. Who knows? And now, I must get to my meeting."

Briskly, Viv opened the door, and Stella scrambled out.

She had much more insight on the family now than she'd had at the beginning of the ride. Now she knew what they were capable of and had a better picture of the complex dynamics.

The rain was easing up, and she had her bearings and knew how to get back.

She followed the route that Viv had pointed out, taking in the imposing architecture and the magnificent big trees of the historic district without really seeing any of it, because her mind was fully occupied by what she'd learned. Howard had a powerful reason for hating Vaughn and had already committed one crime in revenge.

How could she get him alone and question about this, she wondered as she left the historic district and walked back the way she had come.

But, as she reached the Marshalls' mansion, she realized there was a more urgent matter than confronting Howard.

Two gray, mid-range Fords were parked outside the main house. They looked like the cars the detectives drove.

She felt sure that the police had been summoned to a meeting with Gordon Marshall and were being pressured to accept his version of events. What if the likable Detective Bradshaw was there? He seemed to be her only hope for staying out of jail.

What was being said behind that thick, high front door?

Stella decided she was going to head straight into the house and confront them.

CHAPTER TWENTY THREE

Stella pushed the front door open and headed inside. Where would the meeting take place? She listened but couldn't hear any voices.

Hesitating in the hallway, glancing from left to right, she guessed such a meeting might take place in a private study, somewhere that felt secret and hidden away, rather than in the more accessible main lounges. At any rate, the lounge where the ladies had been playing bridge the other day was empty.

That had to mean they were up to something. Why wouldn't a meeting with the police be held in the most convenient place?

Feeling unsure, and wishing she knew the house better, she headed left, deciding to search this wing as fast as she could and then start on the other.

But as she prowled down the spacious corridor, she heard footsteps behind her, walking fast.

Spinning around, Stella saw Howard. He was hurrying through the hall at a half-run, and as she watched, he headed outside. He was dressed in running gear. Now she remembered that Cecilia had said Howard loved running and went out in the afternoons.

She paused, torn by indecision. This was a perfect opportunity to get him alone, away from the influence of his family. She might not get another chance. But on the other hand, the police meeting might be over by the time she got back.

Biting her lip, Stella made the call. Catching the killer was more important.

She turned and hurried out of the house again, running up the main driveway, starting to panic that she might not catch up with the tall, long-legged Howard. The gate swung open, and she hesitated, looking in both directions. Which way had he gone?

There he was, to the right. She saw the orange flash of his shirt in the distance and set off in pursuit. He was going fast, and she quickly realized she wasn't going to catch up with him any time soon. The best she could do was try to keep him in sight until she was far enough from the house to be able to wait safely for him to return.

Jogging down the road for a few hundred yards, she was relieved to discover a huge park at a crossroad. This was definitely runners' territory. There was a track that looked to go the whole way around the park's perimeter. Howard must be running laps and that meant he'd pass by the starting point.

Walking over to a bushy tree, Stella waited behind the cover of its branches.

This was going to be a desperately important meeting. To have the best chance of success, she needed to tune into the way Howard was feeling. After what Viv had told her, she knew that would be complex. His emotions would be volatile. There would be a lot of anger bottled up inside him and perhaps guilt, too. He might not even agree to speak to her. He'd looked furious with her earlier, sitting next to his father in the breakfast room.

There he was. She felt a thrill of excitement and nerves when she saw him approach. Head down, arms churning, he was wearing earphones and immersed in his own world.

"Howard?" she called loudly, stepping out of her cover and onto the paved track.

He glanced up and his face changed when he saw her. Intense concentration was replaced by resentment.

"What are you doing?" he snapped, but he slowed to a walk, breathing hard.

"I wanted to ask you something."

"You came here for that?" He stared at her incredulously, wiping sweat off his face. "What makes you think I'll speak to you? You murdered my brother."

Stella thought quickly. If she didn't say the right thing, Howard might simply run off. She'd never catch up, and back at the house, he'd refuse to speak to her.

He could be the killer. So she had to stay away from the subject of the murder for now.

Killer or not, Howard had a sense of fairness, she remembered, even if it was buried deep. She recalled his comment to Haydi, that he thought the family shrink had been acting unethically. Perhaps she could start the conversation there. That topic would surprise him, which would hopefully jolt him out of his current mindset.

"Something you said a while ago made me think you might be willing. You thought Dr. Lloyd was being unfair by talking about his patients. Correct?" she said in a casual voice.

Howard blinked. As she'd hoped, he was surprised enough to answer.

"Well, yes. Doctors aren't supposed to do that."

"But none of your family seems to mind."

"I'm not my family," Howard shrugged.

"You seem to care about unfairness," she said.

He nodded, looking confused, as if he was trying to work out how the conversation had reached this point. Time to tip him off balance again, and get to the point, she decided.

"Anyway, I came to talk to you because I found out something," she said conversationally.

He glanced at her again and this time she saw a flicker of apprehension in his eyes.

"Really? What?"

"Do you want to take a walk?" she asked, indicating the paved pathway. Then she set off, before he answered, leaving him with no option but to follow. Because now, he was curious and worried.

He caught up with her, striding alongside.

"What is it?"

"I found out you were engaged a while back."

For a moment, she picked up raw shock in his eyes. Then he shrugged and answered casually, "Yeah. It didn't work out."

"There was a reason for that," Stella said.

She didn't look at him but instead, matched her stride with his and waited for him to speak.

"Zoe wasn't right for me," he muttered.

"That's not what I heard. I heard that she cheated on you with Vaughn," Stella kept her voice sympathetic.

Howard shrugged. "It was nothing. She was a slut. Probably screwed around with a few others while we were dating."

Stella noticed the 'probably.' There was no proof of anything except what had happened with his brother. Of course he was angry and ashamed. How could she get inside his mind, and encourage him to talk more freely?

"How did you find out?" she asked. Details would force him to confront it.

"I caught them," he said, with a strange-sounding laugh.

Stella didn't have to fake the surprise in her tone. "What? You walked in on them?"

He nodded.

"Oh, Howard, I'm sorry. That must have been hectic."

She was pretty sure that Howard wouldn't have gotten much sympathy from the family. Loyalties would have been divided. Most likely, Zoe had been blamed, further complicating Howard's ability to deal with things.

"Yeah. It wasn't great. I was pretty upset. Look, she was very drunk. It was at a party. We had a small fight over something I can't even remember now." He shrugged again, as if trying to rid himself of the misery and memories.

"Did Vaughn like her? Why did it happen?"

"He always said she was hot. But that's not why he did it. He basically did it because he was jealous. Being the oldest, he was always the first. First one for everything. I was breaking his rules by being engaged. I could see he was angry from the time I told the family."

"His rules?" Stella asked, probing deeper into how Howard felt about that.

"Yes. Vaughn was a bully. I know I shouldn't say that, because he was your fiancé and now he's dead, but he was, like, such an alpha. He'd lose his sense of humor completely when things didn't go his way. And he could never, ever admit to being wrong."

"Not even after cheating? Did he not apologize?"

"He never apologized. He said it was her fault, she'd come onto him. But it wasn't, I know Zoe wouldn't have done that. It was him. He was ugly and jealous, and he ruined everything for me! Everything! He never could keep his hands off a pretty blonde. No matter who it was. I've seen it before then and since. He didn't care. I know he's dead and I shouldn't speak badly of him, but he'd have done the same when he was married to you. I reckon you had a lucky escape."

Hurt and rage resonated in Howard's voice. Stella felt sorry for him, but at the same time, aware that he was boiling with suppressed emotion. He could have snapped, taking a violent revenge on the man who'd bullied him and stolen his fiancé and future away.

But had he?

"Did you torch his car to get back at him?"

Howard shook his head impatiently. "I didn't do that," he said, sounding exasperated. "The family thought I did, of course."

Stella found this response interesting. Up until that point, Howard had been truthful. Now, he was sticking to his version, despite the evidence of the gasoline can. Was this a lie? Perhaps he worried that if he admitted to one crime, she'd believe he was capable of another.

"You know the family is blaming me for Vaughn's murder," she said, hoping to draw him out on this topic.

"Yes, I know that," he said warily.

"Did you hear, or see, anything that night?" Stella asked.

Howard shrugged. "I wasn't around that night. So I didn't see anything."

"Where were you?" Trying to sound casual, Stella asked the important question. Surely Howard, such a strong suspect, couldn't have an alibi?

"At a friend's house in Darien. Four of us were doing an online gaming session and ended up playing until morning. I came home thinking I would be able to sleep all day, only to find my bro was murdered and all hell had broken loose."

Stella felt crushed by disappointment. She had the perfect suspect, who was angry enough and had a motive to commit the crime. But he'd been gaming, with friends, the entire night. She knew what gamers were like and how intensely they played.

"I guess the police asked you about that?" she quizzed him, wanting to check the story was true.

He nodded. "That detective made me prove that I was away from home. I had to show them all the game logs, and the food delivery orders, and they took statements from my friends also."

Frustrated, Stella realized this was a cast-iron alibi. Worse still, she was lagging behind the police. They'd already struck Howard off the list while she was floundering to find out the facts.

Trying to find a bright side, she guessed this confrontation had resulted in one not-so-bad outcome. The earlier suspicion had vanished from Howard's face. Unburdening to her had created a tenuous trust between them. She guessed it wouldn't last, but for now, she felt she had one contact in the family who wasn't an actual enemy.

"I'll head home," she said. "Take care."

"You, too," Howard replied, and then looked startled, as if his own words had surprised him.

He broke into a run and set off on another lap of the park, while Stella jogged back to the Marshalls' house. On the way, she decided that she was going to continue her investigation of the family by focusing on the next brother.

Elmer was unstable. She'd sensed it and seen it. Also, he was a spendthrift who'd blown through whatever allowance he received. She remembered Kathy's snide comment while they'd been on the boat.

Drugs were a powerful force. The need for the money to obtain them could override common sense and morals. Elmer could have begged Vaughn for money in the past and been refused. Or he could have wanted more of the inheritance and trust fund for himself, including the property portfolio that got passed down to the eldest son.

Perhaps this need had driven Elmer to kill.

CHAPTER TWENTY FOUR

Viv had told Stella that Elmer lived in his own suites, with their own entrance. Therefore, Stella logically reasoned, she must be able to find where they were by walking around the family's house.

Without being caught snooping. That thought sent a shiver of anxiety through her.

A self-contained set of rooms would have to be on the ground floor and would probably be in one of the wings. Stella decided it would be better to wait until early evening, when lights would be on, and she could peek inside without being seen in turn.

While she waited, she checked her phone, noticing that she'd received a few mails while she was out and about, but she'd had so little airtime loaded that she guessed not all had downloaded.

There were a couple of job rejections, one request for further information, and a message from Rebecca.

"Hey, Stella, we're very worried. We heard on the news that there'd been a murder and it sounded like it was your Vaughn. I've tried to call a few times but can't get hold of you. Is it true? Are you okay? Please let us know if you need any help at all, or a place to stay. We're here for you."

Stella felt teary as she read the words. Her friend's loyal support felt like a beacon of light. As soon as she could, she promised herself she would call.

She messaged back, sketching out the facts briefly.

"Yes, it was him. Nobody knows who did it. I'm in a horrible situation now but I don't feel in danger and the police are investigating. I have to stay locally for now and there's no phone reception here, but I will get in touch asap. Please don't worry about me," she ended it, knowing that of course Rebecca would worry more when she received it.

She pressed send and it lodged in her outbox. Hopefully she'd be able to send it soon.

In the meantime, it was late afternoon and the gauzy sun had sunk behind a bank of clouds. It was time to hunt for Elmer.

Pulling on a dark jacket, Stella headed out of the cottage. She made her way to the house, memorizing what she knew of the interior as she tried to get her bearings. She decided to start by walking around the outside, watching and listening for any clues.

It only took a few minutes before she heard the noise.

It was coming from one of the rooms at the back of the home's eastern wing. Loud, thumping music, raised voices, the raucous cries of people who were partying.

She crept up to the window and took a look inside. Her heart flip-flopped with excitement as she saw him there.

Elmer sat between two women on a three-seat couch, roaring with laughter. The coffee table was stacked with beers, whiskies, and mixers. There were three other friends in the room. She didn't recognize any of them. Nor did she see any of the family there.

Elmer certainly didn't seem to be in mourning, Stella noted, watching him for a few moments. Then exploring further, she found a glass-paned French door nearby. It was closed, but when she eased the handle down, she discovered it was unlocked.

She tiptoed into the hallway and glanced around. A door opposite, standing ajar, led to a large, well-furnished bedroom. It was clean but untidy, with clothes strewn over the neatly made bed. Beyond was a kitchen, a guest restroom, and then the lounge.

She closed the door gently and sidled back to the window where she had a view of the lounge. She decided to wait a while. If Elmer left the lounge to get food for the guests or use the restroom, she'd have a chance to speak to him alone.

Stella had no idea what mood Elmer would be in. Would he be talkative, aggressive, raucous? Perhaps it would depend on what he'd been taking. She remembered how wild and fearless he'd been on the yacht, laughing as he vaulted the rail. Drugs could make him more unpredictable, and he might act without thinking.

That could have been how Vaughn got murdered, she realized with a chill.

If she managed to get him alone at all, she'd have to be careful. Elmer was an unknown entity, and she had no idea of the best way to approach him. Preparing herself for a long wait, Stella leaned against the wall.

Then, to her horror, she heard the buzz of the golf cart approaching, and headlights cut the gloom. The security guard was patrolling.

Quickly, Stella slipped into the house again. Would the guard pass by? She hoped he would simply drive along the paved path, but he didn't.

The golf cart braked outside the French door.

Swearing under her breath, with her heart racing, Stella retreated into Elmer's bedroom and pushed the door closed. What was going on?

Heavy footsteps tramped inside.

Stella inched to the side of the bedroom door, so that if it opened, she'd be behind it. Trying not to move or even breathe, she wondered what would play out. Was the guard going to break up this gathering, or why was he here?

Above the noise from the lounge, she heard muttered voices outside. Then, to her horror, the bedroom door swung open. She flattened herself against the wall as unsteady footsteps crossed the room. A drawer opened and closed. Then the footsteps returned.

More low voices and the crackle of paper.

"Yeah, sure. Come past tomorrow again, no problem," she heard Elmer laugh, a slur in his voice.

Stella closed her eyes. So the guard was also enjoying Elmer's contraband. That hadn't taken long. Would he leave, and would Elmer go back to his friends now?

No.

Elmer stumbled into the bedroom again, humming to himself, and this time, he turned and closed the door. He came face to face with Stella and they stared at each other in horror before Elmer recoiled, staggering back.

His hair was mussed, and his eyes were bloodshot. He clutched a fifty-dollar bill in his hand.

"What the hell are you doing here?" he snarled, recovering his balance and his aggression.

Stella felt sick with fear at this hostile reaction. The situation was on a knife-edge of disaster. If the guard heard Elmer and came back, she'd be in terrible trouble. But if he didn't, she might be in danger.

Sensing that fear would trigger even more reaction from him, she forced herself to keep calm and controlled, meeting his aggression with serenity.

"I wanted to ask you something. I was hoping we could have a quick chat." Slowly, she spread her hands, palms up, a sign of peace and openness.

"I don't want you here," he insisted. In a louder voice, he added, "Get out! Now!" Then he shouted, "Dan! Come here!"

He was obviously calling the guard.

The time for slow, reassuring body language had passed. Stella leaped in front of the closed door, leaning against it so he couldn't wrench it open.

"One minute," she said firmly. "A minute of your time."

She didn't hear anything from the other side. Hopefully the guard had made a quick getaway with his stash. Now all she had to do was manage Elmer's aggression.

But then, reeling back, Elmer spat out, "Just leave. I won't speak to you. Get away and don't hurt me!"

To her astonishment, Stella realized Elmer was terrified. Of her? She'd thought he was angry, but it was the flip side of fear showing through. Underneath it, Elmer was a coward.

"Why would I hurt you?" she said, keeping her voice calm and unthreatening. "I'm not a killer."

"Of course you are," he said, peering distrustfully at her through narrowed eyes.

"Of course I'm not. Why would I do such a thing?"

Elmer blinked. "You're asking me? You're the one who knows why, right?"

"I'll tell you a secret," Stella said, dropping her voice to a confidential murmur. Frowning, Elmer stepped closer.

"I was planning to leave Vaughn. I'd decided it wasn't working out. In the morning, I was going to break it off and walk away."

Elmer thought this through, before giving a reluctant nod. "Okay, so what then?"

"Would I have killed him if I wanted to leave? Of course not. Now I'm in all sorts of trouble and the police think I did it. I know it wasn't me, so I need to find out who it was. To clear my name," Stella explained.

"You think it was me?" Elmer asked incredulously. "That's why you're here?"

"Not at all. I just want to ask you some questions," Stella said.

"The police did that too. They asked me a whole bunch of questions about where I was that night."

"Why? Do they suspect you?" she asked.

Elmer shrugged, looking uncomfortable. "Yes, they did. Because of money, I guess."

"Can you explain?" she probed, hoping he'd shed more light on the situation.

"Well, I have a trust fund. We all inherited at the age of twenty-one. But mine's almost used up. I made a few mistakes. Crashed a few cars. Friends borrowed money from me."

Stella guessed he meant his drug user friends. Those who hadn't helped themselves to the household's contents.

138

"What will you do when it's finished?" she asked. "Does Vaughn's trust fund get divided up between the others?"

Elmer shrugged and she picked up a hint of desperation in his eyes.

"I have no idea. At any rate, they won't let me starve." He laughed uncertainly. It wasn't starving he was worried about, that she could see.

"Do you have an alibi for that night?"

"Like I told the police, I was in my room. I was messaging friends and organizing some meet-ups."

He looked at the floor. He was hiding something; she was sure of it.

"You were alone?"

Now she saw desperation in his eyes.

"Look, I wasn't exactly alone. I was with a friend. A good friend. She came around for a drink and ended up staying much later. Overnight, in fact."

"Did the police talk to her?" Stella asked curiously.

"I begged them to keep it under wraps. That Detective Brady, or whatever his name is, said they had to confirm with her, but they'd try keep it confidential," Elmer said miserably. "She's married to a friend of Mom's. Her husband was out of town on business. She was very angry about this. She said it was obviously a home invasion and that we could also have been in danger if they'd broken in here looking for stuff to steal. I promise you, I didn't do it. I didn't even hear anything. Look, I'll show you our messages."

He pulled out his cellphone and opened a chat thread. Stella looked down as he scrolled through.

She saw a message organizing the meet-up and another saying, *"I'm here!"*

After that the tone changed.

"What happened, E-baby? I heard there was a murder? Are you okay?"

And then, yet again, another change in tone.

"Why the hell did you tell the police I was with you the whole night? I told Luke I was away at a spa. Now they want to question me!"

Reading through the increasingly frantic and hostile communication, Stella felt a sense of unreality. Did everyone in this family cheat? At any rate, Elmer had an alibi, but thinking of the family brought another issue to mind. Perhaps while Elmer was in honesty mode, he would explain it to her.

"Can you tell me about something else that happened a while ago?" she asked.

"What?" Elmer regarded her warily.

139

"I heard you were in a car crash and the police saw it happen. What was the story there?"

Elmer shrugged. "Yeah, I made a bad mistake. I was drunk at the time. My dad handled it. He knows the officer in charge and he – he was able to explain to him that it was all a mistake."

"How did he do that?" Stella asked, intrigued.

"I wasn't driving. Just looking for my house keys, so I could get a cab home. But I knocked the car into drive and it rolled forward and damaged some other cars."

Stella felt floored by the flimsiness of this blatantly untruthful story. And the police had accepted it. In fact, she wondered whether they'd come up with it, together with Gordon Marshall.

Because constructing a fake story while collaborating with the police, was so much more acceptable than having your son face the consequences of a DUI charge.

"My dad paid for all the repairs in full," Elmer added, sounding defensive. "The police insisted on it."

Since when was that a job for the police? It must have been one of the conditions for dropping charges, or making the docket disappear, or whatever had happened to allow this crime to vanish off the radar. Stella could imagine how furious her own father would have been if these shenanigans had happened in his precinct.

Knowing the full story made her feel even more wary of the Marshalls. If they could obliterate such a serious offense, they clearly had a very close relationship with the local police.

Was Bradshaw local, she wondered. A homicide detective might not be from the most local precinct. Was he outside this sphere of influence?

"Thank you for explaining," she told him. "I'd better go. Your friends will be wondering where you are."

Elmer looked startled, as if he'd forgotten all about his friends. Then he glanced at the cupboard again.

"Yeah. You'd better go now. Just look out for the guard, he's around. My dad told him to watch my place and watch your place. I know my family are trying to get the cops to arrest you. But they've also been on my back. Dad keeps shouting that it was most probably one of my friends, looking for valuables. He's blaming me for all of this, too."

"Thanks for telling me," Stella said, surprised by the information.

So Gordon believed that the killer was one of Elmer's friends, but was still trying to pressure the police to arrest her in order to shield his son.

Stella hadn't thought her opinion of the family could sink any lower, but a new rock-bottom had been achieved. Now she could see why Gordon was so hell-bent on getting her in jail.

She tiptoed out of the house, keeping a lookout for the guard.

As she headed back to the cottage, she thought about what Elmer had said. Nothing obvious had been stolen. Her laptop hadn't been touched and nor had the phones. But what if it had been a break-in, and something else had been taken? She hadn't done an inventory and had no idea what valuables were in the cottage. For all she knew, Vaughn could have drawn a lot of cash before heading home.

Could she find anything missing if she searched? How would she even know?

Stella headed into the main bedroom.

Vaughn had so much of value. All his clothes, his shoes, his jackets, his electronic equipment. All of it was worth good money, above and beyond the cash in his wallet.

The clothing he'd worn that night had been removed along with the bedding and mattress. She guessed he'd dumped it beside the bed before climbing in, and that it had ended up bloodied and damaged. The police might have taken it away, either to dispose of it or as evidence. Either way, she didn't know where his wallet was now.

Any other valuables?

Her gaze was drawn to the box on the bookshelf, containing the one expensive item she owned, the engagement ring.

Stella reached for the box and snapped it open.

She drew in her breath in a horrified gasp. The ring was gone.

"This can't be!" Stella whispered incredulously. How was it possible that someone had taken it? Who could have done so?

Had it been stolen and sold for drugs? Was it stashed away in a servant's pocket? Had one of the contractors pocketed it?

Her mind spun as she considered the options.

Had there in fact been a robbery? If only she hadn't been knocked out by the sleeping tablet. She might have slept through the commotion under its sedating influence.

Staring around her in panic, Stella felt thoroughly spooked. The immaculate bedroom felt unfriendly and sinister. More than ever, she felt surrounded by enemies, and that the people who wished her harm were a step ahead.

Although she wasn't supposed to, and had been warned about leaving the area, Stella knew she had to speak to a friend, for her own sanity. First thing tomorrow morning, she decided, she was going to call Rebecca and find out if they could somehow meet up.

These four walls felt claustrophobic, and Stella had an uneasy feeling they weren't the only things that were closing in on her.

CHAPTER TWENTY FIVE

Early the next morning, Stella tugged out the chair she'd wedged under the door. She walked into the cool, fresh dawn, locking up behind her, feeling a sense of deep relief to be heading off the grounds.

As she reached the gate, she heard a car approaching and turned hurriedly. A large black Mercedes SUV was powering up the driveway. She saw Rodriguez at the wheel. He stared straight ahead, without acknowledging her, and she felt a stab of fear that he might have told his employers she'd been asking questions.

Who was in the back? Worried, Stella glanced into the tinted window as the car passed.

Through the darkened glass, Gordon stared angrily back. Then, with a jolt, the car stopped, and the window buzzed down.

Stella's heart sank as she turned reluctantly to face him.

"Where are you going? The police told you not to leave the premises," he snapped.

In a polite tone, Stella corrected him. "They told me not to leave Greenwich, because I have to be available for further questioning if needed."

Gordon gave her a knowing look that caused Stella's mouth to go dry.

"It's not questioning you need to worry about. This has gone far beyond that." He leaned out of the window and spoke in a low, threatening tone. "I've heard you've been asking questions, snooping around, trying to implicate one of us in your place. So I've called in some favors. You're going to be arrested soon. If you try and run now, it will only happen faster. I'd stay put if I were you."

He buzzed the window up. The car purred out of the gate and turned smoothly onto the road.

Stella stared after it in a panic.

She had been wondering if she could risk hiring a car and driving straight to Rebecca's place. It was now clear she couldn't. One step beyond the borders of Greenwich would provide a valid reason for the Marshalls to get her arrested.

They had such influence, such power. She felt crushed by fear.

Leaden-footed, she trailed to the main road and waited until a bus came along, headed for town. She climbed aboard and went to the back. There, she called Rebecca.

"I'm on a bus heading into Greenwich center. Can you meet me somewhere? Is there any chance you can get off work?"

"Sure," Rebecca said decisively. Stella realized her friend sounded vastly relieved, as if she'd been waiting anxiously for her to get in touch. "I'm leaving right now. Message me when you find a place and I'll get there as fast as I can."

Disembarking in town, Stella headed down the street. The town center was charming, with wide, tidy sidewalks and tall trees wreathed in bright summer green. The immaculately maintained buildings were a mix of perfectly preserved historic structures and new, ultra-modern ones. Remembering that this city was home to many hedge funds, she wondered briefly if Uncle Mike had his headquarters located nearby. Not once had she seen Vaughn's workplace or even known its address but thinking she might be walking past it made her feel even more hunted.

She noted that almost every car parked alongside the road was a luxury model and this reminded her of the wealth Vaughn's family commanded. She felt intimidated by the sheer scope of the resources they had at their disposal, and the ways in which they were prepared to use them. Gordon was so confident he had things wrapped up with the police, he'd even told her as much. In desperation, she thought of Detective Bradshaw, imagining him tucked away with Gordon in an oak-paneled study, coming to a smiling 'agreement' that would see her land in jail.

They had all the power, she had none, and they were out to get her. Worse still, she was coming up short on every one of her leads. Someone had murdered Vaughn, but even using a process of elimination, she was no closer to discovering who.

She turned into Greenwich Avenue, admiring its colorful flower boxes and exquisite store frontages. The art displayed in the windows made her feel bitter regret that things hadn't been different. She and Vaughn should have taken an outing to town and explored this street together on the day they arrived, enjoying the paintings and the atmospheric sidewalk entertainment. But the moment he set foot on the Marshalls' home soil, he'd been back under their control.

Turning down a side street, she took a seat at a chic café, choosing a table set apart from the others, near a large planter filled with colorful shrubs. Then she messaged her location to Rebecca and waited anxiously for her friend to arrive.

*

Half an hour later, Rebecca hurried up to her table. Stella scrambled to her feet just in time to receive a gigantic, warm hug.

"We've been so worried about you. I felt as if a weight had been lifted off me when you called and said you could meet up. Are you alright? What happened?"

Stella couldn't find the words to speak. Her throat felt constricted, and she was struggling to hold back sobs. She never cried in front of other people. It brought to mind her mother's taunts. *"Cry baby. You little cry baby."*

"Vaughn was murdered," she finally managed in a near-whisper. "He was stabbed to death while I slept next to him. Now I'm a suspect and I feel like my life is falling apart."

"What? Stella, are you serious? That's horrific. Did you not wake up? You weren't hurt or threatened?" Rebecca's voice was tight with concern.

"We both took sleeping tablets. They were part of a whole cocktail of meds that the 'family shrink' prescribed for me. I didn't touch any of the others. They would have turned me into a zombie."

"That sounds unethical," Rebecca sounded shocked.

At that moment, the waiter arrived.

"This is my treat," Rebecca said firmly. "And you look as if you're a few square meals behind. How about a slap-up brunch and milkshakes?" she suggested.

When they'd ordered and the waiter had left, Stella continued, leaning close to her friend. The place was starting to fill up and she didn't want their conversation overheard by any listening ears.

"Prescribing me crazy meds is not the only unethical thing that's been happening," she murmured, feeling relieved to finally unburden. "The Marshalls have the police in their pockets and they're pressuring them to accuse me of the crime."

"What?" Rebecca whispered back. "That's totally illegal. It's defeating the ends of justice."

"That seems to be the family hobby," Stella said.

Rebecca shook her head, looking furious. "That Gordon Marshall is bad news all round. Someone needs to expose him and take him down."

"Vaughn changed so much when he got back home, and they had him back in their clutches," Stella agreed sadly.

"I can imagine," Rebecca leaned over and rubbed her shoulders.

For a moment, Stella wondered if she should tell Rebecca about the pregnancy. She decided not to. At this time, she couldn't bear to voice that worry to anyone.

"Who did it? Do they have any leads?"

Stella shook her head. "All the family seems to hate each other. But again, it could have been a robbery. Vaughn never locked the front door and Elmer, the middle son, has a serious addiction problem. The family enables him and covers it up, with the help of the police."

Rebecca sighed anxiously. "That's not good. Not good at all."

"They think they can buy any outcome they want."

"Of course they do. But this is murder. It's way more serious than a DUI, Stella. They'll surely have detectives from outside the local precinct involved."

"I'm worried they will be able to corrupt them, too. Or override them somehow."

Their food arrived – a sumptuous spread of fruit, cheese, smoked salmon, and cold meats. Double-thick chocolate milkshakes in tall glasses completed the spread. Tense as her situation was, Stella realized she was starving. She hadn't eaten properly in days.

Sipping the thick, sweet milkshake, she thought of Detective Bradshaw. Maybe, despite her fears, he was an honest cop. Rebecca might be right, and the Marshalls might only be pressuring the officers they knew. But then, she worried how easily the rot might spread.

"You said the family hates each other. Do you think any of them hated Vaughn enough to kill him?" Rebecca asked thoughtfully.

"I've spoken to both his brothers. They both had a potential motive, but both unfortunately have confirmed alibis."

"And the sister?"

Stella made a face, thinking of Grace's condescending attitude.

"I can't see a reason for her to hate him enough."

Rebecca cut a croissant open and forked salmon inside.

"What about if she's just a psychopath?"

"Grace?" Stella frowned doubtfully, but Rebecca seemed sold on her own idea.

"I mean, think about it. You did your thesis on serial killer behavior. I remember our chats about how normal the killers act when they're not actually slaughtering people, and how clever they are at concealing their dark sides."

146

"Yes, that's all true. I'm just not sure it's relevant to Grace," Stella said.

"That's a pity. But it might be relevant to someone else."

"It might," Stella said.

Rebecca's words had reminded her that nobody normal would grab a knife and head into a bedroom to murder a sleeping man in cold blood. If it hadn't been a break-in gone wrong, then her friend was right. This had been committed by a psychopath and she would have to look out for any signs.

The food was comforting and invigorating, just like her friend's company. Stella felt vastly relieved to be with someone she could unburden to, and to know that her loyal friend had her back, no matter what.

"You surely can't stay there any longer," Rebecca said, sounding worried.

"I have to. The police have told me I can't leave the area and I can't risk getting into trouble at this point."

"Then you need to stay in a guesthouse. Look, I know money's probably an issue. We have quite a bit saved. We can cover a guesthouse for a few days, no problem. Let's look for one in the area and get you there today."

"No. Thanks, but no. I want to stay where I am."

"You do?" Rebecca stared at her as if she were crazy. "Why?"

"Because I have to find out who did this. I can't live with this hanging over me for weeks, or months, or even years. I can't let the family buy off the cops, so I end up being accused of it. That would destroy my future."

Rebecca nodded slowly. "Crazy, but I see your point. It's the rest of your life at stake," she agreed reluctantly.

"I'm not going to let this crooked, bullying family get away with what they've done." Lowering her voice even more, Stella leaned closer to her friend over the now-empty plates. "My dad always said the worst thing in the world is a corrupt cop, but it's a two-way street and usually starts with the cop being corrupted. Someone takes advantage, they agree to a suggestion, and then it's a slippery slope and there's no going back."

"That's absolutely true," Rebecca confirmed. "Your dad would be the first one to have fought something like that."

"I guess I'm his daughter," Stella said, pretending a courage she didn't feel inside. But she had to try. It would be avenging the person

147

Vaughn could have been. The person he'd never had a chance to become.

In fact, as she thought about that, Stella had an even more audacious idea.

Imagine if she did more than find the killer. What if she could manage to expose the family's nefarious ways, and finally make them answer for their crimes?

She didn't know if it would be possible. She was only one person, and they were wealthy and influential, with their tentacles buried deep.

But deep down, she was her father's daughter. Her current predicament had forced her to acknowledge that truth. He would have done the same. Whatever it took, she had to try.

CHAPTER TWENTY SIX

By the time the waitress brought the check, which Rebecca insisted on paying, it was already lunch time. Stella felt guilty she'd spent too long with her friend. Time was running out for her, and Rebecca needed to get back to work.

"Can I give you a ride to the house?" Rebecca asked as they stood up.

"No, thanks. You'd better hustle back to the office," she said.

They hugged goodbye, and Stella hurried back down the main road to the bus stop on the opposite side. She was relieved that a bus heading out of town came along almost immediately.

She spent the ride deep in thought, planning her next move. What should she do? Who should she speak to? What secrets were the family still hiding that she had yet to uncover?

Climbing off the bus, she strode back down the street, relieved that none of the Marshalls were in sight as she buzzed the gate open.

But as the cottage came into view, she saw something even worse.

There was an unremarkable sedan parked outside its front door. The police were back. Walking up to the cottage, Stella felt she was heading to her doom.

Detective Bradshaw was standing by the door, on his phone. Disconnecting the call, turned to her, looking angry and she felt her stomach constrict.

"Ms. Fall. Where've you been?"

Feeling dizzy from stress, Stella forced herself to stay calm. She hadn't left the area, but she suspected that the detective might have been deliberately misinformed.

"I was in town. I met a friend for brunch."

"The Marshalls told me one of their friends saw you outside of Greenwich. Mrs. Marshall called me in a panic, saying you were going to hire a car and were planning to flee the state."

Stella couldn't believe the extent of this barbaric lie. They were doing everything they could to sow doubt and smear her name, not to mention forcing the police's hand to lock her up as soon as possible.

"Fleeing the state? I didn't step outside the city center."

"I've just been trying to call you and it went straight to voicemail." He frowned at her suspiciously. "We asked you to remain contactable at all times. Is your phone turned off?"

"You could definitely ask the family about that. They're the ones who cut the wi-fi and signal booster to the cottage, as well as disconnecting the hot water. That's why I have to leave the property to make calls and get mails," Stella retorted. "Ironically, if you'd called half an hour ago when I was in town, it would have connected, and I would have answered."

Bradshaw shook his head, looking frustrated.

"Next time you leave the premises for any reason, tell me where you're going and when you'll be back. If there is a next time, because we're under pressure to wrap this up as fast as we can."

Stella feared that spelled disaster for her. Bradshaw's stony glare did nothing to reassure her.

"I need to go over some details in your version. Can we sit down inside?"

Stella longed to ask him if he'd been called to a meeting with the Marshalls. Had they tried to pressure him? Would he tell her if they had?

Don't panic, she told herself. You can't be convicted for a crime you didn't commit. Nobody has the power to do that. But again her thoughts returned, fearfully, to the missing ring. Where was it, and would it provide the evidence needed for proof?

She felt taut with worry as she sat down opposite him.

"You showed me the drugs you were prescribed. I photographed the labels."

"Yes?" Stella said warily. She didn't like where this was going.

"They are very powerful anti-depressants but can cause psychotic side-effects in certain patients."

"I didn't take them," Stella emphasized.

"My sergeant counted the tablets. There are some missing from each container."

"I told you, I threw them out of the window while we were arguing." Now Stella was wishing she hadn't. The rain would have dissolved them by now, without a trace to be found.

Detective Bradshaw stared at her doubtfully. "I only have your word for that."

Feeling a flash of anger, Stella spread her hands expressively.

"All I took was a sleeping tablet. After researching that cocktail, there was no way I was going to take them. They had bad side effects. I think the plan was to keep me sedated so I didn't cause more trouble for the family," she stared at him challengingly.

Bradshaw nodded as if she'd confirmed something to him.

"Tell me again about the argument you had the night before the murder."

That was when she told Vaughn she was pregnant. She couldn't blurt that out now. It would be dynamite.

"Vaughn got home drunk, at around ten. He started bullying me to take the meds. I refused. I pressured him to move out. He resisted. That was when I told him I was done with him, and I was going to leave. We both started yelling. He lost his temper and picked up the knife. I panicked and ran to the bedroom."

As she spoke, Stella felt cold at how guilty this made her seem. For a moment she imagined herself standing in court, with a jury listening to this version.

It was incriminating through and through, and Bradshaw's harsh expression confirmed this.

"Any other reason for the fight?" he asked. Stella felt terrified that he'd sensed she was holding some information back. Quickly, she tried to explain without giving her pregnancy away.

"Vaughn was under stress because his parents were threatening to disown him after I had an argument with his mother. I think that's why he lost it. They were trying to force him to stay in line. Force him, medicate me. That's how they work." Stella stared at him cynically. "The fight didn't last long. Vaughn followed me to the bedroom and started apologizing. We both realized things had gotten out of hand, gone too far, and there wasn't a way to come back. Everything seemed broken beyond repair. Going to sleep seemed like the best option."

"And you woke in the morning at what time?"

"I didn't see. It was only just light outside."

"What did you do when you woke?"

"I'd decided to leave him. I had worked out that the engagement was a very bad idea. When I woke, I felt as if I'd made the right choice. I planned to tell him I'd made up my mind and that he couldn't change it."

Stella sighed, filled with regret at how close she'd been to doing that. Nothing Vaughn could have said would have stopped her. She knew that for certain.

"And then?"

"I felt groggy from the sleeping pill. The sheets were wet and smelled terrible, but it took me a minute to work out what had happened. I realized there was blood on me. I saw – I saw Vaughn had a knife sticking out of his chest. I panicked. I knew he was dead. It didn't feel real. It felt impossible."

"You didn't wake in the night at all?"

His face looked set and stern. Stella found she couldn't clearly recall what she'd said the first time. Perhaps this account differed, and they would use it to bring her down.

"I don't remember waking but I think my sleep was troubled. I wish I'd seen something. Like I said, the meds didn't help," she said sadly.

"Was the bedroom door open or closed when you woke up?"

"It was open. Vaughn never closed it. We were the only two in the house, so I guess there was never a reason to," Stella explained.

"And the front door?"

"Closed, but not locked."

"That was normal?" Detective Bradshaw quirked a brow as if wondering how such a thing could be possible.

"It was. We were on a fenced property with an electric gate. I guess Vaughn felt safe and thought nobody would ever break in."

There was more to it, she thought, but she struggled to voice her feeling that Vaughn's immense wealth carried entitlement along with it. He thought that locking doors was irrelevant, because nobody would ever dare to take from him what he had.

It was more than confidence. It was arrogance. And most probably, the fact that his parents owned the local police had only cemented his attitude.

Stella wished she could explain this but decided it was better not to.

"And you? How did you feel about this behavior?"

Stella bit her lip. "I didn't really think about it. There was so much else to take in. Coming to Greenwich was a huge culture shock," she explained apologetically. "But, even in Chicago, he forgot to lock the door some nights. He rented a penthouse apartment and there was a private elevator. I worried, because it was in a city, and you always lock up in a city. I grew up on a farm in the middle of nowhere and that's one of the things I remember my dad telling us when we visited friends in town."

Bradshaw nodded. For a moment she thought he might smile.

"Did Vaughn fight or argue with anyone recently?"

Shrugging, Stella answered as honestly as she could. "The whole family seemed to operate in a state of conflict. It was normal for them to fight. They did it all the time. Vaughn was the same. Well, he wasn't when I met him, but he defaulted back to it when he came home."

152

"I see."

"We never argued in Chicago. But here, we started to. I know it doesn't look good that we were shouting at each other before this happened. But that was becoming my normal."

"Okay." He jotted something in his notebook, before ending the recording. He sighed. "There's a mountain of evidence piled up against you. I don't have to tell you how guilty you look. We didn't bring you in straight after the murder because there were so many other people on the same property. But so far, all our leads have fizzled out, and everyone we've suspected has an alibi."

"What about Cecilia?" Stella asked.

She didn't know if Bradshaw would answer. Could a mother find it in herself to murder her own son? Had Cecilia been so enraged by Vaughn's potential defiance that she'd lost her temper and taken things into her own hands?

He stared at her stonily.

"Both Cecilia and Gordon Marshall have confirmed alibis for the night of the murder."

They must have been out, at one of the endless social functions this family seemed to thrive on, Stella thought in despair.

"Why aren't you bringing me in?" she asked. Perhaps this was it, and he was here to make an arrest.

Bradshaw grimaced.

"The only reason this hasn't been wrapped up is that we've been provided with inaccurate information in quite a few of the interviews. It's delayed things, as we've had to cross-check it."

Stella guessed the Marshalls lied as a matter of course. Why behave any differently during a police interview when the police were in your pocket anyway? Probably most of the lies had been about her. She supposed they'd thrown everything they could at the detectives, whether true, exaggerated, or wildly inaccurate. Thankfully it had played out in her favor so far.

She wondered if combing through this tangle of falsehoods had alerted the detective that there was more to this, and that the family was trying too hard to get her in jail. Perhaps that was why he seemed so frustrated with the case, and why he hadn't yet arrested her on suspicion. At any rate, she hoped so.

"I can't stall much longer. We have only a few leads left to follow up," he said coldly. "I've already been told – in fact, ordered – by the local station commander to arrest you. But I won't do it until I am

153

satisfied the case has been properly wrapped up. Thank you for your time, Ms. Fall."

Stella felt breathless with shock as Detective Bradshaw walked out. A moment later, she heard his car start and he drove away.

She let out a depressed sigh. Trailing into the lounge, she slumped down on a chair and buried her head in her hands. This couldn't look worse for her. Never had she felt more trapped.

Hearing the front door open, her adrenaline surged all over again. She jumped to her feet and hurried to see who'd arrived.

To her horror, she stared at Cecilia. Flanked by Kathy and Grace, the blonde woman gave her a vicious scowl.

"I see we just missed the detective. What a pity," she said, her voice harsh and ragged. Stella had never seen such hatred in another person's eyes.

"We hoped we'd catch him and be able to explain what we found out," Kathy said spitefully. "We've exposed your background, thanks to the investigator Gordon hired."

"What?" Stella exclaimed. She'd forgotten about this and felt appalled that they'd actually pried into her past.

"It seems your father was a small-town detective and he disappeared without a trace? Is that correct? I see from your expression it is," Kathy continued with triumph filling her voice. "I guess that must have scarred you deeply. We had no idea that, having been abandoned by the family's breadwinner, your upbringing was quite so poor. You really did come from nothing, didn't you? No doubt, it set you onto this path."

"It's obvious why you would want to find a man with money, and get it for yourself at all costs," Grace lashed out.

Stella watched them, feeling turned to stone.

Never had she dreamed that the Marshalls would be taunting her with the most painful incident in her life, the catastrophe that had changed her future and defined who she was. But worse was to come.

"Based on this very strong motive, we were then discussing the fact that you are pregnant. We feel Detective Bradshaw needs to know this important truth about my son's killer," Cecilia spat.

Feeling dizzy, Stella stumbled back. Her shoulder bumped against the wall, and she leaned on it, grateful for its support, unable to meet their smug, accusing stares.

They knew everything about her. Everything. It was all out in the open and they were going to twist every fact to suit their own ends.

"I'm not sure. I had a scare," she stammered.

"Of course you did it on purpose," Kathy said. "You hoped that pregnancy would secure you an easy route to our money. And when you realized your plan wouldn't work, you became angry and killed Vaughn."

"You're such a gold-digger," Grace spat, contemptuously.

"We owe you nothing, you little tramp," Cecilia added.

"It didn't happen that way. I can't believe you're even saying such a thing," Stella protested. Her hands felt icy cold, and adrenaline was making them shake.

"When the police hear this, they will feel differently," Kathy confirmed.

"It makes no difference to the facts," Stella insisted, but they weren't listening.

"They have promised they'll make an arrest by the weekend. Gordon told me just before he left for golf," Cecilia said. "It might be even sooner thanks to the valuable information we've helped them with. It pays to use the best people, we've found. It's amazing what money can buy."

Her tone, and her words, were vengeful.

"Come on. Don't waste any more time on her," Kathy advised her, taking her arm. The trio turned and walked away.

Watching them go, Stella had no idea what she should do next.

The family had made their final moves and she was at the point of being checkmated. That was what it felt like. Cecilia had watched her like a queen staring down a helpless pawn.

In the short time she had left, was there anything she could do to save herself?

CHAPTER TWENTY SEVEN

Stella was shaking as she walked back into the cottage, and she blinked hot, humiliated tears away. She felt small and crushed. Her most private secrets had been exposed and used against her. The Marshalls were using their power and vast reach to incriminate her by whatever means possible.

And what could she do to stop them – one person – alone, broke, and vulnerable? Now, the resolve she'd felt when leaving Rebecca seemed impossible. She could never manage to expose them. They would crush her if she tried.

The most she could hope for was to get away and clear her name.

Remembering that she'd loaded more airtime, so mails would have downloaded while she was out, she checked her phone.

She gasped as she read the first one.

"Dear Ms. Fall. We received your resume last week. We were highly impressed by your background and qualifications. We have an urgent opening for a junior jury consultant, and we would like to interview you tomorrow, at two p.m., at our offices in New York City. Please can you advise if you are able to make this appointment?"

The mail continued with some background information on the company.

Stella felt totally conflicted as she read it. The once in a lifetime opportunity she'd had in Chicago, that she never thought would come her way again, had done so. She'd been offered a second chance.

Was there any way she could take it, she agonized? Her mind raced as she considered all the possibilities. It felt as if she was exploring a maze, but every option she took led to a dead end.

There was no way she could present herself for the interview tomorrow. She didn't dare leave Greenwich after the police had already been told she was trying to flee and were now scrutinizing her even more closely. And how would she explain to a future employer that she was involved in a murder investigation that might land her in jail?

With bitter regret, Stella realized that it wasn't going to be possible to take this job. She felt as if she was hammering the nails into the coffin of her jury consultancy career. There might never be a third chance.

Even so, she had no choice but to write a well worded reply that due to her fiancé's sudden death, she had family commitments that would make it impossible to attend the interview.

Once she'd written it, she trailed out of the house, walked down the driveway, and along the road until the signal improved enough for her to send it. As she headed back inside, she had never felt more hopeless in her life. She needed to think clearly, but the ability to do so seemed out of her grasp.

Stella went into the second bedroom and huddled there, curling on the bed, wishing she could shut the world away. Eventually, she slipped into an exhausted doze.

When she woke, she was surprised that it was already early evening. She must have been shattered to have slept for so long in the afternoon. Perhaps rest was what she'd needed. Although she still didn't have a clue about what to do next, she felt stronger and readier to fight again.

A sudden thought occurred to her. While battling with her thesis, she'd had some of her best insights while doing mundane housework. The routine actions freed her mind and allowed her subconscious to take over. She could use some help from her subconscious now. How could she enable this process?

The cottage was as tidy as could be, but Vaughn's belongings were still in the master bedroom. It didn't seem as if any of the family was planning to do anything with them, so perhaps she could pack them up.

Preparing herself for the memories to surge, she walked into the room.

Surprised, she stopped, staring at the bed. The mattress had been replaced and the bed freshly made up with new linen. The harsh smell of disinfectant had faded, and been overlaid by a more pleasant, lavender aroma. Someone had spent some time cleaning and rearranging. Perhaps this had been done earlier, while she was out seeing Rebecca.

Even though she hated that people could walk in and out of the cottage at will, she felt grateful that the room looked another step removed from the bloody crime scene she remembered. It would make it easier to work here.

Taking a deep breath, she opened the first cupboard, pressing her lips together as the faint scent of cologne and leather wafted out. It was a reminder of Vaughn, one that she didn't particularly want.

She took armfuls of clothes out, placing them on the crisp, starched covers, and lined up the shoes next to the bed. Perhaps all of this gear could be bundled up and donated. Then she reconsidered. Even though she didn't think Cecilia Marshall had an emotional bone in her body, there might be some garments she wanted to keep. Vaughn's old school sweater, for example – a smart, navy blue garment with a red and white stripe around the V-neck. Surely that was something a mother would want, to remember her son by.

Setting the sweater aside, Stella moved on to the next pile. These were pants. There was no emotional value inherent in a pair of pants, surely? They could all go onto the charity pile.

Except as she moved the pants, she realized there was something heavy in one of the pockets.

Curious, she reached inside and pulled it out. Then she stared in puzzlement at the slim, new-looking phone inside.

Vaughn's phone! What was it doing here? Surely the police had taken it, she thought, feeling utterly bewildered.

Then she remembered the police had taken it. It had been on his bedside table. So how had it ended up here?

It took far too long for her perplexed brain to work out the obvious and yet impossible truth. This was a second phone, hidden away in his pants pocket and turned off.

She'd never known about it. Never had Vaughn used a different one. This was very weird.

Experimentally, Stella turned it on, wondering if she might be able to unlock it. Vaughn used a code for his normal phone which she knew well. They'd laughed about it every time she'd used his phone to order food deliveries. Vaughn had joked that there were clearly no secrets between them, and she'd felt a glow of happiness about that.

Now, it was clear that there were, in fact, secrets.

She typed in the code and waited, breathlessly. It seemed like an age before the phone unlocked.

Tension knotted tighter inside her as she checked the list of numbers called. Had Vaughn been having an affair? He'd only been back a few days. Surely that was impossible.

Shaking her head, Stella realized she wasn't sure of anything anymore.

As she scrolled through the list, she saw that there had only been a few calls made and received, and they were all recent – within the last couple of days of his life.

She didn't recognize any of the numbers. Briefly, she considered dialing them, before deciding against it. How could she dial a number without knowing a thing about it? It would be better to check through all the other content in the phone first.

There were messages. Suspiciously, she opened the folder and read through.

A couple of them were acknowledgements of meetings. She saw a pin drop for a home address a couple of miles from the Marshalls. The texts were terse, not the tone she would expect from a lover. They seemed more businesslike.

Perhaps he'd just done business on a different phone, she thought, with a flash of relief that she'd worked out the reason for its presence. This might have been his work phone, which would account for him ignoring her calls on his personal phone.

Yes, it must be business. Here was a meet-up message from Jeff, Kathy's son. She remembered Kathy had mentioned he was also working for Uncle Mike's firm. Jeff had texted Vaughn to come to his home address.

Reading the rest of the text more carefully, Stella felt her skin prickle into goose bumps. This wasn't just a business phone. This was different. As she took in the words, she realized why Vaughn had it and what he had used it for.

"I don't believe it," she whispered.

The evil – the rot inherent in this family – had infected him, faster than she'd ever thought it would. And now, she had to act.

This was more than just a puzzle solved. It could be a message from the killer. Now she knew where he was and how she could find him.

CHAPTER TWENTY EIGHT

At dawn the next morning, Stella headed out of the house. She felt taut with nervousness and anticipation. Her mouth felt dry, and her stomach was churning.

The home she was looking for was a couple of miles away. As she reached the main road, a bus swept up to the stop ahead, its headlights piercing the early grayness.

She jumped aboard, and in five minutes, reached the stop closest to Jeff's house. Unlike Vaughn, he didn't live with his parents, although she was sure the stranglehold grip of his family was equally strong. His home was a double-story mansion that was way beyond what any normal man in his twenties could afford.

As she walked up to the gate and pressed the buzzer, she wondered what she would say if she was questioned. Frantically she thought of a reason that might get her inside.

But, to her surprise, the gate swung open immediately. Perhaps Jeff was expecting a delivery, or for a maid or gardener to arrive.

Feeling as if she'd gotten past an important hurdle, Stella headed up toward the house. She knocked on the front door and was greeted with a shouted, "Come in."

That was Jeff's voice, she realized with relief. And he was definitely expecting someone else.

Pushing the door open, Stella saw Jeff in a spacious room through an archway to the right of the hall. She guessed it might originally have been a reception lounge but was now repurposed as a gym with gleaming cardio machines and an impressive selection of weights. With his back to the door, dressed in a T-shirt and shorts, Jeff was hefting weights during what was clearly an intensive workout.

"Don't do the bedroom yet, I still have to change," he called out breathlessly. "Start with the guest rooms and the lounge. I'll be out of here in half an hour."

It was time to enlighten him that he was speaking to the wrong person. With a rush of nerves, Stella walked into the gym. She breathed in the smell of floor polish, underscored by fresh sweat.

"It's me," she said.

The wall to Jeff's right was one enormous mirror. He glanced into it and saw Stella there.

The weights clanged to the ground. He spun around and glared at her.

"You just walked into my house? What are you doing here?"

"I need to speak to you urgently."

"You do?" His eyebrows rose incredulously. Clearly thinking along the wrong tracks, he added in disparaging tones, "I can't help you. You're in big trouble with Vaughn's folks. I'm staying out of things. I suggest you leave, now. Or else I'll call them and tell them you're here," he added threateningly.

He looked down at his weights. Lifting one, he prepared to resume his workout.

"I haven't come to ask for help," Stella said.

Now, the note in her voice alerted him that there was more to this visit. He turned toward her again, and she saw doubt in his eyes.

"Why are you here, then?"

"I want to know why you and Vaughn were setting up an insider trading deal," Stella said.

She fought for calmness as she spoke but could hear her voice shake.

She'd thought she had known her fiancé. But she hadn't known him. She'd thought she had understood what he was capable of and where his moral boundaries lay, but she'd been terribly wrong.

The dumbbell thudded down once more, so hard that the floor vibrated.

Bunching his fists, Jeff stared at her.

"What the hell are you talking about?" He strode toward her. "How dare you accuse me of such a thing! That's defamation. I'm going to call my lawyer, and you're going to get sued so badly you'll be obliterated. You're not going to get away with this."

His wrath was a palpable force. She felt violence simmering in him and knew he was on a knife-edge.

"It's not slander, Jeff. I have proof. I found the phone you used," she told him quietly. "I saw the messages. I saw what you discussed about the new regulations due to be passed that would cut the costs of oil and gas exports. I saw the list of companies you planned to buy shares in."

She guessed, cynically, that there was nothing like having connections with an ex-senator to source that information.

161

"You what?" He made a grab for her purse. Before she could stop him, he'd wrenched it from off her shoulder, jerking it so hard that she staggered sideways.

"It's not in there," she shouted. "I didn't bring it with me. It's not in the cottage either. I've hidden it elsewhere. You'll never find it, and even if you try and hurt me, I'm not telling you where it is."

Uttering a string of foul expletives, Jeff dropped her purse.

"The deal would have made you both millions. I read the messages. You were going to buy shares today or tomorrow according to the texts."

Staring at him relentlessly, she watched him slowly crumble.

His shoulders slumped. He sighed deeply. The fury left his face and was replaced by fear. His gaze darted left and right, and then he stared at the floor near her shoes.

"It was just a prank," he muttered.

She recognized that pathetic, last-ditch attempt at a lie.

"I don't think so. From the message, it's clear you were about to action it. You had it all planned out."

His features briefly tightened. "Why didn't that moron clear his inbox?" he muttered. Then, finally, he looked at Stella.

"Okay. You got me. Yes, I was going to do it."

"A criminal offense," she reminded him.

"A criminal offense," Jeff repeated, as if he didn't like the taste of the words. "Yes, I planned it and no, I don't want to get into trouble for it. So what do you want from me?"

The hitch in his voice was audible. His bravado was dissolving by the moment.

"I want you to promise me you won't go ahead with it. If you do, I'll know. And I'll report you."

"Deal's off," he acknowledged in a low voice.

"I don't want anything else from you."

He frowned at her, looking surprised.

"Apart from some information."

"What?" he asked warily.

"What made you think of doing this?"

Jeff looked down at the polished floor and didn't speak.

"Could Uncle Mike perhaps have done something similar in the past?" Stella asked innocently.

"He might have done," Jeff muttered. "He didn't know about this, though, okay?"

Stella nodded, filing the information away, feeling a sense of bitter satisfaction that she might be able to get Uncle Mike investigated and closed down.

"Next question. Where were you on the night Vaughn was killed?"

"Why do you ask that?" Jeff sounded dismayed.

"If you were prepared to break the law to set this whole thing up, you might have decided to break it again, to avoid splitting the profits."

"Never!" He sounded aghast as he shouted out the word.

"You could have murdered Vaughn, is what I'm saying," she clarified.

"No way. How can you think that? I would never have done such a thing. Vaughn is family. He's my friend."

Stella tilted her head, making her disbelief obvious. "You'll have to give me more of a reason than that," she said.

"Okay, okay," Jeff gabbled. "There are more reasons."

Stella said nothing but waited for him to keep talking. He was flushed, and his hands were shaking. He was completely rattled by this confrontation, and she didn't think he was coherent enough to lie under such pressure. Hopefully he would spill out the facts.

"Well, first reason is that Vaughn was the go-to man. It was originally my idea, but he was the one who was going to action the plans. Not me."

Stella raised her eyebrows, feeling appalled.

"So he would have been the guilty one if you were caught?" she asked.

"Look, we discussed it," Jeff said defensively. "We had contingency plans for if it did happen. His dad carries more clout and could have kept him out of jail."

Shaking her head, Stella said, "And the second reason?"

"He had the connections to deal with the money. I mean, we couldn't just bank it. It had to be –" he hesitated, clearly unwilling to spit out the incriminating word.

"Laundered, is what you mean?"

"Yes. He had those connections. He was going to run it through a friend's company, and he had various other solutions. We'd have gotten most of it back, I mean, it was all a workable plan. But I wasn't dealing with that side."

Stella's heart sank. Vaughn hadn't just dabbled in this world. He'd plunged in headfirst.

Why, she wondered. It wasn't as if either of the men lacked for money.

But then, with a horrible feeling, she remembered the threat of disinheritance that Vaughn's family had brandished. Had that been why he'd agreed to action this reckless, criminal plan? Had he been looking for a get-rich-quick solution that would have allowed him to escape the family's stranglehold and retain his wealth?

What a mess, Stella thought sadly. What a tragic mess.

"I can provide proof if you want," Jeff said anxiously. "I'd just rather not put it in writing. But I can tell you."

This had been such a promising lead and now it had fizzled out. Feeling crushed by disappointment, Stella fought to stay calm and show none of her emotion at all.

"What were you doing on the night of the murder?" she asked. "Do you have an alibi?"

He looked confused. "I was out with Vaughn and Mike. We were socializing with clients. When the meetings were done, we went home. Vaughn's driver dropped me off because I was pretty trashed and couldn't drive myself. I went to fetch my car the next day."

So he'd also been blind drunk, and went home without his car. With a despairing inward sigh, Stella finally let go of him as a suspect.

"Look, I'm going to lose big-time now, because I've already committed myself financially," Jeff further explained. "I transferred the money to Vaughn already and because he died, I can't get it back. Perhaps you saw it go through?"

Jeff must have put it into an account controlled by Vaughn. She was surprised that he thought she would know about it.

"I don't know which account it was," she hedged.

"Perhaps if you find it, you can wire it back?" Now he sounded pleading.

She shrugged, thinking hard. Jeff was cooperating with her now, thanks to these unusual circumstances, and in this nest of scorpions she needed all the friends she could get.

In a flash of inspiration, she came up with an idea.

"I can't move it. If the police look into his accounts, they'll want to know about money going in and out. Have you thought of that?" she asked.

Jeff looked horrified.

"No! You think they'll search them? That means they'll see the first transfer. They'll know it's from me."

"You'll have to give a reason for it being there,"

"Will you tell them a reason for it, then? If they ask you?" He stared at her anxiously.

"I can do that. You were buying something from him?" she suggested, wishing she knew what the amount had been.

He looked relieved. "Yes. That would work. A vintage car? Maybe the Lotus? He told me on Monday he'd ordered it from a dealer. He was seriously amped about it."

Stella nodded, feeling sad that she'd not known about that. Vaughn loved old-model classics and he'd told her he planned to have a collection one day. But he hadn't shared with her that he was acquiring one so special.

"If they ask, I'll say that. I'll say he was selling it to you, but I didn't know the details."

"Thank you. Thank you, I really appreciate that." He paused. "This has taught me a lesson, Stella. It's made me realize this was a dumb plan and that I could have lost everything."

"I appreciate your honesty," Stella said. At that point, the gate buzzer sounded again. This time it must be the maid and it gave her a good excuse to leave.

As she hurried toward the opening gate, she thought about what Jeff had said.

She wished she could believe him, but she didn't. When he'd gotten over the trauma of being caught, she was sure he'd be tempted into another illegal deal. That was just the way he was.

At any rate, financial shenanigans aside, he wasn't a killer. He'd had no motive to murder Vaughn and in fact had needed him for the plan.

As she headed home, Stella felt filled with despair. Was every lead going to fizzle out? Where could she turn next to save herself?

The faces of the Marshalls seemed etched into her mind. Cecilia's haughty sneer. Kathy's supercilious smile. Gordon's arrogant glower. All of them complicit in illegal doings. All of them with something to hide. But who was hiding the biggest crime of all?

When Stella neared the cottage, she saw Cecilia waiting there again. She stood outside the door, staring out across the lawns, with a hand placed on her skinny hip.

There was an expression in her eyes that Stella didn't like at all.

CHAPTER TWENTY NINE

Cecilia glared at Stella. "Where have you been?" she lashed out. "Out again, so early? Did you tell the police you were leaving the house? I understand they need to know where you are at all times, now."

With a clench of her stomach, Stella remembered she hadn't told Bradshaw she was going out. She'd been too focused on the meeting with Jeff, sure that she'd be confronting the killer and that this would all be resolved.

It wasn't, and now Cecilia had something she could use against her.

In fact, looking at her face, Stella feared there was more to come. She didn't trust Cecilia. She had seen how manipulative she was. Her devious intelligence, combined with her limitless resources, made her a dangerous adversary.

"Would you be missing anything?" Cecilia asked. The meaningful tone in her voice had all Stella's suspicions prickling.

"Like what?" she asked.

"Any treasured personal possessions?"

Stella felt her stomach contract. This was about the ring. It had to be. She was sure Cecilia knew where it was. Playing innocent, Stella replied, "I took my ring off a few days ago, if that's what you're asking about. The diamond was loose."

"You didn't lose it anywhere?" Cecilia asked.

Stella felt sick. This trap had closed around her without offering the chance to escape.

"I put it back in its box."

"I think you wore it again." Cecilia countered.

It was her word against Stella's, but Stella had no doubt that if it suited Cecilia, the family would all swear under oath that she'd been wearing it right up until Vaughn had died.

"Are you saying you have it?" she asked, feeling as if she was back in a chess game again. One with life-or-death consequences.

"Yes. It's been found by a stroke of luck, in the exact place where you must have lost it."

"Where was that?" Stella asked, feeling a sense of doom descend.

"It was stuck just inside the garbage disposal unit in the sink. The maid cleaned the sink this morning, and brought it to me immediately, as I asked her to do if she found it anywhere. I was wondering how a ring could have ended up there. Vigorous hand washing comes to mind. If someone was washing their hands in a panic, late at night, for some reason, then it might have come off."

She stared at Stella in triumph.

This was the worst possible outcome, Stella realized.

She'd been framed for this – by someone. Either the killer, or Cecilia herself. She suspected Cecilia, personally, but no matter who had done it, the placement of the ring in the garbage disposal was a calculated maneuver to make her look guilty.

"I've told the police already. I called them immediately. The detectives have already been here, examined the site, and taken the ring as evidence. They noted that you were not at home and had therefore disobeyed their instructions." She leaned closer to Stella, her voice oozing with pure poison. "I told them about your pregnancy, of course. I'm not one to give personal secrets away, but I'll do anything to get my son's killer arrested."

Stella felt emotionally assaulted by the pure blast of evil radiating from Cecilia.

Somehow, she had to find the strength to withstand it, and fight back.

"If you pressure the police into arresting me, just because it suits your motives, you do realize the killer will never be found?" she said. "Maybe you don't mind that and I'm beginning to think so. It seems like you don't really care who murdered your son as long as you can make me suffer for it."

Cecilia recoiled. The smugness on her face vanished. In its place was raw fury.

"The police said this evidence will be sufficient for an arrest. They should be back any time now and expect to find you here."

Turning, she marched away. Her footsteps receded, and only the floral tinge of her perfume hung in the still morning air.

Stella let out a despairing sigh.

Which police? Was this Detective Bradshaw? Or the local police, being pressured to convict her for the family's sake?

The world had turned against her. Her investigation had stalled, the evidence against her was insurmountable, she'd disobeyed police instructions, and was about to be arrested.

She had no answers and was out of options.

Feeling desperate, she paced up and down the corridor. She guessed she'd appear in court after her arrest. How would she find a lawyer who could defend her against the top-caliber legal team the Marshalls would use?

Stella felt appalled as she realized the Marshalls would hire a jury consultancy firm, just like the ones she'd applied to join, in order to give them the best possible outcome. She knew exactly what kind of people they would choose. They would select jurors who sympathized with the interests of the very wealthy. They'd look for people from the local area, who would more easily believe that this crime must have been committed by a stranger and outsider.

There was nowhere else she could turn.

When she walked into the bedroom, she saw the piles of clothes she'd set out on the bed had been removed. The cupboards were empty, too. Vaughn's possessions must have been taken back to the main house. When the maid cleaned and tidied earlier, she must have found the ring at the same time.

Or had it worked that way?

Which maid would it have been?

Stella thought some more about the housemaid who serviced the cottage. The job belonged to Anya, the attractive blonde. She remembered her shock when she'd seen Anya head into the bathroom, about to discover the test.

But the strange thing was, Stella remembered now, that Anya had seemed even more horrified than her.

Vaughn hadn't wanted the slim, pretty Anya working in the cottage. That had seemed weird and illogical. And he'd never said why. If Stella hadn't been so overwhelmed by everything else that was going on, she'd have asked Vaughn why.

Now, Howard's words rang in her head.

"He never could keep his hands off a pretty blonde. No matter who it was."

"Oh, no," Stella whispered.

The evidence had been in front of her, waiting to be seen. Only now, with her eyes finally opened, did she understand what must have happened.

Anya was on duty today, but where would she be now? Who would know?

Stella rushed out of the bedroom. With the police on their way back, every moment counted now. Where in this huge property would

168

she have gone? Who would be willing to tell her since the staff had closed ranks and were saying nothing?

Glancing into the kitchen, she noticed the water glass and coffee cup she'd used yesterday had been washed and placed on the drying rack. Stella took the glass and refilled it, gulping the water down. Then she headed outside.

It was only as she reached the front door that she realized the significance of what she'd done.

Every time she'd arrived home, the house had been immaculate. Everything had been put away and nothing had been left out to dry.

The cup and glass on the rack meant Anya hadn't finished her work. She'd been interrupted, either because she'd found the ring, or because Cecilia had instructed her to remove the clothes.

That meant she'd be coming back. All Stella had to do was wait, and hope she returned before the police arrived.

*

Tension knotted inside Stella's gut as the minutes passed. She moved from the lounge to the bedroom, and then to the second bedroom, deciding where would be the best place to confront Anya.

If she returned. She might not come back. Cecilia could have sent her out on another errand. Anya could have said she was feeling sick and needed to quit for the day. Someone else might come along to finish up. Or the police might arrive to arrest her, and that would mean she'd never have the chance to confront the housemaid.

Worst of all, Stella knew there was a chance she could be wrong, and as the minutes went by, doubts crept into her mind.

Finally, she heard the click of the front door and soft footsteps entering.

Was it Anya?

Standing quietly in the second bedroom, Stella held her breath, listening.

When she heard the clink of a coffee cup, she knew it was time to act. Gathering her courage, she walked quickly out.

It was Anya. She was in the kitchen, drying the cup. She glanced around and jumped when she saw Stella.

"Morning. Did you take the clothes to the main house?" Stella asked conversationally.

"Yes, ma'am," Anya said.

"What are they going to do with them?" She wanted to open up the conversation with an easy question, and also felt genuinely curious.

"I don't know. I was told to pack them away in Mr. Marshall's old bedroom," Anya said.

Stella decided to go for the shock factor now. She wanted to jolt Anya into a confession.

"Tell me about you and Vaughn," Stella said. "I know he slept with you."

"What?" Anya's voice was high and shrill. "I don't know what you mean."

She turned to stare at Stella, and her wide, blue eyes were filled with fear and guilt.

"Don't lie. I know you did. You can't deny it," Stella pressured her.

Anya's face crumpled.

"It was before you arrived. Months before he left for Chicago. And it only happened twice," she whispered.

"It's okay. I'm not angry about it. But there are things I want to know," she added.

"You don't," Anya warned, in a voice that chilled Stella.

She felt her spine contract with goose bumps. "Why do you say that?"

Anya looked down. "It's better you forget about it. Just like I have done."

Her rhythmic Ukrainian accent was strong. There was a clear note of warning in it.

Stella remembered to the way Anya had looked when she'd seen her in the bathroom. She'd appeared shocked. In fact, horrified. At the time, Stella had feared that had meant she'd seen the test. What she hadn't thought was why that should have caused such a reaction. Why should there be such a strong response, unless seeing it had opened up old wounds?

She felt horrified as she made the next, logical guess.

CHAPTER THIRTY

"Did he get you pregnant?" Stella asked in a gentle voice.

Anya let out a shuddering gasp. Wordlessly, she nodded.

"Oh, Anya." Stella felt a rush of sympathy. "I'm so sorry. What did you do?"

"I got rid of it," she whispered.

And then, seeing the agony in her eyes, remembering her tortured expression as she'd walked out of the bathroom, Stella asked, "Was it your choice?"

The atmosphere in the kitchen felt still and expectant. As if a fuse was burning down. It had that feeling, Stella thought. Then Anya's face crumpled. Her shoulders began heaving as she let out harsh, gasping sobs. Stella sensed that floodgates had opened, and a whole torrent of misery was bursting out.

"Of course not! Not my choice at all. I didn't have a choice in anything, from the moment your fiancé decided that I was cute, and he would like to know me better." Though ragged, her voice sounded angry, as if she was repeating the words he'd told her. "I had no say, from that time. Then when this happened, the family blamed me. It was all my fault. I was the slut."

"What?" Stella said, feeling appalled.

Through her tears, Anya shouted out the words.

"It was as if I had committed a crime. They called me irresponsible, said I had tried to do it for the money. I must get rid of it at once, they said. There was no way I was getting a cent from them. The only money they would pay was for the family doctor to get this done. The very next day, I got driven to his rooms."

Stella felt sick to hear this. Anya's evident distress convinced her that it was true. But one fact in this disturbing account didn't make sense at all.

"Why did you keep working here? Why didn't you leave?"

Through her sobs, Anya spat back, "You think I had a choice in that?"

"What do you mean?" Stella asked, feeling ill with dread.

"I only wanted to go home to the Ukraine. But they told me they knew I would try to damage their reputation," Anya said, confirming

Stella's worst fears. "It is the way they treat us, because we work so closely with them and see what they do. They hire foreign workers, and they keep our passports. They take them away 'for admin' and never give them back."

"No!" Stella exclaimed, feeling utterly blindsided.

"Before you know it, you are a slave. You have no rights. And then something like this happens."

Stella could imagine how frightened and powerless she had felt.

"What did they say when you tried to leave?" she asked gently.

"They said I was here illegally and if I left, they would report me to the police immediately, and I would be jailed, blacklisted and deported. That my bank account would be frozen, and all my money would be seized. That was the only thing I had. The only thing I was living for. My savings, so that I could send money home to my family."

"But they had your passport?"

She shrugged. "They denied that of course. They said I had never given it to them. Their word against mine, who would be believed?"

Cold horror filled Stella. She could not believe that they had gone to such lengths to protect their reputation. The cold-hearted abuse of power, the infringement of human rights, was off the scale.

It was clear now that Vaughn, her beloved, had been two different people. There was the man she'd met in Chicago, free for the first time in his life and finding himself at last. And there was the man he'd gone back to being, corrupted by his family's evil, sucked in by their immense, entitled selfishness.

Worst of all, he'd forced this vulnerable girl into a position where she had been broken. No wonder she had finally snapped. She must have believed she had nothing left to lose.

"Is that why you killed him?" Stella asked.

"No! No, no, no!"

With a scream of combined grief and rage, Anya lunged for the knife rack and grabbed the biggest and sharpest of the remaining blades.

"No!" Stella shrieked in turn.

Terror surged through her. Anya, out of her mind with guilt and grief, was going to try to kill a second time. But as she lunged to grab the other woman's wrist, Stella realized she wasn't trying to stab her at all.

With all her force, Anya was trying to turn the knife on herself.

"No, please! Don't do it! Stop! Help!" she screamed. The other woman's strength felt way beyond normal as she turned the blade toward her chest. Stella knew she couldn't hold her. She gasped for breath, hanging on for dear life, knowing that the wickedly sharp edge was inches away from inflicting a lethal wound, and that in the struggle she could easily get cut herself.

Her wrists were trembling, and she was losing the fight against a woman powered by desperation, who had nothing left to lose.

And then there were hands grabbing her, hands from behind, pulling her away.

"Get her! Get her, quick!"

Detective Bradshaw and one of his officers pushed their way into the kitchen. They seized Anya, tugging her away from Stella. The policeman wrestled the knife from her grasp even as the detective hustled her out of the room and into the safety of the hallway.

Stella gasped for breath. She was shaking all over from adrenaline after what had just played out.

"Are you okay?" Bradshaw asked, sounding rather breathless himself. "You're not hurt?"

In the wild struggle, the blade had veered within an inch of her. In fact, it had sliced a gash in her sleeve. But she wasn't hurt. She took a moment to make sure, to confirm that there was no sting or sudden welling of blood.

"I'm okay, I think," she said.

"We heard what she said," he confirmed. "We radioed for backup immediately."

Stella collapsed onto a hall chair. Her legs felt as if they couldn't hold her up any longer. The scene played and replayed in her mind. The arc of the knife blade was seared in her memory.

"We're arresting her on suspicion of murder. There's now extremely strong supporting evidence, thanks to your bravery. We'll need a statement from you later and will be in touch as soon as we've dealt with this."

"I will. But wait, please. Did you not see what happened?"

Too late, Stella realized that to an onlooker, Anya had seemed to be attacking her.

There was no time to explain what had really played out, because the detective had run out of the cottage in response to a radio call. Stella was hustled by one of the other police, in a rushed yet kindly manner, to the spare bedroom. He closed the door, muffling the shrieks and screams she could hear from outside. The sound chilled her, prickling her skin into goose bumps. She'd never heard such agony pouring out of anyone.

Although, she remembered now that she had. Wrapping her arms around herself, she recalled how her mother had acted after her father disappeared. She'd never known what she would come home to after school and had always dreaded walking through the door.

Would she be met with vicious anger, or by her mother sobbing brokenly, prone on the bed? The one time, the bath tap had been left running and the tub had overflowed.

Stella bent over, breathing deeply as she relived the old trauma.

Was Anya guilty? Or was that terrible sorrow she heard in her cries a sign of the worst unfairness of all – being arrested for a murder she didn't commit?

She felt racked by indecision. What should she do? She should at least call Bradshaw and explain what had really happened. It might not be enough to save Anya, though, given the new evidence, and the lack of any other suspects. Besides, what if she was really guilty, and Stella was just misreading the situation?

As she agonized over what to do, Stella became aware that everything was quiet. The police had taken Anya away.

Now it was decision time.

She opened the bedroom door and let out a surprised shout as she came face to face with Gordon Marshall.

"What are you doing here?" she snapped.

Gordon was briefly discombobulated by her cry. He jumped back, looking startled, and less in control than she'd seen him before.

He made an effort to recompose himself, brushing a hand over his neat hair.

"Excuse me for walking in, but the front door was ajar," he said in a voice filled with oily charm. "Given that an arrest has been made, I thought I should come by immediately."

"Why?" Stella asked. He'd never spoken politely to her before. She felt deeply suspicious.

"Obviously it will take our family a while to recover from this shock. We never dreamed that hiring a bad apple would have such tragic consequences. We knew Anya was a liar but had decided to give her a second chance and keep her on regardless. Little did we know how she would repay our generosity."

He sounded as if he was talking at a press conference, Stella thought, feeling bewildered as he continued.

"We'd like to get things back to normal as soon as we can. Now that she has been arrested, we presume the police will not require you here any longer. So I want to help you to move out. I will book you in

174

for a week, all expenses paid, at an excellent guesthouse a few miles from here. It's close to town and to public transport. This should allow you to get back on your feet sooner." He smiled at her. She was impressed by how his eyes crinkled in false warmth.

"That's very kind, but I'll make my own arrangements from here," Stella said firmly.

"So, can we send a driver round in half an hour? Will that give you enough time to prepare?"

"No!" the word burst from Stella's mouth, causing him to look surprised again. Thinking quickly, she made up a plausible reason. "The police said they can't clear me until the arrest has been processed and that could take the whole day."

Gordon's lips tightened. "I see. So you're saying you want to stay here until then?"

"Yes. If that suits you," Stella said politely.

"Understood," Gordon sounded reluctant. "You can stay for one more night. First thing tomorrow, you must vacate the premises for good. I will send a driver at nine."

"Thank you, but I'll call a cab," Stella said.

Gordon turned and strode away.

Stella waited until he'd gone and then closed the door firmly. She walked to the dining room table and sat down, leaning her elbows on the polished wood, cupping her face in her hands as she thought furiously.

Anya had been arrested, but Stella was certain that she wasn't guilty. Her reaction had been grief, rather than rage. She'd been crushed and broken, battling to survive her terrible circumstances. Stella didn't believe her capable of walking into the cottage at night, to murder Vaughn in cold blood.

But now she'd been arrested and that put the Marshalls in a precarious position. Gordon's words had confirmed it. They must be worried Anya would tell the police how she'd been treated. So now, she saw, their strategy had changed. They wanted Stella out of the picture as fast as possible. Then she was sure, the Marshalls would be collaborating with their police friends to discredit Anya and make sure she was swiftly convicted.

That made Stella even surer Anya was innocent, but she needed to prove this beyond doubt. She'd bought a few more hours, and in that time, she'd have to find the real killer.

CHAPTER THIRTY ONE

Where to start, Stella thought in a panic. How to start?

The only physical clue that she'd uncovered so far had been in Vaughn's clothing. It hadn't come to anything, but perhaps there might be other evidence stashed away in his possessions.

Anya had packed the clothes away in Vaughn's old bedroom. She'd never been there but knew where it was. Cecilia had mentioned it was in the west wing, next to the family gym, and that fact had stuck in her mind.

Determinedly, Stella headed out of the cottage and made her way to the main house.

The corridor she needed was behind the main staircase. Hearing voices from the lounge on the right, she kept to the left of the stairs and hurried past, walking as quietly as she could.

Then she set off down the corridor.

Before she even reached the gym, Stella could hear it was in use. The personal trainer was on site, and she heard cries of encouragement coming from the wide-open doorway.

"Come on Grace. Count 'em down. Another set of eight and this time I want you touching my hand every time. Ready and… go!"

As the man counted down, Stella hurried past the doorway. Beyond it was another closed door. This had to be Vaughn's room.

Opening the door quietly, she felt a surge of regret. Looking at this neat bedroom, decorated in royal blue and white, where Vaughn had slept and played and dreamed, made her wish things could have turned out differently for him.

He'd had a good side. She'd seen it. But what chance did he have?

All she could do now was to try and find who the real killer was. At least, that way, justice would be done.

Closing the door behind her, she saw the room was tidily decorated, characterless. No trace of Vaughn's personality remained.

She opened the cupboard and was rewarded by the sight of neatly packed clothes. Again, a faint hint of his fragrance in the air. She felt her skin prickle into goose bumps.

Quickly, she removed the piles of clothes. What was she searching for? She didn't know. Anything that might be hidden in a jacket or stashed away in a pants pocket. She pulled garment after garment out, crumpling the fabric, hoping to feel the crackle of paper, or the weight of something solid inside.

Frustration built as she found nothing. Nothing but the clothing, neatly folded, the jackets tidily arranged. A total lack of anything that could help her.

Eventually, all the clothes were in a scrambled pile on the bed. She stared at them, feeling panicked. She'd wasted precious time checking the room and had uncovered nothing.

Above the now-empty clothing shelves, she saw a shelf piled with personal items. Photo frames, a paperweight, a couple of rolled up posters, sports memorabilia. Out of desperation, she decided to search through these items, even though none of them were from the cottage and they must have been stored away months ago.

She picked up the first photograph and almost dropped it in surprise.

Here was something she hadn't known about.

It was a heart shaped silver frame of a younger Vaughn, smiling into the camera, cheek to cheek with a radiant young woman.

Stella knew the woman. She recognized her. She just hadn't thought, or known, that she'd been involved with Vaughn in the past.

Feeling curious, Stella opened the frame and took out the picture.

On the back, in a bright blue, curly script was written: "To The Love of My Life and Husband to Be! Together Forever is My Promise to You. Nothing will Break us Apart."

As she stared down at that loopy azure writing, and looked at the date on the photo, Stella found herself remembering how the timeline had played out.

She recalled how Howard had denied setting Vaughn's car on fire. He'd sworn he hadn't done it, and yet the gasoline can had been there, in the Marshalls' garage, waiting to be found. Had it been planted there? It was something she'd never considered at the time because she'd not known anyone who could have a motive.

But now, looking at that photo, she saw there was. Suddenly, the evidence was forming a pattern, and it was showing her, clearly, what she'd been missing all along.

She had the information she needed to lead her straight to the killer's home. Grabbing her purse, Stella rushed out of the room.

*

Ten minutes later, Stella climbed out of the cab and approached the front door of the attractive home in south Greenwich. She felt breathless and unsure, as if this had all happened too fast. As she rang the bell, she felt cold with nerves.

This had to be right – but what if it wasn't? What if something went wrong?

The door opened, and there stood Haydi. For a moment, she gave Stella the exact same strange look she'd given her in the pharmacy. Then a quizzical half smile warmed her pretty face.

"Well, hey! It's you? What a surprise! How did you know where I live?" she said. Then she rolled her eyes. "Oh, of course. Silly me. I gave you my card that day at the pharmacy, when I was inviting you to my next dinner party.

"You did. I apologize for the surprise visit," Stella smiled, although her stomach was churning.

"Come inside." Turning, Haydi led the way. "I know why you must be here. It's because of the whole tragedy with Vaughn. What a terrible thing to go through. I feel so sorry for you. Do you need a place to stay? I can offer you my place if you need it, as I'm leaving on vacation tomorrow."

Stella followed her inside and Haydi veered right, heading into a modern lounge with white leather furniture. A real fireplace formed the centerpiece of the far wall. The window looked out over the swimming pool, and art was displayed on the walls.

"I recognize that artist," Stella said. "Kate Cooper, I think."

"You're right," Haydi laughed. "That's clever of you. Please, sit."

"That's Vaughn's favorite artist. I guess you introduced him to Kate's work in high school, when you were dating?" Stella asked, perching on one of the leather couches that flanked the old-fashioned fireplace.

Haydi sat opposite, leaning back and looking relaxed.

"Actually, it was the other way round. Vaughn introduced me to her work, and I loved it so much I've looked out for it ever since," she explained. "But I don't think that's what you were asking. You were confirming if I dated Vaughn, right? There's nothing to hide there. It's common knowledge we were high school sweethearts."

"And then what happened?"

Haydi shrugged. "He broke it off. He said I was too emotionally manipulative. Unfortunately, I'm the affectionate type and he was going through an independent phase."

"That must have been hurtful."

"I was sure he'd come back to me eventually," Haydi said, sounding confident.

"You were? But then he went and dated someone else."

Now Haydi was frowning.

"Mary-Ann, yes. I knew that wouldn't last though. Clearly, they were wrong for each other."

"It was a shame his car got torched soon after they got together," Stella remembered, watching Haydi carefully.

She nodded. "That was such a shame," she said, her voice filled with sympathy. "Vaughn really did love that Mustang."

Stella started to feel frantic. All she had was a hunch, and the puzzle pieces of what had happened in the past. There was no actual evidence linking Haydi to the crime. No evidence linking her to any of the crimes, thanks to the Marshalls' interference in the torching of the Mustang. So far, this visit was nothing more than a coffee date, although no coffee had been offered.

And Haydi was holding her nerve and showing no signs of confessing.

Perhaps she was wrong, Stella thought, as a terrible self-doubt descended.

Then she caught herself. She was not wrong. How could she be? They wouldn't be sitting here, having this weird normal, but yet not-normal conversation, if she was.

Or would they?

She remembered how Rebecca had reminded her about psychopaths, and the discussion they'd had about how they good they were at concealing their violent tendencies. Her mind raced as she tried to figure out how she could use this knowledge.

"I came here for an important reason. I wanted to ask for your help."

She hoped her spur-of-the-moment plan would work.

"Of course. I'll gladly help you," Haydi smiled.

Stella lowered her voice. "You know, ever since that night when Vaughn was killed, I've been having terrible nightmares."

Haydi nodded. "That's understandable, of course. I remember Cecilia said you were seeing their family psychiatrist. He gave you meds to help you, if I recall. Do you think you should visit him again?"

"I don't think that will work. You see, the reason for the nightmares, I think, is that I did see something that night."

"You did?"

"I didn't take all the meds that the shrink prescribed. If I had, I doubt I would have woken at all. But I only took a sleeping tablet.

"Is that so?" Haydi's gaze intensified. All her attention was focused on Stella's words.

"There was definitely a moment when I woke up," she lied.

"Do you believe you saw something?" Haydi leaned closer.

"Yes. I saw a glimpse of a face. And I knew I'd seen it before. I sensed who it was. But in the morning, I just couldn't remember. It went right out of my mind. I told the detectives that I'd try everything to help them, but nothing has worked. Since then, like I said, I've been having nightmares."

"How weird. Oh, Stella, poor you."

"Stella sighed. "So anyway, I came to ask you if you knew of anyone who might be able to get me through this."

"Such as?"

"I don't know. A good hypnotherapist, maybe? Someone who could take me back to where I was that night, so I could remember for sure?"

There was a long silence. Haydi was looking thoughtful.

Stella's stomach felt so tight with tension she thought she was going to be sick. Would this work?

And then, Haydi's face brightened.

"I do know of someone, and I will give you their details. But I've also had another idea. If you recognized the killer's face then you must have seen them before, right? Or they wouldn't have been familiar to you. Perhaps it was a friend of Vaughn's?"

Stella nodded thoughtfully. "Yes. Perhaps it was."

"I have our old school yearbooks stashed away in the cabinet in the hallway. You could take a look through them and see if you recognize anyone. Perhaps the sight of the right face would help you to remember."

"Oh, Haydi. That's a brilliant idea! I'm sure that would help." Stella smiled at her gratefully. Inside, she felt a flicker of nervous excitement. Haydi was taking the bait.

"Come on. Let's start looking. The sooner you and the family can get this tragedy behind you, the better."

Haydi sprang to her feet and gestured in a friendly way.

"Go ahead," she said. "You get the books. Grab them, bring them all in here, and I'll get my laptop open so we can look online as well."

You get the books.

180

Such an innocent request, Stella thought, yet at the same time, rather strange. Her spine prickled as she realized Haydi was baiting her own trap.

And suddenly, she guessed what the other woman was planning to do.

There was no way of avoiding it if Stella wanted Haydi to show herself as the killer. She would have to walk straight into the trap and hope she was quick and clever enough to save herself.

Feeling dizzy with tension, Stella headed back to the hallway. There was the elegant wooden cabinet. Kneeling, with her back to the lounge, she opened the doors and stared down at the bottom shelf, which was piled with old books and magazines.

She reached over to the pile. Her spine was prickling. All her senses felt heightened. Adrenaline was coursing through her.

A tiny shadow behind her, a shift of the light.

"Now!" she thought.

She dived to the left just as the fire iron slammed down.

It flew past where her head would have been and smashed into the wooden shelf, so hard that splinters scattered and its wicked, pointed tip lodged deep in the wood.

With a scream of rage, Haydi tugged it out.

"You really thought I'd confess? As if! Why would I do that, girlfriend? Why didn't you take all your meds and stay asleep, like you should have done?"

Stella jackknifed away, slipping on the polished tiles, trying to use the open cabinet door as protection. But Haydi kicked it aside, laughing crazily. She raised the iron and the heavy steel bar whirled toward Stella again. Screaming, she writhed aside. The weapon missed her by a hair and Haydi giggled again.

"How stupid are you to come in here and ask me who the killer was? Of course it was me. How dare Vaughn turn his back on me and make like I never existed? I promised myself that eventually he'd pay me the attention I deserved."

"Please, don't do this," Stella begged.

"Do what?" Haydi stared triumphantly down at her. "I'm not doing anything. I'm having a nice relaxing afternoon before my vacation."

"Just let me leave," Stella implored. There seemed no way to reach her. Her eyes were as cold as those of the killers she'd interviewed for her thesis. She was one of them. Just well hidden.

"You'll be leaving," Haydi reassured her. "Not alive, though. I'll fix it, you watch! Nobody will look for you and nobody will care. You'll disappear without a trace, and everyone will forget you."

Stella was barely listening. Her eyes were fixed on the fire iron's wicked point. At any moment, Haydi was going to use it again and she was all out of options. She was trapped, huddled in the corner of the hallway. There was no time to scramble to her feet and nowhere to run. How could she keep Haydi talking a moment more?

"Was it the pregnancy test that made you kill him?" she asked.

"Of course. That complicated everything. The thought of babies made it too permanent, and I lost my temper," Haydi added, breathlessly. "But there won't be a baby, will there? Because you're going to die now. How does that feel?"

Haydi's voice was taunting. The poker crashed down again, and Stella curled tight with a scream of terror. Haydi hadn't even meant to hit her. She'd deliberately smashed it onto the cabinet. The wooden edge splintered away.

"Wait. Just wait," she whispered. She desperately needed more time. Perhaps she could kick Haydi's legs, and get her off balance, but as the thought came to her, the other woman danced back, squealing with laughter.

"I can't wait to hammer you to a pulp," she threatened. All the earlier playfulness had vanished from her voice. "It's going to be so much fun."

She raised the fire iron again with deadly intent in her eyes.

And then, behind her, the door crashed open. Haydi spun around.

Detective Bradshaw stood there, his gun aimed at her.

"Hands in the air. Drop your weapon."

The poker clattered to the ground and Haydi let out a vicious curse.

Stella watched her deflate, the killing rage ebbing away.

Keeping her carefully in the weapon's sights, the detective stood aside. A second officer entered. Moving behind Haydi, he expertly handcuffed her.

"Take her outside. Get her to the car," someone else said.

Detective Bradshaw turned to Stella and held out his hand. She scrambled to her feet. Her legs felt wobbly, and she clutched the cabinet for support, still seeing the fire iron flashing in front of her, feeling a sense of unreality that she hadn't died.

"You could have called me sooner," he said breathlessly. "Giving me a heads-up while on the way to a killer was way too close for safety."

"I called you as soon as I could. Like I said, there's no signal at the house," Stella said. She was surprised by how calm she sounded. She was shaking violently and felt as if her core would never stop quivering from the terror of that experience.

But at least it was over now, she thought. At last, it was all over.

CHAPTER THIRTY TWO

It felt good to be packing up, Stella decided. She couldn't wait to walk out of this place and never return. Stuffing her gear into her shabby bag, she couldn't remember feeling more relieved to be leaving anywhere than to be vacating the Marshalls' cottage at last.

Rebecca was putting her up for a week. She'd insisted on it, saying it would be healing time and that Stella needed to test out their guest bedroom, a converted attic. So that was where she would be going next. She was looking forward to it.

At that moment, there was a tap on the door and Detective Bradshaw walked in.

"All ready? Where are you heading?" he asked.

"To New Jersey to stay with my friend for a while."

"Good." He nodded decisively. "Glad you'll be somewhere safe, with friends. You can expect to feel emotional for a few days. We have a counselor if you need to talk to anyone. Here's her number. Please, have a couple of consults. Trauma debriefing will help you now."

"Thank you," Stella said gratefully.

"You might be wondering what's happening next," he said.

"Yes, I am," Stella admitted.

"We've laid charges against Haydi already. Multiple charges, including murder, attempted murder, housebreaking, theft, and a few others also. She's in jail already and bail is unlikely to be granted. Given the circles she moves in, she's far too much of a flight risk."

"That's good news," Stella said, feeling relieved that the psychotic woman would not be able to cause any further harm.

"And we've released Anya. She's going to testify that she was trafficked by the Marshalls, because that's what her treatment amounts to. At this exact moment I have a team of officers in the main house. They have a warrant to search the premises and will be starting with Mrs. Marshall's office, which is where Anya said the passports are kept."

"You think the charges will hold up?" Stella said, feeling encouraged that the Marshalls might finally be brought to book for their atrocities.

"Hopefully, yes. And Mike Marshall is also being investigated by the Securities and Exchange Commission. They're going to be scrutinizing all his firm's trading records and data."

"Wow," Stella said, feeling jubilant that the whole family would be brought to book.

"And, finally, we're also auditing the local chief of police, and are already uncovering evidence of the corrupt relationship between him and Gordon Marshall. I have no doubt that we'll be able to add items to the charge list on both sides. There are people within the department, lower down, who have testified to what occurred and provided proof. A couple of them stood up to the bribery and bullying in the past, and said no to it, but were too scared of losing their jobs to take any further action."

Stella felt filled with relief. Finally, true justice would be done. It might be too late for Vaughn, but at least the family could no longer exert its chokehold of corrupt influence elsewhere.

"Am I free to go?" she questioned, wanting to make absolutely sure before she stepped out of the gate for the last time.

"You are," he nodded with a hint of a smile. "Need help with your bag? Let me carry it outside for you."

He picked up the heavy bag and Stella followed him to the door.

But, as the detective stepped out, Cecilia was waiting.

She looked different than when Stella had last seen her. Her hair was untidy, and the Teflon coating of arrogance had been stripped away. In her face, and her demeanor, she saw raw dread. Finally, Cecilia was being forced to confront the consequences of her actions, and her family's crimes.

"Detective?" she tried in a husky voice, offering a quivery smile. "Do you have time for coffee with us in our visitor's lounge? We'd like to discuss a few matters with you."

Even now, even broken, she was still trying to influence the police, Stella thought, feeling a sense of unreality.

"I'm busy, ma'am. Save your words for the courtroom," Bradshaw replied abruptly, and Cecilia flinched as if she'd been slapped.

She stared appealingly at Stella as she walked out.

"Please. Honor Vaughn's memory. It's all we have now."

Stella was about to snap out that it was a bit too late for that because she'd given her statement to the police already and had been brutally honest about everything, including Vaughn's misdoings as well as the family's. But, staring back at Cecilia, Stella felt an unexpected moment of regret. Things could have been so different if she, and her

185

family, had chosen to use their power and wealth for good. It was too late now, and they'd be suffering consequences they'd never dreamed of.

"Our time together in Chicago was the happiest in my life," Stella replied truthfully. "I'll always remember it that way, and it will have a place in my heart."

The same could not be said for Greenwich, but she wasn't going to lie.

Cecilia stared at her for another, silent moment. Then she gave a small nod before turning away and trailing back to the house.

"Here we go." Bradshaw placed the bag on the wooden bench near the driveway.

"Thank you," she said.

"Well, if you're moving out of state, I guess this is goodbye. Thank you for everything you've done. And I'll keep you in the loop about the family," he said with a wry smile.

"I appreciate all your help. And that you believed in me enough to drop everything and race to Haydi's house when I called," Stella said.

"Just doing my job," he shrugged modestly. Then he added, "You know, if you're thinking about a career direction, you should consider the investigation field. You seem to have a talent for it. When you're over this, and you've finally gotten past what this family did, why not explore some options? I'll gladly put in a word for you if you want me to."

He turned and strode toward the main house while Stella stared after him in surprise. A career in investigation? Without even meaning to, she'd come full circle, following in her father's footsteps.

But there was one last problem that she had to confront first.

*

Three days later, Stella sat opposite the doctor, fidgeting with anxiety as the woman paged through the file and tapped keys on the computer.

"We have the results back," she said.

Stella nodded, holding her breath as she waited for the hammer blow to fall. This was a situation she'd never wanted to be in, ever. Difficult and painful life decisions lay ahead, and she wished for the strength she needed to make them.

"Negative," the doctor said, shaking her head briefly as she regarded her compassionately. "You're not pregnant, Ms. Fall."

Stella nearly fell off her chair with shock.

"What? Are you sure?"

"Very sure. The blood test we use is highly accurate. More so than the basic home test, which can sometimes give a false positive, or a false negative. You could have had a false positive result due to a urinary tract infection, or simply due to your hormones at the time, which can be affected by stress."

Stella felt stunned by the irony that the false positive test had brought everything to a head. The terrible fight between herself and Vaughn. Haydi's decision to murder him. The family's corrupt behavior exposed. That one faulty result had led to a whole cascade of consequences.

"Other than that, you're run down. You're low on iron and vitamin B, and you're a few pounds underweight," the doctor said. "You need to take a good multivitamin and I'll prescribe some supplements that will help rebalance your body in a healthy way. I'm sure that within a week or two, you'll feel much better."

She pushed the sheet across the table.

"Thank you," Stella said.

She stumbled out of the doctor's rooms feeling utterly shocked. She wasn't pregnant. She never had been.

As she left the building and headed across the road to the pharmacy, Stella realized she was crying. Unstoppable tears of relief were streaming from her eyes. Her last possible link to the Marshalls did not exist and now she was truly free of them.

She bought the supplements from the pharmacy, and as she left, ready to head back to Rebecca's house, her phone rang.

Surprised, Stella saw it was Clem on the line. He must have got back from his vacation and be checking in on her.

Standing in the pleasant afternoon sun, Stella took the call.

"Are you okay after everything?" Clem asked, his voice filled with worry. "I've just read my mails and caught up on the news. Do you need any help?"

"I'm okay. It was rough, but I got through it. The killer was arrested, with my help, and I believe that they've already laid several charges against the family. They're in a lot of trouble," Stella said feeling thankful for Detective Bradshaw's dogged determination.

"I'm glad to hear it. You never deserved to be in a situation like that. Well done for getting out of it – and helping the police. So what do you plan to do next?"

"I'm staying at Rebecca's for a few more days. After that, I'm not sure."

She was grateful beyond words for the supportive environment of Rebecca's home. The first night she'd screamed herself awake, remembering the sight of Vaughn's body, and the terror she'd felt trying to evade Haydi's maddened lunges. But she was starting to feel stronger.

In fact, she thought that she'd grown through this terrible experience. It had taught her valuable lessons about her own strength and abilities.

The problem was that it had derailed her career objectives. No longer did she dream of working for a jury consultancy. Having been through what she had, Stella had decided that wasn't where her calling lay.

"I might go back home for a while. I need to regroup and find a new direction in life. I want to work somewhere that I can make a real difference, but I don't know where that is yet."

The idea of returning to that grim, dusty farmhouse made her shiver. She never wanted to see her mother again. But the house was the only place she could go. She couldn't impose on Rebecca for longer than a week, even though she'd been invited to stay as long as she liked.

"That's great news," Clem said, sounding relieved.

"It is? Why?" What was so great about being in total indecision, Stella wondered.

"I have a recommendation for you. Before I went away, I shared your thesis with a few of my colleagues. I thought they'd be interested in the insights. In fact, they were more than interested."

"What do you mean?" Stella felt complimented and curious, all at once.

"You have an offer from the FBI Academy. They want to take you on as a trainee agent."

"You're serious?"

Stella couldn't believe it. The FBI Academy?

"Of course I'm serious. And before you argue with me, yes, you are ready for it," Clem said with a hint of humor. "They need your skills. Trust me, you'll be making a real difference there."

"How long do I have to think about it?" she asked, stalling for time, but Clem's exasperated sigh told her time was a scarce, in fact nonexistent, commodity.

"These opportunities don't come along often. As you know. So, if you feel drawn to it now, take it. You won't regret it, Stella. It's where you belong. And these people move fast. If it's a yes, they want to fly you to Quantico next week for an in-person interview, and sign you up immediately, so there'll be no need to go back home."

Her future? With the FBI?

The unknowns terrified her. Would she have what it took?

Self-doubt loomed large. Her mother's critical words were seared in her mind. But now, Stella realized, they didn't have to define her forever.

Maybe she did have what it took. Perhaps this ordeal had proved that she was a strong person, her father's daughter, who at her core had always longed to see justice done.

"All right," she told Clem. She felt nervous and unsure, but hopeful, as if she was finally accepting a calling that she'd never thought she'd be ready for. "You can tell them yes."

NOW AVAILABLE!

HIS OTHER LIE
(A Stella Fall Psychological Suspense Thriller—Book 2)

HIS OTHER LIE is book #2 in a new psychological suspense series from debut author Ava Strong, which begins with HIS OTHER WIFE (Book #1).

Stella Fall, still reeling from the trauma of her deceitful fiancé and her failed engagement, has decided to pursue her dreams, follow in her father's footsteps, and throw herself into law enforcement. Upon graduating from the FBI's academy, she isf placed in the FBI's Connecticut field office. It is not long until, by sheer chance, she finds herself assigned to the case of her life—and thrown right back into a world she hoped to never see again—of couples, affairs and high-end suburbia.

A newlywed is found murdered in her bed in her new home, in the town she just moved to with her husband. All seems too picture-perfect in this town for Stella, with the immaculate homes, smiling wives, flaunting of wealth, and obsession with appearances. It is not long until she realizes all is not what it seems.

Who wanted this popular newcomer to town dead? What was the popular card game she attended? What secret are all of these wives hiding?

The case becomes personal for Stella, the memories hitting way too close to home for her. Stirring up her past trauma, she struggles to hang on until she can solve the first big case of her new career. The stakes couldn't be higher. And the killer is still out there.

Will newly-minted FBI Special Agent Stella Fall be able to tap her brilliant mind and figure out what this town is hiding?

A fast-paced psychological suspense thriller with unforgettable characters and heart-pounding suspense, HIS OTHER LIE is book #2 in a riveting new series that will leave you turning pages late into the night.

Book #3—HIS OTHER SECRET—is also available.

Ava Strong

Debut author Ava Strong is author of the REMI LAURENT mystery series, comprising three books (and counting); of the ILSE BECK mystery series, comprising four books (and counting); and of the STELLA FALL psychological suspense thriller series, comprising three books (and counting).

An avid reader and lifelong fan of the mystery and thriller genres, Ava loves to hear from you, so please feel free to visit www.avastrongauthor.com to learn more and stay in touch.

BOOKS BY AVA STRONG

REMI LAURENT FBI SUSPENSE THRILLER
THE DEATH CODE (Book #1)
THE MURDER CODE (Book #2)
THE MALICE CODE (Book #3)

ILSE BECK FBI SUSPENSE THRILLER
NOT LIKE US (Book #1)
NOT LIKE HE SEEMED (Book #2)
NOT LIKE YESTERDAY (Book #3)
NOT LIKE THIS (Book #4)

STELLA FALL PSYCHOLOGICAL SUSPENSE THRILLER
HIS OTHER WIFE (Book #1)
HIS OTHER LIE (Book #2)
HIS OTHER SECRET (Book #3)

Manufactured by Amazon.ca
Bolton, ON